BRIAN
THE MURDERS N

BRIAN FLYNN was born in 1885 in Leyton, Essex. He won a scholarship to the City Of London School, and from there went into the civil service. In World War I he served as Special Constable on the Home Front, also teaching "Accountancy, Languages, Maths and Elocution to men, women, boys and girls" in the evenings, and acting in his spare time.

It was a seaside family holiday that inspired Brian Flynn to turn his hand to writing in the mid-twenties. Finding most mystery novels of the time "mediocre in the extreme", he decided to compose his own. Edith, the author's wife, encouraged its completion, and after a protracted period finding a publisher, it was eventually released in 1927 by John Hamilton in the UK and Macrae Smith in the U.S. as *The Billiard-Room Mystery*.

The author died in 1958. In all, he wrote and published 57 mysteries, the vast majority featuring the super-sleuth Antony Bathurst.

BRIAN FLYNN

THE MURDERS NEAR MAPLETON

With an introduction by
Steve Barge

DEAN STREET PRESS

Published by Dean Street Press 2019

Copyright © 1929 Brian Flynn

Introduction © 2019 Steve Barge

All Rights Reserved

The right of Brian Flynn to be identified as the Author of the Work has been asserted by his estate in accordance with the Copyright, Designs and Patents Act 1988.

First published in 1929 by John Hamilton

Cover by DSP

ISBN 978 1 913054 41 0

www.deanstreetpress.co.uk

INTRODUCTION

"I believe that the primary function of the mystery story is to entertain; to stimulate the imagination and even, at times, to supply humour. But it pleases the connoisseur most when it presents – and reveals – genuine mystery. To reach its full height, it has to offer an intellectual problem for the reader to consider, measure and solve."

THUS WROTE Brian Flynn in the *Crime Book Magazine* in 1948, setting out his ethos on writing detective fiction. At that point in his career, Flynn had published thirty-six mystery novels, beginning with *The Billiard-Room Mystery* in 1927 – he went on, before his death in 1958, to write twenty-one more, three under the pseudonym Charles Wogan. So how is it that the general reading populace – indeed, even some of the most ardent collectors of mystery fiction – were until recently unaware of his existence? The reputation of writers such as John Rhode survived their work being out of print, so what made Flynn and his books vanish so completely?

There are many factors that could have contributed to Flynn's disappearance. For reasons unknown, he was not a member of either The Detection Club or the Crime Writers' Association, two of the best ways for a writer to network with others. As such, his work never appeared in the various collaborations that those groups published. The occasional short story in such a collection can be a way of maintaining awareness of an author's name, but it seems that Brian Flynn wrote no short stories at all, something rare amongst crime writers.

There are a few mentions of him in various studies of the genre over the years. Sutherland Scott, in *Blood in Their Ink* (1953), states that Flynn, who was still writing at the time, "has long been popular". He goes on to praise *The Mystery of the Peacock's Eye* (1928) as containing "one of the ablest pieces of misdirection one could wish to meet". Anyone reading that particular review who feels like picking up the novel – out now from Dean Street Press – should stop reading at that point, as later in the book, Scott proceeds to casually spoil the ending, although as if he assumes that everyone will have read the novel already.

It is a later review, though, that may have done much to end – temporarily, I hope – Flynn's popularity.

> "Straight tripe and savorless. It is doubtful, on the evidence, if any of his others would be different."

Thus wrote Jacques Barzun and Wendell Hertig Taylor in their celebrated work, *A Catalog of Crime* (1971). The book was an ambitious attempt to collate and review every crime fiction author, past and present. They presented brief reviews of some titles, a bibliography of some authors and a short biography of others. It is by no means complete – E & M.A. Radford had written thirty-six novels at this point in time but garner no mention – but it might have helped Flynn's reputation if he too had been overlooked. Instead one of the contributors picked up *Conspiracy at Angel* (1947), the thirty-second Anthony Bathurst title. I believe that title has a number of things to enjoy about it, but as a mystery, it doesn't match the quality of the majority of Flynn's output. Dismissing a writer's entire work on the basis of a single volume is questionable, but with the amount of crime writers they were trying to catalogue, one can, just about, understand the decision. But that decision meant that they missed out on a large number of truly entertaining mysteries that fully embrace the spirit of the Golden Age of Detection, and, moreover, many readers using the book as a reference work may have missed out as well.

So who was Brian Flynn? Born in 1885 in Leyton, Essex, Flynn won a scholarship to the City Of London School, and while he went into the civil service (ranking fourth in the whole country on the entrance examination) rather than go to university, the classical education that he received there clearly stayed with him. Protracted bouts of rheumatic fever prevented him fighting in the Great War, but instead he served as a Special Constable on the Home Front – one particular job involved warning the populace about Zeppelin raids armed only with a bicycle, a whistle and a placard reading "TAKE COVER". Flynn worked for the local government while teaching "Accountancy, Languages, Maths and Elocution to men, women, boys and girls" in the evening, and acting as part of the Trevalyan Players in his spare time.

It was a seaside family holiday that inspired him to turn his hand to writing. He asked his librarian to supply him a collection of mystery novels for "deck-chair reading" only to find himself disappointed. In his own words, they were "mediocre in the extreme." There is no record of what those books were, unfortunately, but on arriving home, the following conversation, again in Brian's own words, occurred:

> "ME (unpacking the books): If I couldn't write better stuff than any of these, I'd eat my own hat.
>
> Mrs ME (after the manner of women and particularly after the manner of wives): It's a great pity you don't do a bit more and talk a bit less.
>
> The shaft struck home. I accepted the challenge, laboured like the mountain and produced *The Billiard-Room Mystery*."

"Mrs ME", or Edith as most people referred to her, deserves our gratitude. While there were some delays with that first book, including Edith finding the neglected half-finished manuscript in a drawer where it had been "resting" for six months, and a protracted period finding a publisher, it was eventually released in 1927 by John Hamilton in the UK and Macrae Smith in the U.S. According to Flynn, John Hamilton asked for five more, but in fact they only published five in total, all as part of the Sundial Mystery Library imprint. Starting with *The Five Red Fingers* (1929), Flynn was published by John Long, who would go on to publish all of his remaining novels, bar his single non-series title, *Tragedy At Trinket* (1934). About ten of his early books were reprinted in the US before the war, either by Macrae Smith, Grosset & Dunlap or Mill, and a few titles also appeared in France, Denmark, Germany and Sweden, but the majority of his output only saw print in the United Kingdom. Some titles were reprinted during his lifetime – the John Long Four-Square Thrillers paperback range featured some Flynn titles, for example – but John Long's primary focus was the library market, and some titles had relatively low print runs. Currently, the majority of Flynn's work, in particular that only published in the U.K., is extremely rare – not just expensive, but seemingly non-existent even in the second-hand book market.

In the aforementioned article, Flynn states that the tales of Sherlock Holmes were a primary inspiration for his writing, having read them at a young age. A conversation in *The Billiard-Room Mystery* hints at other influences on his writing style. A character, presumably voicing Flynn's own thoughts, states that he is a fan of "the pre-war Holmes". When pushed further, he states that:

> "Mason's M. Hanaud, Bentley's Trent, Milne's Mr Gillingham and to a lesser extent, Agatha Christie's M. Poirot are all excellent in their way, but oh! – the many dozens that aren't."

He goes on to acknowledge the strengths of Bernard Capes' "Baron" from *The Mystery of The Skeleton Key* and H.C. Bailey's Reggie Fortune, but refuses to accept Chesterton's Father Brown.

> "He's entirely too Chestertonian. He deduces that the dustman was the murderer because of the shape of the piece that had been cut from the apple-pie."

Perhaps this might be the reason that the invitation to join the Detection Club never arrived . . .

Flynn created a sleuth that shared a number of traits with Holmes, but was hardly a carbon-copy. Enter Anthony Bathurst, a polymath and gentleman sleuth, a man of contradictions whose background is never made clear to the reader. He clearly has money, as he has his own rooms in London with a pair of servants on call and went to public school (Uppingham) and university (Oxford). He is a follower of all things that fall under the banner of sport, in particular horse racing and cricket, the latter being a sport that he could, allegedly, have represented England at. He is also a bit of a show-off, littering his speech (at times) with classical quotes, the obscurer the better, provided by the copies of the *Oxford Dictionary of Quotations* and *Brewer's Dictionary of Phrase & Fable* that Flynn kept by his writing desk, although Bathurst generally restrains himself to only doing this with people who would appreciate it or to annoy the local constabulary. He is fond of amateur dramatics (as was Flynn, a well-regarded amateur thespian who appeared in at least one self-penned play, *Blue Murder*), having been a member of OUDS, the Oxford University Dramatic Society. Like Holmes, Bathurst isn't averse to the occasional disguise, and as with Watson and Holmes, sometimes even his close allies don't recognise him. General information about his background is light on the ground. His parents were Irish, but he doesn't have an accent – see *The Spiked Lion* (1933) – and his eyes are grey. We learn in *The Orange Axe* that he doesn't pursue romantic relationships due to a bad experience in his first romance. That doesn't remain the case throughout the series – he falls head over heels in love in *Fear and Trembling*, for example – but in this opening tranche of titles, we don't see Anthony distracted by the fairer sex, not even one who will only entertain gentlemen who can beat her at golf!

Unlike a number of the Holmes' stories, Flynn's Bathurst tales are all fairly clued mysteries, perhaps a nod to his admiration of Christie, but first and foremost, Flynn was out to entertain the reader. The problems posed to Bathurst have a flair about them – the simultaneous murders, miles apart, in *The Case of the Black Twenty-Two* (1928) for example, or the scheme to draw lots to commit masked murder in *The Orange Axe* – and there is a momentum to the narrative. Some mystery writers have trouble with the pace slowing between the reveal of the problem and the reveal of the murderer, but Flynn's books sidestep that, with Bathurst's investigations never seeming to sag. He writes with a wit and intellect that can make even the most prosaic of interviews with suspects enjoyable to read about, and usually provides an action-packed finale before the murderer is finally revealed. Some of those revelations, I think it is fair to say, are surprises that can rank with some of the best in crime fiction.

We are fortunate that we can finally reintroduce Brian Flynn and Anthony Lotherington Bathurst to the many fans of classic crime fiction out there.

The Murders near Mapleton (1929)

"Sir Eustace Vernon did not die as we had believed. He was not killed by a train passing over his body. He has been killed by a shot through the head from a revolver. Fired from behind."

MOST GOLDEN AGE authors wrote a Christmas tale or two. *Hercule Poirot's Christmas* by Agatha Christie, *Dancing Death* by Christopher Bush, *An English Murder* by Cyril Hare, *Tied Up In Tinsel* by Ngaio Marsh, the list goes on and on. The setting is ideal – a group of family and friends brought together in a country house, where the tensions can reach boiling point and murder can pay a visit. Add in the bonus, usually, of the house being surrounded by unbroken snow, and you have the setting for a classic whodunit.

It only took four books for Brian Flynn to tick this box with *The Murders Near Mapleton*. Published in 1929 by John Long in the UK, and by Hamilton MacRae in the US, it sees the friends and family of local hero Sir Eustace Vernon gathered together on Christmas Eve to see in the season. Something is troubling Sir Eustace – his daughter is convinced that he is scared of something. By the next morning, two of the household lie dead. But as one of the bodies was discovered by a passing Anthony Bathurst, luckily they have a sleuth on hand to try and sort things out.

The Christmas theme is almost incidental, however, with the only real link to the tale being threatening messages hidden inside bonbons. Perhaps that last sentence needs a little explanation.

Christmas crackers have long been a festive tradition, fancily decorated cardboard tubes containing a motto or joke and a small present. When they were invented by Tom Smith in 1847, they were referred to as "bon-bons". The simple reason for this is that Smith had been a sweet seller, and he simply took his usually wrapped sweets (with the wrapper twisted at both ends) but inserted a message between the sweet and the wrapper. He developed these quickly into the more recognised version of the cracker, referred to initially as the Cosaque, but soon adopting the name used today. Some people continued to use the name "bon-bon" however – it is still in common usage in Australia – and one of those places was the Flynn household. It is difficult to find out how widespread the name "bon-bon" was elsewhere, but there were still numerous mentions in the national press at the time, falling off in the 1940s. However, the modern reader, hearing of messages hidden in bonbons, may well think of sweets, so hopefully this clears up that potential confusion. One can speculate that the title was changed to the somewhat underwhelming "The Murders Near Mapleton" from "The Red Bonbon Murders", suggested as the name of the case in the story, to clear up any confusion at the time. Why Flynn chose not to hyphenate the word, which seems to be the standard way of writing it, is another question.

One other point to note here is another coincidence with Flynn and a similar plot idea from another writer, namely Gladys Mitchell. Without going into detail – I will leave the reader to discover it for themselves – there is a common trait shared by victims in this book and one from Mitchell released in the same year. Flynn certainly had no contact with Mitchell, so the ideas presumably formed independently. The two stories told by the writers about their victims are very different, but one wonders if there was a story in the national press that inspired their starting points.

The cynical reader may raise an eyebrow at another tale featuring a country house party and a missing treasure, but Flynn has concocted another thrilling tale that will puzzle readers from beginning to end, with another surprising (but fairly clued) ending. *The Murders Near Mapleton* was published by John Hamilton in 1929 in the UK, and by Macrae Smith in the US in the same year, but to the best of our knowledge has never been reprinted since. It is an absolute pleasure to be able to bring it back to readers after ninety years.

Merry Christmas!

Steve Barge

Chapter I
THE BEGINNING OF THE TERROR

Sir Eustace Vernon straightened his shoulders and raised his glass. "Another toast, ladies and gentlemen, before the ladies leave us! A toast, I think, that we should always drink at Christmas-time! One that should never be forgotten." He spoke very gravely and one by one the company of his guests ceased their gay and irresponsible chattering and looked towards him, with expectant eyes, down the long and brilliantly lighted table. For he was a man of much distinction. "I will ask you all," he announced very quietly, "to charge your glasses and drink to the 'empty chairs.' To those dear ones who once were with us but who have now 'passed on,' as we shall 'pass on' when our time comes." The medley of suddenly grave voices floated towards him—echoing the words of his toast. "Thank you, ladies and gentlemen." Sir Eustace sat down. But his handsome face showed signs of perturbation. The merry chatter of the company recommenced, although the thoughts of more than one had changed and travelled far.

"What's come to your uncle, these days?" asked a debonair young man of his charming neighbour at the table.

The girl addressed darted a quick glance at her companion with her pretty eyes a-flutter. "What do you mean, Terry—tell me—have you—"

"Noticed anything?" he broke in again, before she could complete the sentence. "Yes—I have noticed something. Most decidedly! And what's more, Helen—I don't think I should be very far wrong if I said that you had noticed something yourself."

Helen Ashley looked carefully round her more approximate neighbours before she answered. Lowering her voice she caught Terence Desmond's arm lightly, and admitted the truth of his words. "You're quite right, Terry, I have! It's been coming on him, too, for some time—if you mean the same thing that I mean. But tell me—what is it you've noticed? Tell me exactly."

Desmond was about to reply when a voice sounded at his elbow. "Yes, please, Purvis. Fill up again—please."

The butler filled his champagne glass with becoming dignity.

"No more for me, Purvis," refused Helen Ashley. "What were you going to say, Terence? Please forgive me if I seem unnaturally insistent—but the truth is I'm dreadfully worried about Uncle Eustace."

"Let me think. How long have I been here, Helen?"

"Not quite a week," she answered. "But long enough—"

"To notice a good many things and to get into his bad books very thoroughly—eh?" he replied—the laughter showing in his blue eyes. Helen looked serious. Desmond went on. "I think he's *frightened*, Helen. That's the impression he's given me all the time I've been here. To use an ordinary expression, 'that he had something on his mind' would be beside the point—inadequate. It's much more than that and it's different from that. I've seen 'fear' before—many times—and in many guises—and far too many times not to recognize it when I do see it. Your uncle's afraid of something," he concluded—"I haven't any doubt about it, and very badly scared, too."

"I think you're right," agreed Helen Ashley, quietly—"you've summed up the position just as I've seen it. It's getting on my own nerves, too—that's the worst of it." She looked towards the head of the table where the man of the discussion was engaged in an animated conversation with his left-hand neighbour.

"I am just old enough, Mrs. Trentham," he was saying, "to enjoy my Christmas very thoroughly. It is only the young who are bored by Christmas. Doubtless you are bored yourself."

"I certainly haven't been bored at Vernon House," replied the lady—"you are far too charming a host ever to allow anything like that to happen. I think it's a great pity that Vernon House hasn't a hostess." Her accompanying smile was demurely provocative as it rippled across her face. Sir Eustace twirled his grey moustache and smiled in return.

"That could be remedied, Ruby. It's not too late."

A tray dropped from the hands of one of the maids and clattered heavily to the floor. He broke off his sentence—his lips working convulsively and his face ashen grey. "God!" he exclaimed, "*what* was that?" Then he recovered himself to find Mrs. Trentham's eyes regarding him curiously. "My nerves are all to pieces since I had that attack of influenza," he explained lamely. "The result is that any sudden noise like that plays the very dickens with me and knocks me right over. I'm afraid it sounds silly—" He stopped to watch the effect of his explanation upon his companion. Ruby Trentham's eyes fluttered just the suggestion of an understanding.

"Not at all," she remarked. "I think most of you financiers are like that—Morris is almost as bad—and he hasn't even the excuse of a previous illness to fall back upon—whenever he's pulling a big deal through on 'Change,' as he calls it, or engaged on any big business proposition—he's as twittery as a canary—aren't you, Morris?" She turned her beautiful face towards her fat and prosperous-looking husband.

"If you say so, my dear—I suppose I must agree. You've taught me to do that." He shrugged his shoulders. His answer held a touch of sourness.

Although he belonged to the type of man who ardently desires his wife to excite other men's admiration—he liked that admiration, when excited, to confine itself within certain limits. In this connection Contemporary Rumour had it that he viewed Sir Eustace Vernon's interest in his wife with an appreciable disfavour, that tended to grow rather than to decrease.

"I couldn't help hearing what you said, Sir Eustace," interjected a tall clean-shaven man—the vis-à-vis of Mrs. Trentham—"particularly as it happened to fit into my personal province—but you're quite right. '*Flu*' plays the very deuce with people—it's apt to leave so many evils behind—and the victim's nervous system is one of its happiest hunting-grounds. It plays Old Harry when it gets in there." The speaker was Doctor Lionel Carrington—Sir Eustace Vernon's medical adviser—and a man to whom the latter had undoubtedly taken a strong liking.

"There you are, Trentham," exclaimed Sir Eustace—"Carrington to the rescue! He knows me. He understands me."

The doctor smiled an affirmative, just as another speaker took up the thread.

"You are far too modest, Sir Eustace—you underrate yourself and the strains you have imposed upon yourself—the cause of your indisposition is not far to seek. Why talk of "influenza"— have you forgotten the night of January the eleventh last? Surely not! What you did that night will live forever in the hearts of the people of Mapleton."

The voice of the man that spoke rang with emotion, and almost held the fervour of fanaticism. Doctor Carrington turned and looked at him. Father Jewell sprang to his feet.

"Ladies and gentlemen," he cried with dramatic intensity— his voice vibrant with feeling—"and yet another toast before we finish this Christmas dinner. Let us drink a health to the children—the men and women of to-morrow—whose lives Sir Eustace Vernon saved."

His cultured and incisive voice cut like an icy knife down the length of the table. The company took up the toast with infectious enthusiasm. Major Prendergast waved his glass by its stem.

"Hear, hear"—his heavy voice boomed approval—"Sir Eustace Vernon! Sir Eustace Vernon! One of the bravest deeds I ever saw."

Diana Prendergast—a cameo of loveliness—turned her eyes radiant with star-sheen, and laid her hand on her husband's arm. "Be quiet," she said—"Sir Eustace is going to speak. Be quiet! Listen!"

To the others there came the same realization. They were silent again and unanimously sank back into their seats—subsiding gently. Sir Eustace rose. As he stood there at the head of the table, Terry Desmond suddenly became more conscious than ever before in his life that their host was rapidly aging. His baldness was thrown up into startling prominence by the relentless light of the room, and his shoulders drooped perceptibly. But his eyes shone through the glass of his pince-nez as fearlessly as ever; and it was herein that the discerning observer could catch sight of the indomitable courage that had sent their owner to climb the front of a rapidly burning building time after time to save the lives of a dozen children hopelessly entrapped therein. With the Fire Brigade in attendance at another fire, no other course of action could have saved the twelve helpless little prisoners. This heroic feat, coupled with his work for Mapleton, had brought Sir Eustace a baronetcy in the last Birthday Honours' List. Which fact had also caused much heart-burning among the other Aldermen and Councillors of the before-mentioned County Borough. To say nothing of Mayor and Ex-Mayors! Sir Eustace extended his hand towards his guests—a gesture requesting a silent audience.

"Father Jewell makes far too much of an ordinary deed," he said, with impressive quietness. "I merely did my duty as any Englishman would and must have done in similar circumstances—and I was rewarded. It is nothing to mention."

The Mayor of Mapleton—Alderman Alfred Venables—began to feel a sense of annoyance. He felt aggrieved that even at a Christmas banquet of this nature he was unable to escape the shadow of Vernon's baronetcy. He muttered something to his wife—under his breath almost—and glared fiercely at the standing figure of his host.

"My reward," continued Sir Eustace, "was not the honour that His Majesty was pleased to confer upon me. I do not desire that you should misunderstand me." He paused abruptly—with the inevitable result that Alderman Venables' accompanying snort got "well over."

Helen looked across at him with strong indignation in her face. Emily Venables returned her look for look. The amenities of guest and hostess were temporarily forgotten.

Sir Eustace went on. "It was in the eyes of the first little girl whom I was able to get to safety. That is all I have to say." He sat down and picked up the red bonbon of crinkled paper that lay beside his plate. The others saw the action and recognized it as the signal to pick up their own. The noise of the pulling of the crackers snapped through the room. Suddenly Sir Eustace's face went the colour of cigar-ash and his eyes held a strange anxiety. His more intimate neighbours noticed the rapid change in his facial colour. He half-rose in his chair and then sank back again as though uncertain what to do. His eyes sought Purvis. The butler met them and came obediently to his master's side. Sir Eustace motioned him to bend down and then whispered something in his ear in the lowest of tones. Purvis nodded understanding and made his way slowly down the spacious room. Sir Eustace watched his figure pass and then rose again—his body and voice alike a trifle unsteady, and wavering. He spoke with difficulty.

"Ladies and gentlemen," he said—"I should be extremely obliged if the ladies of the party would adjourn at once and if the gentlemen would join them at their discretion. I am compelled to leave you for a little time, but I hope to be with you again very shortly. Please accept my sincere apologies for the apparent discourtesy, but I assure you that it is beyond my control. I would give much for it not to have happened. I have received some very bad news."

The faces of his guests followed him—startled yet sympathetic—as he walked down the room—absent-mindedly as it were and sorely troubled in spirit. For he had carried away from the table two red bonbons in his right hand. Ruby Trentham saw them plainly as Sir Eustace passed through the door. She realized that one was his own and that he had picked up also the bonbon that had been intended for her.

Chapter II
HAMMOND SCREAMS

Doctor Carrington declared afterwards, upon due reflection, that he was absolutely certain at that particular moment of the grim presence of Tragedy. How the conviction came to him he was unable to explain—all the same he was definitely aware of it. However, he appears to have said nothing to that effect. None of his companions is able to remember that he did, which is moderately conclusive. He himself is not sure. Anyhow, the ladies withdrew as Sir Eustace Vernon had suggested and which is more—had obviously desired. About half an hour later, that is to say—about thirty-five minutes past nine—the gentlemen left the dinner-table and joined them. Terence Desmond led the way into the sumptuously-furnished lounge and the others followed him. But by this time—and now very much more pronounced—there was an indefinite something in the air that seemed to hang like a pall over the proceedings and cause almost everything to fall unutterably flat. Conversation was desultory to the extreme. Languishing attempts to revive the spirit and *élan* of the evening were one and all doomed to failure. Two hours dragged slowly by. A card-party was formed after a time—and a game of Auction Bridge started—the players being the two Venables, Morris Trentham and Diana Prendergast. Helen Ashley, Major Prendergast and Father Jewell wandered into the music-room adjoining the lounge, while Desmond and Carrington migrated to the billiard-room, just as the former put it, "to knock the balls about a bit." Each was somewhat above the average in billiards' skill. It may be remarked at this period of the story that the lounge communicated directly with the music-room, which in its turn opened on to the billiard-room.

"What are you going to do, Ruby?" asked Helen, as she herself sat down to the piano—"you seem at a loose end. If you stay in here, I'll sing you something. Tell me something you'd like."

"Thanks—but I've rather a 'head.' It's been coming on for some time now. If you don't mind I'll go and watch the boys in the billiard-room."

The pallor of her face seemed to intensify the truth of her words. She turned and left Helen sitting there.

Thus was the stage of Vernon House set at about a quarter to twelve on that Christmas night for the enacting of one of the strangest cases that ever fell to an investigator's lot to unravel.

Suddenly Helen Ashley looked at the ormolu clock upon the mantelpiece. "Good gracious, Terry," she exclaimed, "look at the time—whatever can it be to have kept Uncle Eustace all this time? If he isn't back by the time it strikes twelve, I shall have to go and look for him."

Terence looked grave. "It certainly is most extraordinary—he's been away now just on three hours. I've been worried about it for some time now. Goodness knows what his news could have been—on a Christmas night, too! When you start on your voyage of discovery, Helen, I'll come with you."

Venables crossed the room towards her. "Mrs. Venables and I must be going shortly, Miss Ashley. Within half an hour, I'm afraid! I ordered my car for twelve-thirty. If your uncle doesn't show up before then, please pay my respects and explain to him—will you? It doesn't do for me to have Mrs. Venables out too late, you know. The night air and her asthma don't exactly—"

At that precise moment, as Alderman Venables was making his historic contribution, there rang through Vernon House a blood-curdling scream. It was a scream of fright—but of far more than ordinary fright. It contained a note of horror and above that a note of stark terror! It came from a person who, in the scream, had entirely epitomized all the gamut of Abject Fear. It seemed to come from the same side of the hall as the lounge—but from the part that lay towards the back of Vernon House.

"Good God!" cried Morris Trentham—"what on earth does that mean? It's a woman!"

Without waiting to answer him the whole crowd of them dashed across the hall, seeking the meaning of the scream. Everything now was silent. Whoever it was that had screamed had no life to scream again. The investigators stopped—uncertain of their next step, uncertain of their exact destination. Lionel Carrington turned to Father Jewell behind him.

"Where did it come from, Father?" he asked with agitated lips—"any idea?"

The priest shook his head helplessly, and to stifle his emotion—caught at his breast with his two hands.

Helen Ashley quietly interposed. "I think it came from my uncle's study," she said—with a tremor in her voice. "Certainly from that direction." She explained more fully. "The room at the end on the right. It leads on to the garden."

"I think so too, Helen," cried Terence Desmond—"come on then—as quickly as possible."

Prendergast and he outdistanced the others and reached the door first. It was locked, and there was no key in the lock on the outside.

"Put your shoulders to it," cried Major Prendergast, as the others panted up. "Keep back, ladies—please. This is a job for men."

The men flung their united weight against the door. "I know a better way than that," cried Desmond. He turned and ran back—through the lounge, music-room and billiard-room—round into the garden. Helen Ashley watched him with anxious and wondering eyes. For a time the door held—defying all the efforts of the men to move it. Strive how they would to dislodge it—the door held. Then it began to yield by inches. But the surrender seemed painfully slow to all of them in their feverish impatience. However, although slow, it was nevertheless sure, and suddenly without imminent warning the door gave to the force of their onslaught. Thus it was that when the entrance was ultimately effected Terence Desmond had already gained access to the room through the French doors leading from the garden. Helen Ashley was conscious of his white startled face confronting her as she surged into the room at the rear of the men and contrary to the instruction given just before by Major Prendergast An instruction which she found it impossible to obey. On the carpet—just in front of the French doors—lay a woman's body—inert—lifeless.

"It's Hammond," exclaimed Helen—"one of the kitchen-maids—whatever's the matter with her? What is she doing in here?"

Doctor Carrington strode quickly and noiselessly towards the girl's body and went down on both knees to make his preliminary examination. The crowd of guests stood round them in an expectant semi-circle—each one reflecting horror and dread in his or her watching eyes. Then Carrington made an announcement that seemed to surprise them all. "She's only fainted," he said, curtly—"smelling-salts—anybody? And will somebody bring me a glass of cold water?"

Diana Prendergast, hovering on the fringe of the crowd at the back, heard the request and quickly satisfied it. Within, a few moments—under the doctor's professional attention—the colour came slowly back to the cheeks of the prostrate girl. Then she opened her eyes—dilated with the terror of her last conscious experience, whatever it chanced to have been.

"Come, my girl," said Carrington—"what's all this about? Pull yourself together and tell us." As he spoke he assisted the still-trembling girl to her feet and subsequently into a chair. A shudder came from her body and she looked fearfully round the room, her eyes wide open and terror-stricken.

"That hand!" she exclaimed. "That icy hand!" She shuddered again. "I shall never forget it. It was awful!" She turned and clung to Doctor Carrington's arm. "Don't let it touch me again, sir," she entreated, "I can't bear it."

"That's all right, my girl," he intervened—"that's all right. Calm yourself and collect yourself. Let's hear what's upset you. The sooner you tell us what it was that frightened you—the quicker, in all probability—we shall be able to help you. Now then—what's it all about?" He looked at her with very close scrutiny.

"I'll tell you," replied Hammond, recovering herself a little, "I was coming up the garden—"

Interruption came immediately. "What were you doing in the garden at this time of night, Hammond?" Helen Ashley's question cut into the tense atmosphere of the room with imperious insistence, and everybody realized that she had put into words the question that had been in everybody's mind.

"I had been to the Kennels, Miss Helen." Hammond looked calmly at her interrogator. "Boris—the wolfhound—hasn't been too well. He's been on special diet for three days. Owing to something or other—Stevens couldn't feed him at his proper time—so to-night, during the evening, he asked me to see to him. I forgot it for a time, but remembered it just now."

"Go on," said Helen Ashley.

"As I came up the garden path—I was surprised to see that the French doors of this room were wide open. The moon was shining beautifully and I could see the open doors quite plainly. It was almost like daylight. I thought it very strange, so I came up to them—just in order to look and see that everything was all right—as you might say. It was quite dark in the room—the electric light was not turned on—so I stood just inside the doors—listening. Suddenly, I thought I heard a peculiar rustling noise—coming from that direction." She pointed to the left-hand corner of the room. A heavy *portière*, suspended from a thick brass rod, marked the entrance to another apartment. All eyes were instinctively turned to it as Hammond told her story. She continued. "I peered into the patch of darkness—it was very dark in the corner there—although I was strongly tempted to take to my heels and run. All of a sudden—a horrible figure dashed out on to me—carrying something shining in its hand. I think it must have been a huge knife. It seemed to flash in the darkness. An icy hand and icy fingers were pressed against my face. Then I screamed."

"Yes—we heard you," said Doctor Carrington grimly—"you certainly did scream all right."

"But who was it, Hammond? Have you any idea?" questioned Desmond, coming to the point.

She shook her head blankly.

"Was it anybody you knew at all?" demanded Morris Trentham, with just a hint of aggressiveness.

"I didn't recognize the figure at all," repeated Hammond, vaguely—"there wasn't time enough—I could only see one thing about it."

"What's that?" queried Major Prendergast, eagerly, "any little point is sure to help us in a matter of this kind. What was the point you noticed?"

"It was a *woman*," replied Hammond.

"What makes you think that?" asked Desmond again.

"I don't think—I know," answered the girl. "I know," she repeated—"because as she dashed past me—in the darkness—I felt her frock or her skirt."

As she spoke the various clocks of house, home, church and building—non-coincident—seconds behind each other and seconds in front—struck twelve. Midnight!

Chapter III
THE TERROR CONTINUES

"Come over here, gentlemen, will you, please?" asked Helen Ashley, very quietly. She was standing by her uncle's table—her face bearing a very strained expression and white as death. The others hurried across to her—Doctor Carrington leading the way. "Look," she said, in a curiously unemotional voice—"look! What is that little patch there on the blotting-pad?" She pointed to the white expanse of blotting-pad that lay on Sir Eustace Vernon's writing-table. All eyes followed her gesture, and from Father Jewell there came a quick and startled exclamation. On the white blotting-paper at which they gazed there had spread a tiny dark red patch. Its shade of colour was not the tint of red ink. That fact was plain to everybody. The terror that it told seemed to lay a cold hand round the hearts of all.

"Looks like blood, certainly," contributed Doctor Carrington. "Be calm, Miss Ashley! You mustn't jump to conclusions, you know. Even now, everything may be all right. Don't immediately imagine the worst has happened—just because of this." He threw a sharp glance in Helen Ashley's direction as though not quite sure of her.

"My uncle," she murmured, "my uncle. I'm frightened."

The cold December air penetrated through the open doors, intensifying the chill of this last discovery. It was strange to see the varying effects that had been produced upon the faces of the different members of the party. Major Prendergast and his wife were attempting to encase themselves within what can be best termed, an aristocratic aloofness—they seemed to be desirous of showing these other people who were with them as sharers in and partakers of the same experience that the word

Fear was not to be found within their vocabulary. Alfred and Emily Venables—plebeian and purse-proud—were at no pains to conceal the extent of their agitation. Mrs. Venables' false teeth chattered audibly, and if the occasion had not held such a fierce hint of dark and dreadful tragedy—Terence Desmond felt that he would have burst into riotous laughter. Laughter which would have been amply justified. "When her tongue doesn't chatter—her teeth do," he thought, grimly, to himself. But at the moment his own face was white with strain and anxiety—and it was easy for an intelligent observer to see that the worry and foreboding were more for the sake of Helen Ashley than for anybody else. Continually his eyes travelled towards her—wistfully anxious. She, however, seemed to have surrendered herself with infinite resignation, to something that she regarded in the light of a Stronger Force—a Higher Power. It had entered her life quite suddenly and for the moment had paralyzed her into a condition of peculiar inactivity. It would pass—she knew—but the time for the passing was not yet. She would have to suffer before that time came.

Father Jewell stood at Doctor Carrington's side—austere in his thin-lipped asceticism—his black cassock adding a touch of the "macabre" to the proceedings. The lines of his face, rigid and severe, betrayed no sign of his present emotions, but in his deep-set—almost sunken eyes—there lurked a brooding watchfulness. They held a fire that at any time might leap into being. The two Trenthams held their place upon the fringe of the onlookers. The self-complacent pomposity of Morris Trentham had undoubtedly undergone some disturbance—a fact that his fat, and line-creased face unmistakably showed. Ruby's eyes were widely distended, and had the French system of "Heart-beat Registration" been brought into operation at that particular moment, the machine—in her case—would have told an alarming tale. Doctor Carrington himself seemed to be fighting to save the doctor from becoming submerged by the man. Terence—watching him carefully—was amazed to see the muscles of his face and jaw set with an almost iron-like sternness. Major Prendergast lit a cigar to steady his nerves and smoked silently. Carrington turned again to Hammond, who by this time had recovered her equanimity and self-possession, with such a degree of success that she now appeared to be the coolest and calmest of the entire gathering.

"You are quite sure that only *one* person came out of the room when you entered it?"

Hammond nodded confidently. "As far as one *can* be sure, sir, in the dark as I was. Pitch-dark it was, too, in that corner." Once again she pointed to the heavy *portière* that she had indicated previously.

"What do you say, Doctor Carrington"—exclaimed Major Prendergast—"shall we investigate? Don't you think it's our duty?" He nodded in the direction of Hammond's finger.

"I think so. I think we owe it to Miss Ashley—I am right, I think, Miss Ashley, in assuming that the *portière* there marks the entrance to your uncle's library? That is so, is it not?" Helen assented mutely. "You have no objection to the Major and me?"—he raised his eyebrows in interrogation.

"None whatever, Doctor," came her quiet reply. "I realize that it is very necessary. If you don't mind, though, I'll remain here until—"

"Certainly, Miss Ashley. I understand your desire perfectly."

He motioned with his eyes to Terence Desmond to stand by the girl in case of need—because he feared what the next few minutes might bring forth. Desmond required no second bidding, and before the Doctor and the Major could enter the inner apartment he had ranged himself by her side. Major Prendergast pulled the *portière* along the rod and the two men entered. For a moment, after they passed through, there was an ominous silence. Then the Doctor's face appeared again round the corner of the heavy curtain.

"Do you mind coming in here a moment, Miss Ashley?" he inquired. She scanned his face with anxious inquisitiveness— seeking to read there what it was he wanted her to see and know before she obeyed his request. He observed what she did. "It's quite all right," he affirmed, reassuringly—"there's nothing at all of which you need be frightened. I want you to help us over something—that's all."

Helen crossed over to him quietly, but swiftly. She passed into the library behind him. The others, with the exception of Desmond, crowded over towards the hanging *portière*.

"Look here, Miss Ashley," said Doctor Carrington—"what does this mean?" The door of a small safe in the wall stood wide open, the key—one of many on a key-ring—in the lock. "You knew of the existence of this safe in the wall here, of course?" inquired the Major.

"Of course, Major Prendergast I have been to it many times."

All the drawers inside the safe were fastened—locked.

"Can you say, by looking at it as it is, if anything has been taken, Miss Ashley?"

Helen shook her head—doubtfully. "I don't know what my uncle kept in here under lock and key," she declared. "I haven't the least idea—but on the face of it—nothing appears to have been touched. As far as I can tell—that is—of course." She shook her head again, more doubtfully. "But where is uncle?" she murmured—"he would tell you—everything looks all in order to me."

Major Prendergast pulled at the handles of the drawers that had been fitted within the safe. They were all secure. "Strange—the safe-door left swinging open like this," he muttered—"the key left in the lock too—looks as though somebody had been here but had been suddenly surprised and hadn't had time to complete what they wanted to. Don't you agree with me, Doctor?"

Doctor Carrington gestured an acquiescence. "Certainly looks like it," he declared. Then he—in turn—shook his head dubiously and almost forebodingly. "But I can't make head or tail of it! Who was it in here that caused Hammond's fright? What was she doing here? And where is our host?"

A sharp exclamation from Terence Desmond still in the room which the Doctor had just vacated arrested his attention.

"Doctor! Major Prendergast! Come back here, quickly, will you, please?"

The agitation clearly apparent in his voice was more than enough to bring the two men immediately to his side. In his hand there fluttered a sheet of white note-paper. "Read this!" He pushed it into Doctor Carrington's outstretched hand and went quickly across to Helen. He braced his shoulders as he took up his position by her. What was coming was about to test her fortitude more than anything that had yet transpired, and Desmond knew it. "I found that down there on the carpet—curled against the base of the table-leg." He put his right arm round the girl's waist with a movement of protection. The others saw the Major peer over the Doctor's shoulder in an abortive attempt to read the message on the writing-paper. For a brief moment there was a tense silence—unbroken save for the breathing of the knot of people in the room.

"What is it?" cried Trentham, sharply. "For goodness sake, Doctor, don't stand there like that—put us out of our suspense, if you can't do anything else."

"It is bad news, Miss Ashley—do you think you—"

Helen intervened with nervous abruptness. "I would much rather know, Doctor Carrington. Anything is less intolerable than this suspense. What does it say?"

"I can't understand what's happened at all. I can't make anything fit properly. On the face of things this letter seems absurd—incredible. Especially to those of us who knew Sir Eustace—intimately. But I'll read it to you." The message that had caused him so much misgiving was not a long one. He read it out to them as they huddled together as people do under the numbing instinct of a gregarious fear.

"Vernon House,
"Rodding,
"Xmas Night.

"My dear Helen and all dear friends!

"Something has come into my life to-night—quite unexpectedly—that I find it impossible to face. I am therefore taking what is, perhaps, 'the coward's way out.'

That question, however, is a matter of opinion. Anyway, I am taking a path that should be quick to lead me to a painless end.

"Good-bye, everybody—and a Happy New Year to all.
"EUSTACE VERNON."

Again, for a moment, no sound broke the silence.

Then Helen Ashley, freeing herself temporarily from the restraining and supporting grasp of Desmond, held out her hand to Doctor Carrington and spoke in a low tense voice.

"May I see the letter—please?"

The doctor handed it to her—at the same time watching her face intently. She examined it carefully, as though clinging to a last strand of hope. Then she shook her head slowly. For that last strand of hope had snapped and failed her. "It's my uncle's handwriting," she admitted. "I thought perhaps—"

Venables came to her side and looked at the letter.

"No doubt of that, Miss Ashley," he supplemented—"I've seen it far too many times not to know it."

Father Jewell broke in impatiently. "If Sir Eustace Vernon has laid violent hands upon himself"—he put his hands to his breast with a curious gesture that seemed to betoken reverence—"and it is reasonable to suppose that he has from the evidence upon the blotting-pad—where's his body?"

"Just what I've been thinking," said the Major.

Desmond intervened excitedly. "Fools that we are to stand arguing in this fashion! He may have failed in his attempt and even now be lying wounded somewhere near at hand."

Prendergast turned quickly to his wife. "Diana! Take charge of the ladies—please. Get them back into one of the other rooms—we men must get to work outside. Poor Vernon may be anywhere in the grounds and needing our help badly. Desmond is undoubtedly right."

Diana Prendergast put her right arm round Helen and motioned to Ruby Trentham and Mrs., Venables. "Come, Helen dear," she said, sympathetically. "Come with us—perhaps the men will find something and everything will be all right after all—come on, dear. You must try hard not to worry."

"Thank you, Mrs. Prendergast. It is most kind of you, I know—but I shan't break down if that's what you mean. Don't be afraid of that. I've too much to think about for that to happen."

"Would you like me to get you anything, Miss?" inquired Hammond, solicitously.

Before Helen could find time to reply—Terence Desmond broke in upon them with another interruption. "We'll get a search-party out then, at once. You take command, will you, Major? Hammond—get Stevens—the chauffeur—to let us have half a dozen of the lanterns that used to be kept down in the old stables—will you? Anybody got a flash-lamp handy?"

"I have," returned Major Prendergast in prompt support—"I always carry one at this time of the year in this part of the country. In fact, I should be lost without it. When the lanterns come—let each man get about a dozen paces from his neighbour and advance in as nearly a straight line as possible. If anybody finds anything—" His words stopped short for, for the second time that night, a piercing scream of horror rang through the stillness of Vernon House. This time it seemed to come from a greater distance off than had the scream of Hammond.

"Good God!" said Prendergast—unconsciously echoing Morris Trentham's words that followed the hearing of the first scream—"whatever's doing tonight?"

Some of the others looked paralyzed with fear. Their recent experience had served to unnerve them thoroughly.

"A Merry Christmas," muttered Alderman Venables, with grim irony in his tone, but Helen, unheeding him, caught Desmond impetuously by the sleeve.

"That came from the servants' quarters, Terry," she said, excitedly. "I expect somebody has found poor Uncle Eustace." Her hands worked nervously at her throat.

"Very likely, Miss Ashley," said Doctor Carrington, with more zeal than discretion—"I had better get down there at once. It's possible that I may be wanted. There may be just a chance—"

"This way, Doctor," said Desmond, decisively—"follow me."

Carrington and Desmond dashed off—Major Prendergast and Father Jewell close upon their heels. Morris Trentham turned to Alderman Venables. "You stay here with the ladies, Venables. It isn't safe for anybody to be alone to-night in this infernal place it seems to me—no matter in what room you may chance to be. You stay with the girls. Somebody should be with them. I'll cut along after the others."

Carrington and Desmond—holding the lead with which they had started—did not have very far to go before they received news that could not be disregarded. Round the corner of the long passage that wended its way to the servants' quarters they almost collided with a girl—running and breathless. White-lipped—white-faced and with fear showing in her eyes! It was another of the maids, and there was no mistaking the extent of her fright. Desmond knew her. It was the maid who had dropped the tray during dinner to occasion Sir Eustace Vernon so much agitation. Also he remembered her from his previous visits to Vernon House. It was Palmer—he recalled her name at the very instant that he stopped her in her tracks.

"Was that you who screamed, Palmer?" he asked peremptorily.

The girl stopped, and swayed towards the two men as though about to fall.

"Hold up!" said Carrington—"hold up! What's amiss, my girl? What's frightened *you*?"

Palmer clenched her two hands and stabbed unsteadily with her fingers in the direction of what Desmond knew was the butler's pantry.

"Purvis!" she exclaimed. "In there—go at once, please!"

The four men needed no further bidding. The door was open. Seated in a chair by the small table was Purvis. His face was livid and bloated. Carrington lost no time. He shook the limp body by the shoulders. There seemed to be complete muscular relaxation. Carrington pushed his thumbs under the eyelids and examined the pupils of the eyes, which were strange-looking and very much contracted. He felt the pulse—put his ear to the heart—and then felt the face, neck and arms. They were all alike—stone cold. Carrington looked up at his companions and shook his head.

"Quite dead," he said. "Poisoned!"

"How?" snapped Prendergast. The excitement and tension of the last few hours had worn his nerves and his manners to shreds.

"Chloral, I fancy," replied the Doctor—"I'll tell you for certain, later. But the symptoms—the muscular relaxation and the strange condition of the eyes—point to poisoning from Chloral Hydrate." His eyes wandered to the table and the eyes of the other men followed him to see immediately what was attracting his attention. On the table stood a glass—empty—of the type known in the trade as "a pony." Carrington picked it up and held it to his nose. He sniffed round the rim. "Whisky—I think. Chloral Hydrate crystals are peculiarly pungent, both to smell and taste. Neat whisky may well have been used to disguise them. Extraordinary business—don't you think, gentlemen? All of it! It means communicating with the police now—there's no help for it I'm afraid."

"What do you think, Doctor?" said Father Jewell, reverently crossing himself as he gazed at the dead body of Purvis, "is it suicide?"

"Quite probable, Father, I should say. There is no reason to suspect anything else—as far as I can see. But the police had better see him just as he is. Desmond, 'phone to Mapleton, will you? Tell Inspector Craig that Doctor Carrington wants him immediately at Vernon House—tell him a case of a sudden death requires investigation as the attendant circumstances are somewhat peculiar. We others had better get back to that business of Sir Eustace. Don't tell him—Craig, I mean—anything about Sir Eustace yet—let that wait until he arrives here. It will be easier to explain then—perhaps we shall know more. It's all most disturbing. One doesn't know what to do for the best. But there's one thing, we must certainly go to see if we can find poor Vernon—just as we intended before we struck this last ghastly business. Come, Major!"

Terence Desmond nodded his agreement with Doctor Carrington, and then gave a sharp exclamation. "What's that?"

he cried. He pointed to the inside pocket of the butler's dress-coat. Something red showed—just protruding from the depth of the pocket. Father Jewell bent down, and following the direction of Desmond's indicating finger inserted his fingers into the pocket and drew out the red object that Desmond had noticed. It was a bonbon.

"Curious," declared the Major—"strange thing to carry in one's pocket."

But the Roman Catholic priest was curiously examining one end of the red bonbon. The others watched him fascinatedly. From the crinkled end in question he pulled out a piece of ordinary note-paper. He unfolded it. On it were a few written words. The men bent over Father Jewell's stooping shoulder, eager to see what the words were. They were as follows—"One hour to live: *You pay your debt—to-night!!*" Father Jewell looked fearfully at the four other men. "This is not suicide, gentlemen, as Doctor Carrington supposed. This is murder! Cold-blooded murder! The sooner we get the police here and find Sir Eustace Vernon, the better!" His dark eyes blazed with the vehemence of his words, but Desmond felt a shiver run through his frame.

Chapter IV
SHOCK FOLLOWS SHOCK

"Father Jewell is undoubtedly right," said the Major. "There's no getting away from it. Desmond—get on to Mapleton Police Station at once, and ask for Inspector Craig, as I told you. The rest of us must try to find Vernon—don't you agree, Carrington?"

"Yes. You get along as you suggest. In the circumstances—taking this new discovery into account—I'll stay here with the body until Craig turns up. It will be better for me to do so—officially—you know." Desmond gave a quick nod of assent and dashed off to the telephone. "I'll be with you again, Major," he cried, "in two minutes. If the lanterns are handy, get one ready for me and wait for me to come back to you. Two minutes on the 'phone should be ample. Don't start off without me."

"Very well," called Prendergast, sharply—"we'll leave the Doctor here as he suggests and wait for you by the study windows."

"I don't like the look of things at all, Major," put in Trentham, as the three men made their way back. He glanced nervously behind him. "I'm shivering—and not with cold either. When I think of the body of the butler there, and that room of Vernon's—empty—the safe open—the French doors open—the stain on that blotting-paper and the screams of those two girls—it makes my blood run cold. If I'd known what I know now I'd never have—"

Major Prendergast cut short his flow of recrimination. "Pull yourself together, Trentham. It's a nasty experience for each one of us. For goodness sake remember that it's up to us to find Vernon. 'Shivering' won't find him. It's a question of action now."

The ladies were still huddled together in the study under the somewhat doubtful protection of Venables. Stevens, the chauffeur, was waiting with the lanterns ready for use. Desmond was quick to rejoin the party. He looked inquiringly at Major Prendergast, who was alert to comprehend his meaning.

"Purvis has had some sort of a seizure," he announced. "Doctor Carrington has seen him and is stopping with him for a time while we concentrate upon finding Sir Eustace. Diana! Take all the ladies back to the lounge, will you—please? As soon as we have really definite news, Miss Ashley, we will return to you." Helen inclined her head in silent understanding. "Come, gentlemen! You come as well, Stevens, will you? You may have the chance of being useful."

Slowly and steadily the search-party made their way into the grounds of Vernon House. "Shout, at once, if you come across anything," cried Prendergast, leading the way.

Terence Desmond was immediately conscious of a feeling of complete unreality. It seemed to him that but a few moments had elapsed since dinner, and he felt that he had suddenly stepped out of a real and tangible existence into the grotesque cast of a kind of gigantic pantomime. At the same time his senses were acutely alert and keyed up to the highest pitch, and as he flashed his lantern on the ground in front of him and all around him, he was determined to miss nothing that might tend to aid them in their quest. The moon was up and helped considerably when it scudded from the clouds. All was quiet—the only sound to disturb his ears being the occasional footfalls of his fellow-searchers. He could see them working along in a slowly advancing line of light. The effect was ghostly in the extreme. But no shout of heralded discovery disturbed the clear stillness of the December night. "Must be morning now," he thought to himself, and calculated the time—"although one can't visualize 'morning' out of conditions like these." Keats' lines suddenly flashed through his mind. To his amazement he found himself quoting them aloud—

> "In a drear-nighted December
> Too happy, happy Tree,
> Thy Branches ne'er remember,
> Their Green Felicity."

Midway about the second verse, he stopped. Something just to his right had attracted his attention. His swinging lantern had picked out a dark object lying on the rimed grass in front of him. He bent down to pick it up. To his surprise his hand held a slab of what is usually termed "hard" tobacco. He slipped it into the pocket of his dress-trousers, but finding its shape and hardness distinctly discomforting and interfering considerably with ease of movement, he transferred it to the breast pocket of his dress-coat. He soon reached the brick walls of the grounds, that ran along the Rodding road, and then turned to commence to work his way back six yards or so away from the track he had pursued previously. But to no purpose. There was no sign of Sir Eustace Vernon. Eventually the others joined him, one by one. They had very little to report. Only Trentham had anything of consequence to mention.

"The garage doors are not shut," he said. "Also, Sir Eustace Vernon's car is not in there. Mine is there and another car, that

I take to be the Mayor's—of course I'm not sure that it is. But Sir Eustace's car has gone."

"Sure of that?" queried Father Jewell.

Morris Trentham nodded. "Quite. I know Sir Eustace's car well. It's a 'Wolseley.'—Saloon-de-luxe. I've travelled with him in it many times."

"Perhaps Vernon's gone away in it somewhere. Perhaps to—" Prendergast stopped short, but each one of his companions silently completed the unfinished sentence with the thought that was uppermost in his mind. Then Desmond thought of his find, and at once an alternative theory was born in his brain.

"Perhaps somebody else has gone away in it," he contributed.

"What do you mean?" said Father Jewell. "Who could have—"

Desmond cut in. "I've an idea—just an idea—that's all," he submitted. "Stevens!" He called to the chauffeur.

"Yes, Mr. Desmond."

Terence pulled out the dark cake of tobacco and held it up for the chauffeur's observation. "Do you know anybody round here who smokes tobacco of this description?"

Stevens shook his head negatively.

"You don't smoke it yourself, by any chance?" continued Desmond.

"Not on your life, sir! 'Gaspers' for me, every time. I haven't seen a bit of 'hard' since the—that reminds me, though, sir—although I don't exactly know—" He broke off for a moment seemingly undecided and uncertain.

"What do you mean, Stevens? What is it you want to say?"

"Well, sir, Hammond, the maid, is keeping company with a sailor—I do know that. And sailors have rather a partiality for that kind of stuff. That's what I was thinking."

"Is that so, now? What's this chap's name, do you know?"

Stevens shook his head again. "There you've done me, sir. But he's a Mapleton man, I can tell you that—he's home on 'leaf' now, sir. I could find—"

"What have you there, Desmond?" interrupted Major Prendergast.

Desmond passed his find over for inspection. "I found it on the grass over there—about thirty yards, I should say, from here. I should think it had been dropped fairly recently. It was comparatively dry, despite the state of the grass."

"Extraordinary," commented Prendergast—"hang on to it. You never know. Suppose we go in to see if the police are here yet. They should be. What do you say?"

Father Jewell assented somewhat eagerly. "I don't think we can accomplish much good out here." The others agreed.

Helen Ashley came to meet them as they passed through the doors of the study. Desmond shook his head in denial in reply to her unspoken question. "There's no need for you to worry about the worst—yet," he supplemented. "There's absolutely no trace of anything wrong out there in the grounds," he continued—"all we can think of is that your uncle may have rushed off somewhere by car."

"Why?" queried the girl.

"His car isn't in the garage—so Trentham says—and the doors of the garage have been left open—so we conclude that the bad news he mentioned at dinner may have necessitated a journey of some kind on the spur of the moment. Personally, I think there's no doubt about it, judging the facts as we found them," he added, rather unconvincingly.

Helen turned a troubled face towards him. "I can't think that Uncle Eustace would do anything like that. I can't believe such a thing for a moment—besides, there's that farewell message of his that we've found. How can you explain that away? Then there's this scare about Purvis." She stopped and scanned his face searchingly and critically. "Terence, you're not telling me the truth! Is Purvis dead? Tell me—I'm not a child to be fended off with fairytales. Tell me, Terence—please don't hold *any* of the truth back from me—it's vital with uncle missing that I should know all—is Purvis dead?"

Desmond looked helplessly at his companions—in the hope, apparently, that one of them would throw him a suggestion of help. But unavailingly—none came! He therefore assumed responsibility. He could see no way out.

"Purvis is dead," he said, very quietly and simply. "We left Doctor Carrington with him, and we have sent down to Mapleton for the police. We could do nothing else in the circumstances. We didn't tell you before because we didn't want the other ladies to be upset over it."

"I knew it," she said—"I felt certain of it."

"How?"

"I don't know—something seemed to tell me. I can't tell you what it was. Call it instinct, if you like—or say that I'm 'fey' to-night." She laughed hysterically, and the unaccustomed note that he detected in her voice caused him to look at her sharply and with genuine concern.

"Is the Inspector here yet?" he queried.

"He wasn't when I came away from the others just now—let's go back to see."

But Major Prendergast had forestalled her. As she turned to Desmond with the suggestion he came forward to speak to her.

"Inspector Craig from Mapleton has just this minute arrived," he announced. Then he stopped for a moment, uncertain as to what he ought to say, for he found the situation awkward, to say the least. She waited for him to proceed. "Shall I inform him about—or would you rather Desmond or you yourself—?"

"About my uncle? I think the best thing to be done will be to tell Inspector Craig everything quite frankly—all that we know—and all that we've done—in the exact chronological order in which it has occurred. It should be done as thoroughly and as carefully as possible. If you will be good enough to do so—it will be a kindness."

Prendergast nodded and looked inquiringly at all the others, only to receive similar signs of acquiescence.

The Inspector stood in the hall, having as his companion Doctor Tempest, the Divisional Surgeon. Each was heartily cursing the unkind Fate that had brought him out to a case of this nature on a Christmas night of all nights. Craig had been summoned from the bosom of his family and the warmth of his own fireside, and Doctor Tempest from a most attractive bridge-party at Colonel Ridout's—half-way between Mapleton and

Rodding. They stood waiting for a second or two—irresolutely—having been admitted by the very frightened maid—Palmer. The death of the butler, it will be observed, had seriously disorganized the *régime* of Vernon House.

"What was your 'phone message, Inspector—a suspected murder?"

Craig lowered his voice. "That's what is suspected, Doctor Tempest. The 'phone message was from a gentleman giving the name of Desmond. I didn't take it myself, as you know. He didn't say who it was they feared was murdered—simply would we send up at once? Leastways, that's how the message came to me."

The Divisional Surgeon was about to frame a reply when he caught sight of the four men approaching. "Here we are, Inspector," he said—"now we shall hear all about it."

Prendergast wasted no time. In as few words as possible he told the Inspector all that had transpired just in the manner that Helen Ashley had suggested he should do. Also he added an explanation. "Miss Ashley and the other ladies are in the lounge, Inspector. I am Major Prendergast. I am acting as Miss Ashley's spokesman at her own expressed request. I hope it will not be necessary for you to worry any of the ladies to-night. We have all been thoroughly alarmed, and for them it must have been excessively disturbing and trying."

"I understand. Unless I am absolutely forced I will not trouble them at all. Take me to Purvis. I presume from what you have told me that Doctor Carrington is still with the body?"

"That is so, Inspector."

"Right—we'll get along there then, at once."

For the second time since dinner they traversed the distance to the butler's pantry. Doctor Carrington was standing deep in thought just inside the door. When he saw the *personnel* of the approaching company, he pulled at his lip for a moment as though in doubt as to whether he should come to a decision. It was clear that something was worrying him. Seemingly he reached a satisfactory solution, for as his visitors entered he pulled-to the door silently and closed it behind them. Before Craig or Doctor Tempest could speak, Carrington took charge of the situation. He felt that he was compelled to do so—that he would be failing in his duty if he did not. He spoke very quietly, but very much to the point.

"Prior to you making your examination, Doctor Tempest, and also you, Inspector, I feel that I must give you some very important information. Startling as well as important. Information that I have discovered only very recently. And discovered too—professionally. This body here *is the body of a woman*!"

Chapter V
THE FINDING OF SIR EUSTACE

"What on earth do you mean?" gasped Desmond, complete incredulity showing in his eyes. "That can't possibly be—I've known Purvis for years."

"So have I," retorted Carrington coldly—"as long as you have, I expect. But that fact doesn't alter the case. You simply accepted appearances the same as I did. The person that both you and I and Sir Eustace Vernon and all the rest of the world knew as Purvis—was a woman. We've been deceived. That's all there is to it."

"Very strange," muttered Craig—"and coming on top of what Major Prendergast had just told me of all that's been happening here in Vernon House tonight, it makes it seem very remarkable to me. Still—" He paused for a moment—then thought of the Divisional Surgeon. "Have a look at the body, Doctor Tempest, will you?"

But Tempest's action had preceded the Inspector's words, and he was already bending over the huddled body of the butler. Carrington slipped quickly to his side and bending down spoke quietly in his ear. The others saw Tempest look up and then nod decisively. "That was what prompted me," they heard Carrington say, and then there followed more head-noddings and conferrings between the two men of medicine. Craig picked up the red bonbon from the table and carefully examined the menacing message that had been attached. "I wonder if anybody will be able to recognize the writing," he declared—"I'll keep this for further developments." He pushed the piece of paper into his pocket. "Well, Doctor, what's your verdict?" He addressed Tempest. The latter turned towards him very gravely.

"I entirely concur with Doctor Carrington. This woman has undoubtedly been poisoned. He thinks by Chloral Hydrate. I see no reason, at the moment, to disagree with him."

Craig frowned heavily. "It may be suicide, Doctor, after all," he suggested.

"Quite possibly," conceded the Divisional Surgeon—"but for the fact of the apparent threat in the red bonbon. We'll assume that the message was intended for the person on whom it was found. That certainly tends in the direction of murder—murder for revenge, I should say."

Craig frowned again. "I'm sorry then, Major Prendergast, Doctor Carrington and gentlemen, that I shall have to have a word with Miss Ashley—Sir Eustace Vernon's niece. She's the only person here, I understand, with the exception of the servants, that actually resides here. This sex-mystery surrounding the butler must be investigated. It's most mysterious and I can't tell to where it may lead. You're quite sure that there's no trace of Sir Eustace—there's no place where he may be that you may have overlooked?"

Prendergast gave a quick denial, and Desmond interjected rapidly. "Miss Ashley will not be able to tell you anything about Purvis, Inspector. I am absolutely certain of that. I'm an old friend of hers and I'm convinced that any thought that Purvis was other than he seemed to be—'she' seemed to be, if you prefer me to be more exact—has never crossed her mind. I'd wager my whole fortune on it—not a lot perhaps, but a great deal to me."

"I've no doubt you're right, Mr.—" he paused, seemingly not sure of Desmond's name.

"Desmond," replied the latter.

"Desmond! But if you'll pardon me saying so—your opinion is only 'conjecture.' This mystery about the butler seems to me the kind of mystery that people 'in the know' so to speak, would keep very quiet about. Just because the lady didn't tell you anything about Purvis, doesn't mean that—"

Desmond cut in again impatiently, and with more than a suggestion of frayed temper. "I am in Miss Ashley's confidence," he asserted—"that should be sufficient for you. Still, if you must see her—you must see her. Only for Heaven's sake treat her kindly, I imagine she's about 'through' by now." He turned on his heels and went across to Father Jewell.

"I know my business," returned Inspector Craig, shortly—"we will get back to the room to which I understand you were first called, and please inform Miss Ashley that I should like to ask her a few questions in there as soon as convenient to her. Perhaps you would be good enough to bring her along, would you, Mr. Desmond?" He went to the door and looked at the lock. "We'll lock this door," he declared, suiting the action to the word—"and I'll come back to this room later on. Now, gentlemen!" The others watched him as he placed the key in his pocket.

When Helen Ashley answered the message that had summoned her, ordinarily-observant onlookers might have been pardoned for thinking that Desmond's misgivings and solicitude upon her behalf were unfounded. Outwardly she appeared quite calm, but the truth was that she was vividly conscious of an agony of suspense that had caused a dull and dragging ache in her breast. The Inspector wasted no time over the broaching of his inquiries.

"I am Inspector Craig from Mapleton Police Station," he made his preliminary announcement somewhat more curtly than courteously—but in the excitement and anxiety of the moment, the fact passed almost unnoticed and certainly without comment. "I am sorry to trouble you, Miss Ashley," he continued, "but you will realize that in the absence of your uncle, Sir Eustace Vernon— an absence towards the facts of which I shall be compelled to return—I have no option but to ask a few questions of you." He looked at her—inviting, as it were, her approval and acquiescence. She gave him a slight inclination of the head. It seemed to disconcert him somewhat, but he accepted it and went straight on. "You are aware, I believe, that Purvis, your uncle's butler, has been found dead in the room that he usually occupied, known, I believe, as the butler's pantry. The two doctors here, Doctors Carrington and Tempest, are agreed that death is due to poisoning—but at the moment we don't know by whom or how it was administered." He paused and watched her again, but Helen made no sign from which he was able to construe any definite meaning. Therefore he proceeded. "But beyond that they have discovered another fact that—to say the least—is most extraordinary and er—perhaps—disconcerting. Purvis was a woman!" He shot the last piece of information at her with characteristic rapidity and suddenness. Helen's eyes parted in amazement, while from her lips there came a low gasp of astonishment. "A woman?" Craig nodded—emphatically. "You can take it from me—there's not a vestige of doubt about it—is there, Doctor?" He turned to Doctor Tempest for corroboration of his statement. It came—immediately.

"That is so, Miss Ashley. What Inspector Craig says is perfectly true. The butler you knew as a man—is really a woman."

Helen gazed from one to the other, her mind struggling against the flood of amazement that was threatening to engulf her better and clearer understanding. Eventually—after what seemed to the onlookers a protracted struggle—she surrendered to an urgent desire for help. This she translated into activity by turning towards Desmond and Father Jewell, who were standing together a few feet away from her. "Purvis—a woman," she repeated tonelessly—"I can't understand—"

"The news then is a complete surprise to you?" interrogated the Inspector.

Before Helen could reply, Desmond gave vent to a sharp exclamation of supreme annoyance. "Good God, Inspector," he cried—"it doesn't need a great deal of intelligence to see that! I told you so! Surely you don't—"

"Keep calm, Mr. Desmond—please. And let me point out that I am conducting this investigation and not you. When I want your assistance I'll ask for it. Miss Ashley?"

"The news you have just given me *astounds* me, Inspector. I am still trying hard to believe it. I can say no more than that."

"I see. Now as to this other matter, Miss Ashley. This letter that has been handed to me—I understand it was found in here—you have no doubt that your uncle wrote it?"

"As far as I can judge—none."

"Right! And this is the patch on the blotting-pad—eh, that Major Prendergast mentioned?" He walked across to it. At that moment the door opened to admit the Mayor of Mapleton—Alderman Venables. When he saw what was proceeding the unhealthy pallor of his face became more marked. Trentham held up to him an admonitory hand—the gesture enjoining silence. The worthy Alderman seemed only too pleased to be obedient. He tiptoed noiselessly round the room to the *portière* that had covered the entrance to the library. It had remained as the Major had pulled it upon his entrance. Prendergast watched Craig intently as he examined the small red stain.

"H'm!" he commented—"take charge of this, Doctor Tempest, will you, please?" He stopped and caressed his trim moustache. "The safe you mentioned, gentlemen—in here?" Prendergast nodded art affirmative to his inquiry and the Inspector, avoiding Venables adroitly, passed through into the library. Desmond and the Major followed him—the others remaining where they were.

"H'm," he muttered again—"nothing stolen—eh?"

"Miss Ashley thinks not, Inspector. Looks to me as though Sir Eustace—assuming that it was he who opened the safe—was suddenly disturbed by something and left the door open and the key of the safe in the lock."

"Possible—certainly," returned Craig.

"Probable, don't you think?" countered Desmond. Craig gave him a direct look—a look that might have meant much. "I've learned to distrust the probable, Mr. Desmond—I pay more regard to all that I consider 'possible.'"

A smile played round Desmond's lips as he turned away to follow the Inspector back to the others. "Wouldn't surprise me if he finishes up by arresting me," he muttered to himself—"silly consequential ass that he is."

Then the Inspector's voice cut across his soliloquy and brought it to a precipitate conclusion. "The grounds have been searched, you say? Carefully searched and not just glanced over?"

"That is so, Inspector," answered Prendergast. "We've had a search-party out—been over every inch of the place as carefully as we were able—without any sign of Sir Eustace. But as we told you just now—or rather as I told you—we have an idea that Sir Eustace's car has been removed from the garage."

"Has the chauffeur gone with it?"

"No—no. As a matter of fact he has been with us nearly all the time and actually formed one of our search-party."

"Where is he now?"

"Not far away, Inspector. I can get him for you if you want him." Prendergast made a movement towards the door to put his suggestion into effect, but Craig promptly checked him.

"Don't trouble, sir, for the time being. There's no immediate need for me to see him. It will do very well if I see him later. But it's a most curious business, as you'll all agree, gentlemen. Anyhow—I tell you what—I should like a word with these two maids that appear in the story—Miss Ashley. The two maids who gave the alarm in the two instances—what names were they—"

"Hammond and Palmer," replied Helen—"I'll ring for them to come in here at once."

As she crossed to carry out her avowed intention, there happened one of those strange coincidences that life so often furnishes for us. There was a sharp sound of running feet and the maid Palmer appeared in the doorway where the damaged door hung on its twisted hinges.

"Palmer!" said Helen, but that was all she had time to say, for Palmer herself had news that would not brook delay.

"Inspector Craig is wanted at once on the telephone in the hall, please, Miss," she blurted—"and I was asked to say as how it was most important. It's a proper 'Big Noise' the other end, too, judging by the way he gives 'is orders."

Craig received the information with some show of surprise.

"Stay here, Doctor, will you please?" he said. "I'll go and see who it is and what's doing. But what gets over me is who in the name of goodness can want me here."

While he was away Helen Ashley thought of the ladies left alone in the lounge. "I'm going back to the others, Terry," she said—"I don't know what they're thinking all this time. They must be worried almost beyond endurance. Come for me when you want me—or if the Inspector should happen to want me again."

She slipped away—Doctor Tempest's eyes watching her. Three minutes later Craig was back—graver and with more signs of responsibility than ever. His eyes searched the apartment for Helen.

"Miss Ashley has gone to the lounge," explained Desmond in interpretation of his look.

"It's as well," said Craig quietly. "I've just heard that Sir Eustace Vernon's body has been found on the railway line a few yards from Dyke's Crossing. He must have driven straight there from here and thrown himself under a passing train." For a moment he respected the awed silence that followed his announcement. "A bad business, gentlemen," he then continued—"but what puzzles me is the identity of my informant—it's no less a person than Sir Austin Kemble—the Commissioner of Police. How he comes into the picture beats me entirely. But it's evidently going to be a case for Scotland Yard." He watched the expression on their faces as he made his portentous announcement.

Chapter VI
MR. BATHURST TAKES A SHORT CUT

On the same evening as the events took place that have already been described, Sir Austin Kemble, Commissioner of Police, settled down luxuriously at the side of Mr. Anthony Bathurst and prepared himself with a sigh that might have betokened a measure of discomfiture and also a certain degree of contentment for the forty-five miles drive that would take them back to London.

"Great nuisance not being able to stay the night, Bathurst," he remarked, "and damned good of you to offer to bring me up. Very sporting—I must say. But I've business at the 'Yard' to-morrow that I cannot consider the possibility of neglecting or even delegating."

Mr. Bathurst grunted as his strong teeth bit on to the stem of his pipe, and with a clear road in front of him, immediately accelerated.

"One or two nasty cases at the moment, haven't you?" he interrogated.

Sir Austin frowned. He never liked to be reminded too directly of matters which worried him. At that particular time there were two professional anxieties that transcended all others. One was the strange murder of the boy chorister in Clerkenwell, who had been strangled as he walked home after Evensong on Advent Sunday, and the other a mysterious murder of a pastry-cook at Nunhead. In each instance the assailant appeared to have got away without leaving any tangible clue whatever, and in each case also the last person who had been seen in conversation with the victim had been a tall dark woman. Those at work on the two cases regarded this last fact as an important coincidence.

"A couple of very nasty ones," he replied, when the frown had relaxed somewhat.

"Clerkenwell and Nunhead?" queried Anthony.

"Yes. There's no doubt that somebody's pulling the wool over our eyes in each of them. I've been a good mind to call you in, Bathurst." His eyes flashed interrogation in Anthony's direction.

The latter smiled his unwillingness. "Too busy, sir. I should get sick of a surfeit of cases. One every now and then does me very well." He negotiated a sharp turn as efficiently as he did most things. "I'll take a cut across country here and cross the line lower down."

"Remember where we were just about a year ago, Bathurst?" proceeded Sir Austin.

"Very well, sir. As a matter of fact, the reminiscence flashed through my mind at dinner to-night. When our hostess laughed I was irresistibly reminded more than once of Lady Fullgarney."

His companion chuckled. "Your masterly conduct of the 'Peacock's Eye' case created sad havoc in that lady's heart, I fancy, my boy. Ah well. It's not to be wondered at. You've a way with you, Bathurst, you know! Seen anything of them since we were down there?"

"Saw them in June at Ascot. On the last day of the meeting, I fancy." He reflected for a minute and then continued. "Yes, it was. I ran into them just as the numbers went up for the Wokingham Stakes. And I saw them again somewhere about the end of July. At Lord's during the Rugby and Marlborough match. They had come up to town after Goodwood. Sir Matthew had a young nephew playing. A good boy, too—played a really good 'knock' on a most poisonous wicket. He played for the Lords' Schools against 'The Rest' on August Bank Holiday."

"A Fullgarney?"

"No, Sir Matthew's sister's boy, I believe—Conway Beresford, by name—hallo—what's this?" He pulled up abruptly—almost without warning.

"What's the trouble, Bathurst?" asked Sir Austin.

"Level-crossing, sir. And the gates are against us. There's another car waiting there, too." Bathurst had stopped his own car a few yards to the rear of the one that was waiting, and Sir Austin thrust out his head and looked out. Then he glanced at his watch.

"This is Dyke's Crossing, Bathurst. I know where we are. We're just about equidistant between Rodding and Mapleton. I remember coming down here over a 'poisoned-pen' affair, somewhere about five years ago—a country wench fancied herself as a censor of morals." The words had scarcely left his lips when the shriek of an engine heralded the passing of an express. The iron giant flashed by attended by a whirling company of dancing sparks. After what seemed an interminable wait, the gates of Dyke's Crossing swung open slowly but surely. They clicked together with that sound of undisguised relief that seems to be the unique property of the gates of level-crossings. Bathurst naturally waited for the car in front to cross. But as it never moved, he decided to start his own. As he crossed the two lines of rails he threw a remark to his companion—"What's that car doing there at this time of night—and Christmas night at that?"

Sir Austin flung a backward glance over his shoulder in the direction of the object mentioned. "Can't see anybody in it," he muttered—"queer—don't you think?" He pushed his head out again for the purpose of taking a closer look at their surroundings. As he did so a white shaft of shimmering moonlight, cold and clear, and straight from the White Lamp of the sky, flooded the track that they had just crossed and exposed it all with a merciless and relentless glare. Sir Austin gave a sharp, but smothered, exclamation. "Go straight over, Bathurst, will you—and pull up?" he said in a strange voice. "There's somebody there!"

"Where?"

"On the line there. The body of a man in my opinion. The moon showed it up, for a second, as plainly as though it had been broad daylight. I could see it quite plainly."

Anthony looked grave. "Or what's left of a man—more probably—after what we saw go by a moment ago. Poor devil—if he tried to stop that lot." He drew the car up alongside the hedge that ran by the line. "See there's nothing coming, Sir Austin—never mind about the gates being shut—one's enough of that kind of thing."

Without replying Sir Austin broke through the hedge on to the line and made straight for the spot where his eyes had been able to pick out the shapeless mass that the moonlight had thrown up. Bathurst was quick to follow him. Some twenty yards from the level-crossing lay the body of a man clad in evening-dress. It was badly mutilated, especially about the legs. The right leg had been completely severed from the body—the other leg seemed to be just a mass of bleeding pulp. Strangely though, terrific as had been the impact, the face had scarcely been touched, and in the middle of the track lay a pair of pince-nez, by a miracle of Fate completely undamaged. The face was the face of a middle-aged man, bald, but with a grey moustache. It was a face of fine lines, sensitive and refined, suggestive altogether that its owner was a man of artistic susceptibility. He was in dress-clothes, black dinner-jacket, black bow and black braided trousers. The shoe on the foot of the leg that had been mutilated so badly hung in black shreds, but on the foot of the severed limb the other shoe was in excellent condition. Sir Austin Kemble had great difficulty in the repression of a shiver of horror.

"What a mess of a man," he muttered—"what is it, Bathurst—suicide?"

"Looks like it, Sir Austin—on the face of things. He must have stopped the car down there purposely. Got out and then deliberately come on to the line and waited for the train. Or perhaps a previous one, unless—" He stopped—lost for a moment in a temporary cogitation.

"Unless what?" broke in Sir Austin, with a touch of his habitual impatience.

"Unless he had an assignation with somebody and she hadn't kept the appointment."

"Over-old for a lover, Bathurst. More likely to have been waiting for another man—admitting—that is—your assignation theory."

Anthony laughed with tolerant cynicism. "Some men are never too old for sexual adventure, sir. It's their one link with life. They remain caught in the toils of the 'Life-Force.' At least, that's how they explain it."

"What shall we do with him?" questioned Sir Austin, ignoring a strong temptation to argument, "it seems inhuman to leave the poor fellow here." Anthony nodded and looked round. "Let's lay him in the shadow of the hedge, yonder. We can move him easily. On our way through Mapleton, we can stop at the police station and inform them there of what's happened. They can send an ambulance up here."

"Can't do better, Bathurst. I'm afraid it's going to be a horrible business, though—moving him. Get hold of his shoulders, will you?"

Anthony stooped down and did as he had been directed. Together they dragged the mutilated, lifeless body over the down-line track and reverently laid it in the shadow of the friendly hedge by the side of the line.

"Curse this ghastly moonlight," railed the Commissioner—"it seems indecent somehow in the circumstances. Do you get what I mean, Bathurst? Darkness would have seemed so much more friendly and comforting. Eh?"

Bathurst seemed not to hear—at any rate, Sir Austin was not favoured with a reply. His companion was examining the right hand of the dead man. Suddenly his eyes took on an even more acute appearance, and he dropped on one knee beside the body. Sir Austin regarded him with some measure of amazement. Surely Bathurst had not discerned signs of feeble life still flickering in this bruised and battered body? Sir Austin need have had no doubts. The man was dead—there was no doubt about that fact—but Bathurst's quick and observant eyes had detected something protruding from the inside pocket of the dead man's dinner-jacket. He thrust in his hand and pulled out a red something that Sir Austin, for the moment—peer as he did—was unable to recognize. Bathurst rose to his feet and held it out for inspection—a curious expression on his face.

"Good gracious!" cried Sir Austin—"a bonbon! Strange thing to carry in your pocket! I don't know, though, Bathurst," he retracted, "he may have driven straight from a Christmas party of some kind. It's a seasonable thing. That's the explanation, my boy! Simple enough, after all!"

Bathurst looked at him with a mixture of curiosity and doubt. Then he shook his head slowly and with an infinite wealth of meaning. "There's more in it than that, I'm afraid, sir. And I'm inclined to think there's a good deal more in it than we thought in the first place. Look at this piece of paper here."

From one end of the red bonbon protruded a piece of paper—a small strip of ordinary note-paper, such as can be purchased in any news-agent's or stationer's shop, at a few pence for a number of sheets. On it were two lines of writing. Sir Austin held it so that the moonlight played upon it and made the words easily legible. Then he frowned as the startling nature of the written words came fully home to him. *"One hour to live—you pay your debt to-night."* He handed the paper back.

"Damn it all, Bathurst. We've stumbled into something this time, and no mistake! This is murder, man! Murder! As sure as my name that's what it is! Don't you think so? That body's been found by the wrong men." His eyes gleamed, and Bathurst was able at that moment to separate the man from the Commissioner and to realize that he was in the presence of a real and supreme passion for Justice. He did not reply for a brief period. Then as usual his thoughts flew to the possibility of immediate action.

"Before we run into Mapleton, sir, I'd like to go and have a look at that car. There will never be a better time than now, and this poor chap's past all earthly help. By the way—how far away is that signal-box? How far would you say?"

"From where?"

"From where the body was when you first saw it."

Sir Austin Kemble made a mental calculation of the distance. "Twenty-five to thirty yards," he answered eventually.

"Not far out," replied Bathurst laconically—"a trifle under that I should say, rather than over. Twenty-five yards we'll say, then, at the outside."

He waited for Sir Austin to get into their car again and then drove slowly back over the railway line to where the other car stood—lights still burning—just as when they had passed it a bare ten minutes previously. Mr. Bathurst rubbed his hands.

"I think I'm going to enjoy this little problem, Sir Austin. Two little matters puzzle me already."

Had he been taxed, Sir Austin Kemble would have pleaded guilty to a higher number than that.

Chapter VII
A SHOT FROM BEHIND

Anthony stopped his Crossley on the other side of the railway line. The two men alighted and found themselves by the side of the car that had apparently been abandoned.

"There's a rare lot of this stolen car business going on lately, Bathurst . . . it's a problem that engages far too much of our time at the 'Yard.'" Sir Austin was becoming angry again. "When our best men should be at work on cases that have proved extremely difficult, their energies are dissipated more often than not on these miserable stolen car episodes. Waste of valuable time, I call it."

Without replying, Anthony opened the door of the car in question and peered in. Sir Austin took from his pocket the flashlight torch without which in the winter he seldom travelled.

"Good," said Anthony. "Just what I wanted." His eyes followed the circle of light that his companion turned upon the interior of the car.

"Nothing much in here, Bathurst," grunted Sir Austin—"not a sign of any luggage, rugs—wearing apparel—or anything. No suitcases *here*. You'll have a ticklish job reading anything out of this."

"Looks very much like it," replied Anthony laconically—"shine your torch on the floor, will you, please—on the left of the steering-wheel—thanks."

He stooped down quickly and ran the fingers of his left hand lightly over the surface of the floor.

"Now on the other seats at the back, will you, Sir Austin—ah—what's this?" He pointed eagerly to the back seats of the car. On the light fawn, luxurious upholstery, there could be seen a red stain. In this empty, abandoned car—found under such bizarre circumstances late on a Christmas night—with a dead man lying under a hedge less than a hundred yards away—the stain looked ominous and trebly suggestive. Mr. Bathurst whipped out his magnifying-glass. "Shine the light directly on it, will you, Sir Austin, please?" He scrutinized the crimson smudge with as great a care as possible in the circumstances. "Blood—in my opinion," he muttered. Then his hands swooped to the floor again, directly under the tell-tale stain. They occupied themselves there for a moment or two. Sir Austin saw him shake his head impatiently, jerk it up as impetuously and set his brows in a decided frown. Then the head assumed a challenging tilt. "The light again, sir," he called. "At the other end of the seat here—right at the end."

The Commissioner did as directed, and Mr. Bathurst began to rub his hands again. His keen grey eyes had caught sight of two small patches of fawn that were distinctly dirtier and darker than the upholstery generally. This particular light-putty shade of fawn was such that it quickly showed any trace of dirt and dust.

"What have you got, Bathurst?" interposed Sir Austin, with some eagerness.

"Something I was looking for, sir. Some dust on the seat." He swung out of the car and took his place again by his companion's side. "Extraordinary, Sir Austin, you know, when you come to think of it. An abandoned car—its owner—or driver, at least, we'll say—cut to pieces on the line—and traces of blood *inside* the car. Why blood *inside* the car? Appears somewhat contradictory, doesn't it?"

"It's murder, Bathurst," returned Sir Austin, with an air of judicial finality—"that's what it is—murder."

"There's not a doubt about it, sir. But I wonder if it's a murder exactly as that grotesque red bonbon is intended to—" He broke off—thinking hard for a moment. "I shall have to have another look at that body, Sir Austin," he ventured at length—"this makes a big difference. A vast difference. I rather think we shall discover something very startling—if I'm not making a big mistake." He stopped again, and Sir Austin could see that some point or the other was troubling him considerably. Suddenly his face became animated again. "Lend me the torch a minute, sir. There's one other little thing I want to do." He flashed the light on the two receptacles within the car that held the burnt cigar and cigarette ends. He picked out three burnt cigarette stubs and one cigar end and examined them very minutely. Then he laughed and replaced them. "Just an idea that flitted across my mind—that was all. Not conclusive, by any means—but it was just on the cards that it might have told me something of the utmost importance."

Sir Austin grunted unintelligibly. "What now, Bathurst?"

"I don't think we can do better than to get along into Mapleton as I suggested just now and call at the police station. It doesn't seem to me that we can do any more up here now. I'll leave my second look at the body until later. What do you think yourself, sir?"

His companion reflected for a moment or two. "On the whole I agree with you, Bathurst. But I'll tell you what does occur to me—and very forcibly, too."

"What's that?"

"Will it be wise on our part to leave this car here? Supposing for instance—"

"Supposing what?" Anthony cut in, unceremoniously.

"Supposing it's gone when we return? Seems to me to be quite a likely contingency. Supposing the people concerned come back for it? Will you stay on guard here if I drive your car down into Mapleton? What do you think?"

Anthony rubbed his cheek with the palm of his hand while he gave consideration to the Commissioner's suggestion. Then he shook his head in repudiation of the idea. "I don't think we need trouble to do that. I appreciate your point, sir, but I don't imagine there's the slightest reason to anticipate that any of the people responsible for this business will return to this particular spot to-night. I think it's the very last thing they would think of doing. No, Sir Austin—it will be quite safe to leave matters here as they are—take it from me."

Sir Austin shrugged his shoulders as though only half convinced. But he gave way. "Very well. I'm quite content to rely on your judgment, as you're very well aware, Bathurst. We'll get on to Mapleton, then."

A matter of ten minutes' fast driving brought them to the police station of Mapleton, where Sir Austin's unexpected arrival caused much fluttering among the dove-cotes. A visit from the Commissioner of Police himself, on such a night and under such alarming conditions, was a questionable privilege for which the local powers that be had certainly not bargained. But once having weathered the storm of surprise and semi-anxiety, they were able to cope with his information immediately. The Sergeant in charge was sufficiently intelligent to grasp its significance without any preliminary investigation whatever.

"You've brought us precisely the information we've been requiring, sir. Inspector Craig has just been sent for to investigate something very queer up at Vernon House—Rodding. That's Sir Eustace Vernon's place. I had to dig him out of his home, sir, as a matter of fact. You can guess how pleased he was. I shouldn't be surprised if the information you've stumbled across, so to speak, sir, won't have a big bearing on the matter that they've called him up there about. According to the message that came through for the Inspector, Sir Austin, there's been a mysterious death up at Vernon House. I'll get our ambulance to go up to Dyke's Crossing and I'll also have that car you spoke about brought down here at once."

"Very good, Sergeant," rejoined Sir Austin. "I was going to instruct you to do that myself. In the meantime Mr. Bathurst and I will warm ourselves by the fire in the Inspector's room."

"Fate plays strange tricks, Sir Austin," remarked Mr. Bathurst a few minutes later as he said "when" to a liquid expression of the Yuletide hospitality of Mapleton Police Station—"who would have believed an hour ago, as we were speeding towards home, that we should land up where we are now?"

For a moment Sir Austin was unable to reply—being very much better employed. Eventually he put his glass on the table. "My boy—you never know from one minute to the next. Especially in a game like mine." He caught Bathurst's eye and smiled slyly before making his amendment. "Your pardon, my dear Bathurst. *Ours.*"

Mr. Bathurst returned smile for smile, raised his glass and bowed his tolerant acknowledgment. Taking into consideration the fact that it was Christmas night and very late at that, Sergeant Banks completed his arrangements comparatively quickly, for it did not seem an unduly long time to either Sir Austin Kemble or Mr. Bathurst himself before the Sergeant put his sleek head round the door of the room in which they were so comfortably installed and made his next announcement.

"Everything was as you said, sir," he declared deferentially, "the car you spoke about was still there, in the very place that you described; and we found poor Sir Eustace Vernon under the hedge where you'd laid him. He's in the mortuary now, poor fellow, at the back of this building."

"Sir Eustace Vernon?" queried the Commissioner—"you know him then? You're—"

"Not a doubt about it, sir. I know him very well. He's far too well-known a figure in these parts not to be recognized. I'm very sorry—it's a proper bad job—Mapleton can ill afford to lose a man like him. He was a hard worker for Mapleton. Can't imagine what can have induced him to commit suicide like that."

Sir Austin looked across at Mr. Bathurst. "You think it was suicide then, Sergeant?" he queried, turning to Banks again.

"Why—what do you mean, sir? Surely there can't be two opinions about it? It's Sir Eustace's own car—the car that you thought had been abandoned. I've seen him in it scores of times. He's done himself in all right—you needn't worry over that."

Sir Austin motioned to Anthony, who understood readily the meaning of the somewhat peremptory gesture. He produced from the pocket of his travelling coat the red bonbon, together with the gruesome message that it had contained. Sir Austin extended his hand and took them.

"When I entered, Sergeant, I suppressed certain facts of which Mr. Bathurst and I were aware. I suppressed them with a definite purpose. I thought it best for you to get the body here before I told you all that we knew; what you had to do was quite sufficient with which to be getting on. Now look at these, will you, Sergeant Banks?"

The dumbfounded Sergeant, who had listened with much curiosity, took the bonbon very gingerly. He turned it over without vouchsafing any remark and then gave his attention to the piece of paper that accompanied it. Still silent he looked up, and then his eyes wandered from Sir Austin to Mr. Bathurst.

"Tell him, Bathurst," said the former. "Tell him exactly what happened. Omit nothing."

"That red bonbon, Sergeant, was in the pocket of Sir Eustace Vernon's dinner-jacket. As we were putting the body under the hedge where you found it, I caught sight of it. The moon was shining brilliantly." The Sergeant's wide-open eyes opened yet wider, and his heavily-furrowed brows contracted into a menacing frown. Mr. Bathurst continued his history. "Protruding from one end of the red bonbon, Sergeant, was that friendly little *billet-doux.*"

Sergeant Banks read the message, and forgetful of his company, immediately became the slave of habit. "Not exactly a ruddy Christmas-card to send anybody—I beg your pardon, sir."

Sir Austin frowned. His frown was followed by a cough.

"Get to business, Sergeant—please," was all he permitted himself to say.

"Exactly, sir." The Sergeant pondered for a moment. "Certainly it puts a different complexion on things," he ventured, at last—"but it's a mighty queer business whichever way you choose to look at it."

Sir Austin, however, was growing tired and a trifle impatient. The hour was late and the whisky-bottle empty. "Did I understand you to say that your Inspector is at Vernon House now?"

"Quite right, sir."

"Get on to him then, at once. Tell him what we've discovered with regard to Sir Eustace Vernon. Tell him that *I'm* here. And give him my orders to come back here as soon as he conveniently can. Let that convenience be now! Where's the Divisional Surgeon to be found?"

"Doctor Tempest went up to Vernon House with Inspector Craig."

"Good—tell him he's to come along here as well—his services are needed. At once!"

Banks appeared to hesitate for a moment.

"I'm to tell Inspector Craig that you're here, sir?" he questioned, with more than a touch of reluctance.

"Take me to the telephone, Sergeant," rapped Sir Austin, firmly and finally—"I'll speak to your Inspector myself and settle the matter. Then there'll be no doubt about it and there'll be no possible misunderstanding. Stay here for a moment, Bathurst."

Thus it was that the telephone message reached the Inspector at Vernon House and caused him to adjust his vision of the case. Leaving the body of Purvis in the temporary care of Doctor Carrington, he and Doctor Tempest were quickly back as Sir Austin had instructed. He listened very quietly and attentively to what the Commissioner had to tell him. When Sir Austin reached the point of the red bonbon with its sinister message, he asked permission to speak.

"This is positively amazing, sir," he said. "The butler is dead up at Vernon House—a butler by the name of Purvis. A similar bonbon has been found on the body containing a similar message. And it was found, I believe, in the inside pocket of the dress-coat. The same as you've just described."

Mr. Bathurst sprang to his feet. "I find this most fascinating," he interjected—"may I see the message you mention? Have you brought it with you?"

Craig handed it over and went on. "Moreover, in addition to what I have just told you, Sir Austin, I have made another most startling discovery. Or at any rate, Doctor Carrington did. And Doctor Tempest here can confirm it. Purvis, who has been butler to Sir Eustace Vernon—for many years so I am given to understand—is not a man at all. He's a *woman* or *she* is—rather."

Mr. Bathurst whistled. "By Jove—this gets worse and worse—or shall we say better and better. A woman masquerading as a man—eh?" He rubbed his hands again, to Sir Austin's secret amazement. "Sir Austin," he said—"a word with you." He went quickly to the Commissioner's side and spoke to him quietly. The others saw the latter nod in evident agreement. Mr. Bathurst ranged himself by Doctor Tempest, who nodded very much as Sir Austin had done.

"I'll go now," he said. "Go with him, Bathurst," ordered Sir Austin—"there's nothing like seeing a thing for yourself. Craig and I will await the report in here."

Within a quarter of an hour the Divisional Surgeon returned with Mr. Bathurst on his heels. The former looked very grave, but in the grey eyes of the latter there glowed a gleam of confident excitement.

Doctor Tempest's voice came very deliberately.

"Sir Austin," he announced, "Mr. Bathurst's theory has received very strong substantiation. Sir Eustace Vernon did not die as we had believed. He was not killed by a train passing over his body." Doctor Tempest paused—plainly agitated. "He has been killed by a shot through the head from a revolver. Fired from behind."

Chapter VIII
SAM MCLAREN'S MERRY CHRISTMAS

Mr. Bathurst glanced at Sir Austin Kemble, and the glance contained a wealth of meaning. "Have I your permission, Sir Austin," he supplemented, "to ask Inspector Craig one or two questions?"

"Tut-tut, Bathurst, I've no doubt you'll ask 'em whether I give you the permission or whether I don't. Ask on, my boy."

Sir Austin puffed out his cheeks and the hint of a smile played for the fractional part of a moment round his thin lips, for although he would have been the last to admit it, he had taken Bathurst to his heart. Anthony unabashed returned the smile and turned his attention to Inspector Craig.

"I should be eternally obliged, Inspector," he said, "if you would be kind enough to favour me with a short *résumé* of all you know. It would assist me tremendously at this stage of the case and it might prevent me making a move in the dark, a move which might very well prove to be disastrous."

The Inspector accepted the situation with good grace. "Very good, sir. Please understand, however, that since I've been up at Vernon House I haven't examined anybody. I haven't yet tested anybody's story. I haven't had time to do so. I was about to do so when I got Sir Austin Kemble's telephone message recalling me here. But I'll tell you exactly what I've been told and where I stand. My informant—in the main—has been Major Prendergast. Sir Eustace Vernon—as was his custom, I understand—ever since he has lived in the district—was entertaining a number of guests for the Christmas season."

"Give me their names, Inspector, will you, please?" intervened Mr. Bathurst, quietly.

"Father Jewell, the priest in charge of the Roman Catholic Church in Mapleton—St. Veronica's—Alderman Venables and Mrs. Venables, the Mayor and Mayoress of Mapleton—the Alderman has been on the Council for many years—Doctor Lionel Carrington—a local doctor—and Major Prendergast himself—together with his wife. They are what I will term the 'local people.' In addition to them there were a Mr. and Mrs. Morris Trentham—London friends of Sir Eustace Vernon—and a Mr. Terence Desmond, a friend of Miss Ashley—Sir Eustace's niece. Miss Ashley herself was also present, of course. The first intimation the company had that anything was wrong was during dinner. I believe I am correct in stating that dinner was almost over. Anyhow, Sir Eustace startled his guests by declaring suddenly to them that he had received 'bad news.' As a result of whatever he had heard he left the table. He walked out of the room, as we know now—to his death. Anyhow, the ladies and gentlemen, naturally desiring to make the best of things, attempted to carry on the social round in the absence of their host, to the best of their ability, until, I am told, about a quarter to twelve. Late perhaps—with your host missing all that time—but not late for Christmas night. We're apparently going to be later," he added ruefully, glancing at the clock, and secretly yearning for the attractions of his own fireside.

"What happened then?" cut in Sir Austin.

"A terrible scream was heard from what proved to be Sir Eustace's study. Everybody, of course, rushed there to find one of the maids unconscious on the floor. I haven't yet interrogated her, as I said just now, but I understand from the Major that her story was this. She had been in the garden and found the doors of the study that lead out on to the garden—wide open. This fact struck her as being extremely unusual. She went in to investigate. Suddenly a woman with a knife in her hand jumped out of the darkness on to her and caught hold of her face. The maid fainted with fright. I don't wonder at it."

The Inspector swung round on to Doctor Tempest. "Can I have that blotting-pad, Doctor?"

Doctor Tempest passed it across to him and he in turn handed it on to Anthony.

"That was found on Sir Eustace's table."

"In the study?" queried Anthony.

"In the study. Also, there is another important fact—the safe in a small room adjoining the study was open, but strangely enough—according to Miss Ashley—nothing appears to have been stolen. Nothing at all events that she can name."

"One moment, Inspector," interposed Anthony—"when the various people were attracted to the study by the scream of the maid, was the study door on the house side open or closed?"

"I am sorry, sir," apologized Craig, "I omitted to tell you, the door was locked on the inside. The men who rushed there burst open the door."

"Thank you. Proceed, Inspector, will you? I find it a most interesting story."

Craig produced a piece of paper from his pocket. "This paper was found on the floor of the study—by Mr. Desmond—I'm given to understand. It is pretty obvious from it what Sir Eustace's intentions were."

Sir Austin came over to Mr. Bathurst's side and read the paper with him.

"No doubt about the handwriting, I presume?" questioned the last-named.

"According to my information there is no doubt about it being in the dead man's handwriting. At least so Miss Ashley says. Surely there can be no better witness. But I will continue. The house-party, upon the finding of this letter, became—very naturally—apprehensive of Sir Eustace's fate. So a search-party was immediately organized. It was just on the very point of starting out—they had provided themselves with lanterns, by the way—when a second blood-curdling scream was heard. This time from the servants' quarters."

"From the same maid as on the first occasion?"

"No, Mr. Bathurst. From another maid. Once again, as you may well imagine, investigations had to be made. In the butler's pantry sat the butler, Purvis—dead. Poisoned! A glass was on the table close at hand, and it seemed quite on the cards that the dose had been self-administered. But for the presence of the red bonbon with its ghastly message, which Mr. Desmond noticed in the pocket of the coat. Then to cap matters and to give us a nice comfortable little climax, Doctor Carrington—that's the doctor who was Sir Eustace Vernon's guest, and who happens to be his medical adviser also—discovers that the dead butler *is a woman*. I think that's about all," he concluded, "but it's quite enough to be getting on with."

"I'm disposed to agree with you, Inspector. There can be no two opinions about that. But there's one point at least upon which I should like to feel more sure. This question of the sex of this butler—Purvis. Do you think such a thing was suspected by any of the household at Vernon House? Were you able to observe the effect the news produced upon them?"

"The very thing occurred to me, Mr. Bathurst. So I put the question to Miss Ashley. She lived in the house with her uncle. She seemed as completely surprised at the news as I was myself. Unless she's a very good actress," he added, quietly.

"H'm," muttered Sir Austin—"deuced queer business, Bathurst, whichever way you choose to look at it. What do you propose to do now? I think my suggestion will be to sleep on the problem until to-morrow morning—eh? I'm sure we shan't do better." Anthony thought hard for a brief period. The others watched him intently. Anybody possessing an intimate knowledge of him would have known that something was bothering him. Suddenly his brow cleared somewhat and he looked at his wrist-watch.

"As it's so very late, I think we had better do as you suggest, sir. We can come down again in the car to-morrow."

Hardly had the words left his lips when the door of the room opened again to admit Sergeant Banks. His face reflected the enthusiasm occasioned by a new development.

"Sorry to interrupt you, gentlemen, but something's turned up that appears to me to be most important. There's a man in the charge-room—a man we all know very well in Mapleton—Sam McLaren, the coffee-stall keeper—and he's got a very curious story to tell."

"What about?" demanded Craig, curtly—a little annoyed perhaps at what he evidently considered an interruption.

"He's been attacked—according to his own story—somewhere in the vicinity of Vernon House. It seems to me to be something more than a mere coincidence."

"Bring him in here, Sergeant," ordered Sir Austin, authoritatively—"let's have his story first-hand."

Anthony Bathurst awaited the entrance of the newcomer with intense interest. He felt with a strong certainty that a story that brought a man to a police station at so late an hour as this at the Christmas season would almost assuredly bear the impression of authenticity. The man that brought it certainly presented an unusual appearance. His reddish-ginger hair was streaked with grey and a straggling grey moustache covered his upper lip. His nose was well-shaped, but over his left eye he wore a black shade that caused Mr. Bathurst to be irresistibly reminded of Pew. A shabby lounge-suit of blue serge was stained with dirt and mud, while his face showed unmistakable signs of its owner having recently passed through a severe physical ordeal. In his hand he carried a bowler hat much the worse for either wear or illegitimate treatment—perhaps both. As he entered he put his forefinger to his forehead in respectful salute.

"Good evening, Sam," commenced Craig. "What's all the bother? Sergeant Banks tells us you've been meeting trouble this Christmas."

McLaren let a feeble grin pass over his face—apparently he wasn't in the mood to appreciate the Inspector's pleasantry, which he probably was quite justified in regarding as singularly ill-timed. "Come on, Sam," continued the Inspector encouragingly—"let's have it. Who's been putting it across you?"

The coffee-stall keeper twisted his hat in his hand in a kind of despairing attempt to overcome his nervousness. When he spoke it was with a pronounced Cockney accent. Sam McLaren was something of a local comedian, and his coffee-stall was a well-known Mapleton rendezvous for the lower classes of the town. He jerked his head up with a curiously plebeian gesture and started to tell his story.

"Well, gentlemen," he commenced, "first of all, I'm going back a bit. The 'ole affair started for me abaht a month ago. Sir Eustace Vernon—and there ain't nobody better than 'im in the Cahnty Burrer of Mapleton—Gawd bless him—stopped at my stall and gives me the office that 'e wants a couple of words with me. I'd often seen 'im pass by and 'e always 'ad a friendly sort of nod for old Sam—being one o' the best—as I said just now—so I felt sort of flattered-like—as yer might say. Well, Inspector, he fairly took me by surprise—knocked me all of a 'eap—'e did, and took the wind from my sails. He told me that certain information 'ad some'ow come to his knowledge direckly affectin' yours truly. He said that matters weren't quite complete yet and wouldn't be for a little time to come. But it would mean 'bees and 'oney' for old Sam—which as you may guess, was news that 'ad a very sweet sahnd. I could ha' listened to it for hours. Well—orf goes Sir Eustace—a-raisin' of his old 'battle' and I 'ears no more about 'Hell-dorado' till this very Christmas night wot ever was."

"Battle?" queried Sir Austin, with a puzzled frown. "I don't quite—"

"Hat," explained Anthony—"'tile' becomes 'Battle of the Nile'—abbreviated rhyming slang."

"Go on, Sam!" exclaimed Craig, "let's have the rest—we're anxious to hear it—I can certainly assure you."

Sam McLaren grinned again, but at this statement of the Inspector's he proceeded with more confidence than he had previously displayed. No doubt he regarded it as full of encouragement.

"At twenty minutes to ten to-night—or last night I ought to say—seein' as 'ow it's mornin' now—I gets a message from Sir Eustace. In a way the message wot I'd been waitin' for. Brought by Stevens it was—Sir Eustace's chofer—'e come along to my place in the car. When I see 'oo it was I lost no time in bein' polite. He 'ands me a letter from his guv'nor. I was to go up to Vernon 'Ouse at once and knock five times with my knuckles on the French doors of his study—the room wot you could approach from the grahnds. Well, as you might guess—I didn't waste no time in goin'. My place is abaht 'arf an hour's stretch from Vernon 'Ouse and I was makin' good time along the road, I can tell yer. I was feelin' all merry and bright. I was spending 'the bees' in anticipation. Nah—listen! 'Cos wot I'm goin' to say is worth listenin' to. Abaht a couple of 'undred yards from Sir Eustace's place—just by that there belt of trees on the left of the road—a pair of 'ell-deservin' swine jumps out of the darkness and gives me a couple of 'fourpenny-ones.' The shorter one o' the two gives me a smash under the jaw that made me see a bloomin' Brock's Benefit, and then works a bit of Jew Jitsoo on me with his left hand, while the other catches me a welt on the back o' the bonce that I fair took the count over. Carpenteer never 'anded Joe Beckett a juicier one. I must ha' laid in the ditch there by the side of the road over a couple of hours, before I came to my senses. My 'ead was fair splittin'—buzzin' like a top it was—and I was some time then before I could piece things together properly. I staggered off to the 'ouse to try and find the old toff. I made my way through the grahnds as I'd been told to do, and bless my soul, there was a reg'lar concert-party in the room wot Sir Eustace called his study—but no sign of 'im 'imself. So I comes away—and thinks I can't do better than take a stroll up 'ere—and let you people know all about it—them there swine might ha' killed me." He brushed his nostrils with the back of his hand, after the manner of his class, and sniffed resentfully.

The respective faces of his hearers betokened the varying interests of each one of them. Craig—trained to meet emergencies of this nature—was first to put a question.

"Could you describe your assailants, McLaren? Were you able to get a sufficient sight of them to do that?"

"They were big 'efty fellers, I could swear to that. Both White 'Opes, I should call 'em and no mistake. I couldn't say no more than that. I was fair taken by surprise—you see."

Anthony nodded, as though in entire understanding. "Quite so, McLaren. I can see that readily. But tell me this. I am going to ask you a different question altogether. Can you possibly remember the date when Sir Eustace Vernon came and spoke to you, as you described, at your coffee-stall?"

McLaren knitted his brows—and then shook his head doubtfully. "I've no doubt Sir Eustace himself could tell you—better than wot I could—if you approached 'im. 'Is memory is probably better than mine. You could find out."

"Try yourself, Sam," urged Mr. Bathurst—"I'm rather interested."

The man addressed brushed his straggling moustache with his fingers and screwed his face up in a strange grimace. After a time the contortion passed and his face subsided into the normal again. Anthony felt that Sam had seen better days.

"I can tell yer, guv'nor," he asserted, with the confidence of returning memory. "It was on the last Saturday in November. I can remember it, because I had 'arf an 'Oxford' on 'four 'omes and one away' on the short list and brought it off, too. Yes—that was the day," he added, after more reflection—"because I can remember thinking after Sir Eustace 'ad spoke to me that I was 'avin' a good day—all things considered. 'Four 'omes and one away' on the short list want a bit o' findin' you know—especially—"

"The last Saturday in November," repeated Anthony—"you're pretty certain of that? What time was it when Sir Eustace spoke to you?"

"Abaht a quarter to eleven on the Saturday night, sir. As near that as could be—before the second 'ouse was out from the "Ipp.'"

"The music-hall?" queried Anthony.

"That's it, sir."

At a glance from the Commissioner, the Inspector took up the threads. "Your information is very valuable, Sam. More valuable, perhaps, than you think. Sir Eustace Vernon was found dead to-night on the line near Dyke's Crossing."

Sam McLaren's one visible eye expressed his astonishment. "You don't mean it, Inspector!" he gasped, incredulously.

"Unfortunately, it's only too true. His body is only a few yards away from us at the present moment."

Sam looked round fearfully, almost as though he expected the dead man to materialize at his side, then and there. Then curiosity overcame his sense of awe. "'Ow was 'e killed? Run over?"

Craig hesitated. "We don't know for certain, Sam," he declared—"but he's certainly been run over, poor chap."

"Just my blarsted luck," moaned McLaren—"it's good-bye to what 'e promised me then. It's all as per perishin' invoice. Trust me to be with the 'also rans.'" He added the last remark so lugubriously and with such an expression of despair that Mr. Bathurst had hard work to repress a smile.

"That's a matter of conjecture, McLaren," he exclaimed. "We don't know yet what the nature of your expectations was—any more than you yourself do. All may yet be well for you. Don't cry over spilt milk before the cow's given it to you. Let me have a glance at the letter you received from Sir Eustace this evening. The letter that took you up to Vernon House."

Sam's hand went to his pocket. A second after, his watchers saw the woebegone expression on his face change—and then change again. Bewilderment succeeded anxiety and consternation took the place of bewilderment. Sam then sought succour in the harbour of tradition. He gave way to profanity. "It's gorn," he cried. "It's been 'pinched.' So that's what them two 'ell-deserving swine was after."

Chapter IX
THE SECOND LETTER

"I AM VERY pleased to meet you, gentlemen," Terence Desmond—worried and anxious—bowed to his three visitors. "Miss Ashley and I have been expecting you all the morning, and I'm glad that you have come. When I think that the staggering events of last night are only a matter of a few hours old it seems amazing—not to say incredible. I will tell Miss Ashley you are here. I need hardly say that she is extremely upset. May I rely implicitly upon your discretion, Inspector?" Desmond gazed at Craig apprehensively.

Sir Austin Kemble waved a pontifical hand. "I give you my word, Mr. Desmond, that Miss Ashley will be treated with every possible consideration. Consistent that is, with the Inspector's legitimate investigation of the case as it is presented to him."

Desmond suitably acknowledged the Commissioner's promise.

"None of your uncle's guests are gone, of course, Mr. Desmond?" interrogated the Inspector. Desmond showed a certain amount of surprise.

"Certainly they have, Inspector. Major Prendergast and his wife returned home this morning—as did the Mayor and Mayoress—Alderman and Mrs. Venables. Surely there was no reason for any one of them to remain here? What was there to stop them returning?"

"Aren't they the people who reside in the locality?" asked Anthony.

"That is so," replied Desmond, rather coldly. "Major Prendergast lives less than a mile from here and Alderman Venables in Mapleton—about three miles away. They're very easily accessible."

"That's all right then, Craig," put in Sir Austin—"as long as they're close at hand—we can get into touch with them quite easily. Don't waste time over that."

"Doctor Carrington remained here and also Mr. and Mrs. Trentham. They live in London."

"What about the priest who was here—Father Jewell, was it?" queried Mr. Bathurst.

"He left early this morning, too—but in his case he has promised to return again before lunch. Don't worry about him. He won't run away." Desmond's voice held a note of satire, but he was sensible enough to go straight on. "Do you wish to see the two rooms? Or do you wish to question any of the people? Last night, I believe, you intended to question the two maids concerned in the affair when the interruption came on the telephone."

The answer to the question came from Sir Austin. "We will see Sir Eustace's study first, Mr. Desmond. Mr. Bathurst is anxious to do so as quickly as is convenient to you."

"Very good, sir. If you will be good enough to accompany me—"

Before he could complete his sentence the door opened. Helen Ashley's hand went to her lips instinctively, as though to repress an exclamation that she had been about to make. Desmond seemed to sense this and walked to her side.

"I was about to let you know these gentlemen were here, Helen. Let me introduce them."

She bowed her greeting to the three of them. "I am sorry I wasn't here before," she announced, with a simple dignity. "But please stay here for a moment or two before going to my uncle's study. I have something to show you." She put her hand to her bosom and from the intimacy of her dress took a letter. "I found this letter in my bedroom last night when I went to bed. To be strictly accurate it was actually *in my bed*. When I turned the clothes back to get into bed I saw it there. But, of course, it was impossible for me to see it *until* then. It is from my uncle."

The Commissioner read it and passed it over to the two others. It ran as follows:—

"My dear Helen,

"By the time to-night when you discover this, you will know that I am dead. I am dreadfully sorry—far more than I can ever tell you in words—to have to do what I am going to do, for I know that you will grieve for me. But, believe me, it is inevitable. There is no other way out for me, little girl, strive how I may. So let this be good-bye! It will be a shock to you also to learn that I am far from rich, so that it will be impossible for me to make ample provision for you. But there will at least be something.

I have left no will, but the keys of my safe will be found on my study-table and the parcel in the safe is for you. I have preserved it from the wreck of my fortunes. It should realize several thousand—enough to keep you from want till you become Mrs. Terence Desmond, Take it to Cornelius Van Hoyt—he has wanted it badly for two years, and will give you a better price than anybody else I know.

"Good-bye, dearest Helen—for the last time.

"UNCLE EUSTACE."

"And the safe was empty," supplemented Mr. Bathurst—"we are progressing. Forgive me putting it like that, Miss Ashley—but this letter of yours throws a new light on the affair."

"We both realized that, Mr. Bathurst," intervened Desmond—"so we decided that we should inform you of its existence at the first opportunity."

"Have you any idea to what your uncle is referring? As to what the article mentioned in the letter was?"

"No, Sir Austin. None whatever." Helen spoke with marked emphasis. Mr. Bathurst, meanwhile—in a fit of seeming abstraction was pulling at his upper lip.

"There is a dressing-table of some kind I take it in your bedroom, Miss Ashley?"

"Yes—of course."

"Why, then, do you think, did your uncle put your letter inside your bed? Why not in a prominent place?"

"For safety, I suppose, Mr. Bathurst. Why else?"

"I wonder, Miss Ashley, I wonder! Surely the natural inclination would have been to have left it where you would be sure to see it—on your dressing-table. You would go there naturally—before—"

He stopped again—considering something that had occurred to him. Sir Austin Kemble took a hand again.

"I am told, Miss Ashley, that this curious business of Purvis—the butler here—turning out to be a woman and all that, is as much a surprise to you as to anybody—eh?"

"Why—of course! That is so, Sir Austin. I never dreamed of such an extraordinary state of affairs. I was simply astounded when I heard the news."

"Tell me," broke in Mr. Bathurst again—"of your uncle's life as you knew it. Where did he live before he came here? What was he in life before he retired? Let me hear anything that you deem sufficiently important to be told."

Helen Ashley shook her head with obvious misgiving. "I am afraid I'm going to prove of very little help to you there," she declared. "I came here nearly ten years ago—when my uncle first came to live in Rodding. He sent for me because he said I was the only relation he possessed. When he sent for me I was at a private school in Worthing. I am an orphan. I cannot remember either my father or my mother. They were killed in a railway accident near London one New Year's Day. I was only three years old at the time. But Uncle Eustace told me that my mother was his only sister—to whom he had been devoted. That was why he wanted me to live with him. He brought me up and he was very good to me. It was he who paid for my education while I was at Worthing." The tears rolled very slowly down her cheeks. "He was more like my father than my uncle," she added.

"You can tell me nothing more?" asked Anthony. "For instance," he followed up—"what work had he done? To what profession did he belong? Have you ever heard him refer to it? To any friends or business associates?"

Again Miss Ashley found herself unequal to Mr. Bathurst's demand. "Never—in any way whatever! He never spoke of such things himself, and certainly never encouraged me to do so. Therefore—I understood and never did. I just respected what I knew were his wishes. But I believe—I've certainly always had the idea—that he had conducted some very successful operations on the Stock Exchange. As to his friends—they were usually connected in some way with that sort of work. Mr. Trentham, for example, who is staying here now—and before him a Mr. Paget-Colvin. The latter, I fancy, went in a speculation with Uncle Eustace over something to do with rubber. They each made a lot of money out of it. I think I have heard uncle describe it as a 'Joint Venture.' I can't think of anybody else," she concluded.

"Where is this gentleman now?"

"I don't know at all. I haven't heard uncle mention his name for years."

"Another question, Miss Ashley"—Inspector Craig, who had been exhibiting considerable impatience at the turn that Mr. Bathurst's questions had taken, interposed at last—he felt that it was necessary that he should—"and a very usual question, I'm afraid, in affairs of this kind—had you noticed anything strange about your uncle lately? Anything that you could truly describe as out of the ordinary?"

"At last I have been asked a question that I can answer without any hesitation. My uncle had not been himself for a month now at least. It was beginning to worry me."

"In what way—not himself?"

"He was *frightened*, Inspector. He was a man *afraid of something*! And my uncle was a brave man, too," she declared—the pride glowing in her voice. "You remember, Inspector, what he did at the beginning of the year?"

"I do, Miss. And it grieved me to see him as I saw him this morning. You have my deepest sympathy."

Helen continued quickly, anxious to avoid the pain of memory. "Mr. Desmond, here, can confirm what I say about my uncle's strangeness, can't you, Terry?"

The man addressed showed agreement with a quick and impetuous nod of the head. "As a matter of fact, Miss Ashley and I were actually remarking upon it as recently as dinner last night. There isn't the shadow of a doubt that Sir Eustace was very badly 'rattled.'"

"So his suicide didn't come as a surprise to you—eh, Mr. Desmond?" The Inspector shot the question at him with unexpected suddenness. But Desmond showed no signs of discomfiture. He was quite ready with his answer.

"I wouldn't go so far as to say that, Inspector. Surely to expect a man's suicide is travelling to an extreme."

"Quite so, Mr. Desmond," interrupted Anthony. "And one moment before we go any further. Miss Ashley has just mentioned—with legitimately pardonable pride, I've no doubt, something that Sir Eustace Vernon accomplished 'at the beginning of the year.' Am I permitted to inquire what that something was? I ask, from much more than mere curiosity I assure you."

Helen Ashley told the story of the events of the night of the eleventh of January—simply and unemotionally. But her eyes were an eloquent testimony to the prompting of her soul. Sir Austin Kemble and Anthony listened quietly.

"Splendid work," exclaimed the former, when she finished.

Mr. Bathurst added his own expression of admiration. "A very brave deed, Miss Ashley. It requires superlative courage to face the horror of blazing fire—perhaps the greatest horror that Fear holds."

"Thank you," she answered, with a little touch of dignity—"I know that what my uncle did that night is imperishable. The good in his case *will* live after him. It will be remembered when we are forgotten."

"Yet another question," said the Inspector quietly. "Did your uncle ever mention the name of Sam McLaren to you?"

"Sam McLaren," she repeated after her interrogator—"do you mean the old man at the coffee-stall down in Mapleton?"

"The same—Miss Ashley."

"In what connection do you mean? I've heard him referred to quite casually—just as anybody living near or working near might have been at any odd moment—certainly nothing more than that, I am quite sure."

"You've never heard your uncle make any special reference to him—then?"

She wrinkled her brows—evidently puzzled at the question. "Never—Inspector."

"What's the allusion, Inspector?" broke in Desmond—"what's in your mind about McLaren? I'm at a loss."

"All in good time, Mr. Desmond. At the moment you may assure yourself that I have a sound and solid reason for asking Miss Ashley the question."

Desmond turned away impetuously with an ill-concealed gesture of impatience.

Sir Austin Kemble caught his eye and intervened with a suggestion of sympathy. "Mr. Desmond," he commenced—imperious as ever despite the sympathy that he intended to convey—"and Miss Ashley, too. It is only right that you should know the facts relating to Sir Eustace's death. More than that—it is only fair. We have strong reason to suppose that he did not commit suicide as was generally and reasonably supposed."

He paused—waiting to see the full effect of his announcement upon the two people most concerned.

Desmond looked dumbfounded, and Helen, although plainly shaken at the intelligence, was the first of the two to speak.

"What exactly do you mean?" she gasped. "Please explain."

"There is every reason, Miss Ashley, to believe that your uncle was murdered." Sir Austin made the assertion very gravely.

"Murdered!" Her cheeks and lips were blanched with fear. "How—murdered?"

"He was shot with a revolver—there is strong foundation for thinking that the bullet which killed him was fired from behind."

"Where? Here? Or down there at Dyke's Crossing?"

"That is what we have to discover." Sir Austin bowed his head in solemnity.

Desmond's face registered sheer astonishment. "Are you sure of—"

Sir Austin's uplifted hand checked his question. "In addition to what I have already told you—there remains yet another most extraordinary and astounding feature. Upon his body there was found a red bonbon—similar to that—"

Desmond's impatient curiosity mastered him and forced him to interrupt. "Found on Purvis?" he cried.

"Exactly," returned the Commissioner—"and what is more—containing an identical message—'warning' if you prefer the word."

"Good God!" exclaimed Desmond. "How unutterably horrible."

Sir Austin extended his hand towards the Inspector. "Let me have them, will you, Craig?"

Helen Ashley regarded the two crimson relics of two mysterious crimes with a horror that she made no attempt to disguise. "The one marked 'A' was found upon Purvis. The message she had is marked 'A' also. The 'B's' are those which were found upon Sir Eustace."

Desmond took the latter and Helen the former. Simultaneously almost, there broke from each of them an exclamation of amazement.

"Yes?" murmured Mr. Bathurst—his grey eyes alight with excitement—"you've discovered something—what have you to tell us?"

"This writing—found on Purvis"—Helen got in first—a triumph of femininity—"*was written by Purvis herself.* I'm perfectly certain of it."

Desmond spoke with more weighing of his words. "And this found on Sir Eustace *was written by Sir Eustace himself*—I'm equally certain of that."

The three men to whom these surprising and unexpected revelations were made received them with varying emotions. The Inspector stared incredulously, while Sir Austin's eyes glared in an antagonism for which he would have been at a loss to account. On the contrary, Mr. Bathurst appreciated the situation. "Now that's very interesting," he murmured—"and moreover—distinctly illuminating."

Chapter X
BEHIND THE CURTAIN

Inspector Craig gazed pointedly at the two scraps of paper. Despite Mr. Bathurst's last remark, it might have been observed that he appeared to be neither illuminated nor yet increasingly interested. He looked first at Desmond and then at the white-faced girl. "Each of you, I take it, is quite sure of the statement that you have just made?"

"Quite sure," affirmed Helen Ashley.

"And I," repeated Desmond.

"Very extraordinary," commented Craig slowly—"I don't know that I've ever heard of such a—" he passed his hand through his hair, with a gesture of perplexity, evidently considering some angle of the case that had just presented itself to him. Moving suddenly and rapidly across the room, he said something in a very low voice to Sir Austin Kemble. The latter listened and then nodded sharply. "Certainly—certainly. I entirely agree, and the sooner the better! It would be far more satisfactory to have it here."

"Very good, sir." Craig crossed back to Desmond.

"I shall be glad if you will arrange for all the people who were present here last night to be here again after lunch to-day. From what you have told me it will only mean getting into touch with the local people who have left. Telephone them all, where it is necessary—will you, please? Also ask the London people to stay on for a few hours longer."

"Certainly, Inspector. Everything shall be as you wish. I will let the people in question know immediately."

Desmond slipped out. As he closed the door Mr. Bathurst, who had been thinking deeply since his last contribution to the conversation, turned again to Helen Ashley. "What you told me about your uncle's hand-writing, I suspected. I was able to compare the message on the bonbon with the two letters that he left But this handwriting that you assert is the butler's, Miss Ashley, do you think you could answer me another question—a question that you may perhaps be inclined to regard as a trifle strange? As far as you know, was your uncle very familiar with the handwriting of Purvis—would he know it for certain when he saw it?"

The girl took a little time to reply. "I couldn't say," she answered at length—"that kind of question is very difficult to answer—it concerns another person's knowledge—you see, so that you can never feel absolutely sure of yourself when you answer. But I think it quite likely that he wouldn't—that he mightn't know it. I can't think of any circumstance, for instance, that would cause Purvis to write to him. Certainly—of recent times, I myself can only recall seeing the butler's writing two or three times, and then only because I attended to matters affecting the house. It was an occasion of that kind when I saw it recently which helped me to recognize it just now. It's feasible that my uncle mightn't have seen it for years." She shook her head. "No—it's quite possible that my uncle would not recognize it."

Anthony expressed his understanding of her meaning. "I see. Now tell me something else. Were these particular red bonbons actually on the table at dinner last night?"

"Yes, Mr. Bathurst. Or at least they are similar to the bonbons that were. Of course, I can't say that these very two—"

"I follow you, Miss Ashley. Of course you couldn't go farther than that—naturally."

"What's your point, Bathurst?" interjected Sir Austin.

"Only this, sir—I am endeavouring, if I can, to ascertain the exact meaning of the red bonbons. Are they deliberate or accidental? Significant or fortuitous?"

"H'm—I see. Well—which are they? That's a big point it seems to me. I've been wondering myself."

"I'm not sure at the moment, sir. But I have just the glimmering of an idea—too nebulous and perhaps too chimerical at the moment to discuss or even to consider seriously. Ah, Mr. Desmond—now you've returned—perhaps we might have a look at the study—is it convenient?"

Desmond took them across.

"You broke the door down—then?" queried Sir Austin.

"That is so. Or rather—" Desmond paused.

Anthony cut in instantaneously, quick to sense the other's disclaimer. "Or rather what, Mr. Desmond?"

"The others did. I had no hand in it."

"Why not? Weren't you with them at the time? I understood from Inspector Craig's account—that following upon Hammond's scream—"

"Perfectly true, Mr. Bathurst," came Desmond's response—cool and unabashed. "I came to the door with the others—just as the Inspector no doubt told you, but when we found it locked, I dashed back through the lounge, music-room and billiard-room so that I came round into the garden and entered the room through the open French doors. It was simply a question of trying to save time at a critical moment—that was my sole motive."

"And did you succeed? Did you save time?" Anthony said quietly.

Desmond reflected. "I think perhaps I was the first to enter—but it was by the shortest of short heads—there was very little in it."

"Is this where the blotting-pad was?" questioned Craig.

"Yes," said Helen—"just in the place where you would expect it to be."

"Where was the maid lying?"

"There." Desmond indicated the exact position. Mr. Bathurst walked to the heavy *portière* that covered the entrance to the inner library. "I understand, do I not, that Hammond, the maid, was of the opinion that the woman who frightened her came from this direction? Is that so? I should be glad of an assurance on the point."

"Quite correct," put in Desmond. "I certainly gathered that impression when she told her story. Do you agree, Helen?"

"Oh, yes. I understood her to say that."

"I should like to ask a question here." Craig seemed very definite at this moment. *"What reason did this maid Hammond give for being in the garden at that time of night—that seems to me to require a deal of explanation. Surely it was very late? Did she give any reason?"

"I asked her that question myself," Helen Ashley assured the Inspector immediately. "The same idea occurred to me then and there, as it did, no doubt, to all of us. Her explanation was this, and it was a perfectly simple one. One of the dogs had been out of sorts—a big wolfhound of my uncle's—and had been put on special diet by the vet. whom he had called in to see it. The dog was in the temporary care of Stevens, my uncle's chauffeur, who is passionately attached to all animals, but owing to something that Hammond didn't quite explain, so far as I can remember— Stevens hadn't been able to feed Boris—that's the dog—last night. As a result he had told Hammond to see to it. That was how she explained being in the garden."

Anthony turned to the Inspector. "That coincides with McLaren's statement. Stevens had other work to do. He was prevented from attending to the dog."

As he spoke Desmond felt a sudden stab of remembrance. Consummate ass that he was, never to have thought of it before! He plunged his hand into the pocket of his coat.

"By Jove," he cried—"something I meant to tell you about directly you started this inquiry last night, Inspector, but in the excitement it slipped right out of my mind." He handed the Inspector the cake of hard tobacco that he had picked up in the garden while engaged on the fruitless quest for Sir Eustace.

Craig took it curiously. "A bit of 'hard'!" he exclaimed, "'Dark Willie'—very popular among men of the seafaring class, I believe. And how did you come by this, Mr. Desmond?" Desmond told him.

"In the garden—eh? Still—come to that—anybody may have dropped it. I'll make a few inquiries before I leave here."

"There's just one other point, though," interposed Desmond, "and it was your question about Hammond's presence in the grounds last night that revived my remembrance of having found that cake of tobacco you hold in your hand. On account of a certain combination of ideas, I taxed Stevens, the chauffeur, with regard to it. I thought—vaguely perhaps—that he might know something about it He said he didn't, but he gave me a piece of interesting information. He informed me that Hammond was being courted by a sailor—a Mapleton man. It's just possible therefore—"

Craig intervened confidently and intelligently.

"That she was killing two birds with one stone—eh? That when she went to feed the dog, she was going to combine business with pleasure—and keep an assignation with her lover? Quite likely, Mr. Desmond—quite likely. I felt all along that it was strange she should have been out there at that time of night, and I shall certainly have to investigate it. That seems a much more likely proposition."

As he spoke Mr. Bathurst walked back to the heavy *portière* that had engaged his attention a few minutes previously. For a moment he stood in the entrance to the inner room, lost in thought. Sir Austin Kemble caught his eye, but was sensible enough—knowing the destructive power of disturbance—to contribute no active interruption of his meditation. The Inspector walked through brusquely, stopping before the open door of the safe. Sir Austin followed him.

"The door was open about that much, sir," volunteered Craig, "according to the information given to me last night. The key was in the lock—one of a bunch of keys on a key-ring. It certainly suggests that the person who opened the safe, whoever it was—was taken by surprise in some way and rushed off in a hurry, leaving the keys as they were afterwards found."

"Quite feasible—certainly," declared Sir Austin.

Mr. Bathurst rose from his hands and knees by the *portière* and broke in upon them. "That raises another important point, Sir Austin. No doubt it has already occurred to the Inspector. Something was taken from the safe—presumably after the murder of Sir Eustace. Presumably, too, from what we know, whatever was taken was the special legacy that was intended for Miss Ashley as indicated by her uncle's last letter to her. Now—this is what is disturbing me for the time being—how did the killer know that the keys of the safe would be on the study-table as Sir Eustace stated in that letter. *Did he know—*or *did* *she know*, if it were a woman? Or were the keys discovered by accident? By—shall we say—a chance entrant? Where is Purvis in the cast? Or did Miss—" He stopped suddenly, and Sir Austin Kemble immediately formed the impression that he had begun to follow another line of thought that was probably taking him temporarily across a line of unknown country. Then Anthony's voice startled them all again.

"What a remarkable thing," he remarked pensively, "that a man with every intention of committing suicide is murdered at about the same time as his intended suicide!" He walked impatiently to the *portière* again. "There's something vitally wrong here, gentlemen," he cried with fervent emphasis—his keen grey eyes alive with chafing enthusiasm. "We're missing some cardinal point, surely. I'm missing it, I keep missing it. What is it? Who, for example, stood behind this curtain?" He shook the *portière* impatiently, and the brass rod that held it rattled under the sudden strain to which he subjected it. Sir Austin looked at him inquiringly, but Inspector Craig seemed unmoved by Mr. Bathurst's wave of feeling. It is impossible to respond adequately to that which one does not understand. Terence Desmond and Helen Ashley seemed content to say nothing—it was almost to them, as it were, that they were spectators at a strange play, watching it interestedly, and that here were the principal characters, strangely and unaccountably intimate with them and in close proximity to them.

"How do you know somebody stood behind the curtain, Bathurst?" Sir Austin's slightly pompous voice broke the silence that had temporarily descended upon the entire company.

"Look here, sir." He pointed down to the bottom of the heavy blue curtain. "On the fringe there—on the back there—and in the lower folds—there are distinct traces of cigar-ash. Do you see it? It dropped from a cigar held by a man who stood there, listening, shall we say—watching, shall we suggest? Probably both."

Inspector Craig put a stop to Mr. Bathurst's imaginative flight complacently, but nevertheless distinctly pleasurably. At the same time his voice held a hint of reproof. "I'm sure you'll pardon me, sir, when I'm forced to upset some of the castles you're building so confidently, but you're quite wrong." He paused, as though he had no intention of hurrying over his devastating demolition of Mr. Bathurst's theories. The latter frowned.

"How do you mean, Inspector? How am I wrong?"

"I noticed the cigar-ash, myself, when I examined the library last night. Perhaps you may be interested to see, Mr. Bathurst, that there are signs of ash having been dropped over here by the wall-safe also." The Inspector caressed his cheek, dallying over the full flavour of his enjoyment of Mr. Bathurst's discomfiture.

"Well," demanded that gentleman—"what's your point with regard to that? Explain—do you mind? I'm curious."

"Simply this. I noticed the ash as I told you, and after I got the message from the police station about the finding of Sir Eustace's body, I just had time to make inquiries about it One of the gentlemen here—Major Prendergast—admitted dropping the ash himself when he first entered the library. And what is more important, Mr. Bathurst, I took steps to confirm what he said. I make a point of always verifying my facts. Doctor Carrington, who was with the Major at the time, was able to corroborate what the Major said. He said that when he and the Major first examined the library, the Major was smoking a cigar, and that he—the Doctor—distinctly remembers seeing the ash drop from it when the discoveries they made excited them. The Doctor verified the Major's story completely. So you can try something different, Mr. Bathurst. With all respect, of course."

He caught the disapproving eye of the Commissioner, and added the last sentence quickly. Mr. Bathurst's face showed signs of distinct annoyance. He considered Craig's statement very carefully. Then his face changed and assumed those lines of set determination that Sir Austin Kemble knew of old. He swung round on to Desmond, eager and inquisitive.

"Mr. Desmond," he exclaimed—straight and unerring to his point—"you were here, I take it, when Major Prendergast and Doctor Carrington first entered?"

"I was in the study with them. Hammond had told us that the woman who had frightened her had come from the inner library."

"Exactly—that's what I meant."

Desmond proceeded as his memory grew clearer. "Doctor Carrington asked me to stay with Miss Ashley while he and the Major had their look round in the inner apartment I think he was apprehensive."

"Very good, Mr. Desmond. Now tell me this. When the Major and the Doctor entered was the *portière* in its place—that is to say, masking the whole entrance space, or was it pulled to one side as it is now? Think—it's most important."

Desmond knitted his brows, but the expression on his face was dubious.

"I can answer that, Mr. Bathurst," said Helen, very quietly. "It covered the entire aperture, as it usually did. Because I distinctly remember seeing Major Prendergast pull it to one side when he entered. If you ask the Major he will confirm what I say. That's what you mean, isn't it?"

"Absolutely my point, Miss Ashley. You've helped me considerably."

"That doesn't touch the question of the cigar-ash, Mr. Bathurst," persisted Craig. "You can put that down to Major Prendergast's cigar after he pulled the curtain as Miss Ashley has just described."

"Prendergast certainly was smoking," supplemented Desmond—"I remember it myself. He lit a cigar in the study there."

"And that's the ash off it," asserted the Inspector.

"You still think so?" said Mr. Bathurst. "Well, then, Inspector, we must agree to differ."

Chapter XI
MR. BATHURST TAKES THE FIRST WICKET

Craig smiled with an air of complacent superiority. "By all means, sir! But you'll be convinced I'm right before we've finished, you see if you aren't." He addressed himself to Sir Austin Kemble. "I should like to interview those two maids now—that is, of course, with your approval, sir. In the adjoining room here. Unless you, yourself, think otherwise."

Sir Austin immediately disclaimed any such idea. "I think so too, Craig. Have this girl Hammond in first. She seems to have had the more to do with it."

"That was just my own idea, sir. Then I will have a word or two with the other maid, Palmer, if I have time. After that I propose to send for Stevens, the chauffeur. Following upon lunch we will see the guests. They should be all available by then as I arranged with Mr. Desmond here just now."

"Quite right, Inspector," put in Desmond. "All the arrangements are made for you. Everybody you want will be available by then."

Anthony Bathurst smiled across the room at Craig. "I don't think you can do better. There are one or two questions that I desire should be answered myself. Pardon me, Inspector, however, for just one moment. Miss Ashley—before the maid Hammond comes in here to us—one more question I want *you* to answer for me." He continued immediately without waiting for her reply. "At the dinner-table last evening, when Sir Eustace got up and left you so suddenly upon the receipt of his bad news—who were his immediate left-hand and right-hand neighbours? Can you tell me that?"

Helen nodded affirmatively. "I can—I have a particular reason for remembering. My uncle sat at the head of the table—naturally—as would be expected. On his left he had Mrs. Trentham, and on his right—that is to say directly facing Mrs. Trentham—sat Doctor Carrington. I can picture the table just as it was set out last night."

"Thank you, Miss Ashley. Pardon my curiosity, though—but that rather significant remark that you let drop just now—why have you a particular reason for remembering? What is the particular reason? May I ask you?"

"A very simple one, Mr. Bathurst, but nevertheless one from which you can't get away. My uncle *asked* me to place Mrs.

Trentham next to him. He even made a point of coming to see me regarding the arrangement of the seating for the dinner, and was most insistent throughout that his wishes with regard to Mrs. Trentham's seat should not be forgotten or overlooked. I thought of it immediately you touched on the question."

"H'm," Mr. Bathurst pulled reflectively at his upper lip. "May I ask you how exactly your uncle's desire affected you?"

"Affected me—I don't quite—"

"Well, what I mean is this. Did it surprise you? For instance— whom would you have put as your uncle's neighbour at table had the matter remained in your hands? Were you going to put Mrs. Trentham there?"

Helen puckered her brows. "I see your point," she conceded.

Mr. Bathurst and the others who were watching her might have been justifiably excused for the formation of the opinion that she was according the question a certain amount of serious consideration. At length came the answer, enunciated very carefully.

"When my uncle spoke to me on the matter I had not definitely decided upon the plan of the dinner-seating. I usually leave matters like that as long as possible, so that I didn't have to alter my existing arrangement in order to comply with his wishes concerning Mrs. Trentham. But—since you desire me to answer your question—I don't *think* I should have placed Mrs. Trentham next to him, as he instructed, had it been left entirely to me." She spoke the last sentence very slowly—evidently giving it the most careful thought. Anthony, as was his wont, followed up with rapidity.

"Had you obeyed your first inclinations then, Miss Ashley, whom would you have placed there?"

Sir Austin Kemble flung him a puzzled glance the apposite quality of which Desmond appeared to understand thoroughly. It seemed to him, also, that Mr. Bathurst's examination was taking an unexpected and most unusual line.

"Well, since you've asked me, Mr. Bathurst, I think my own personal inclination would have been to put Diana Prendergast there. My uncle admired her tremendously, and I know that the feeling was to some extent reciprocated. She had sat next to him on many similar occasions, previously. They had been neighbours, you see, for some years."

"Of course—quite a natural feeling. Who was next to Mrs. Trentham—on her other side?"

"Her husband—Morris Trentham."

"And who next to Doctor Carrington—on the other side of Sir Eustace?"

"Diana herself—with Major Prendergast on her immediate right. I was next to him at the other end of the table, facing my uncle."

"I understand, Miss Ashley. I am able now to visualize the whole table. You have told me all I wanted. Stay though! When Sir Eustace spoke to Purvis, immediately preceding his announcement that he had received bad news—can you remember which side of your uncle Purvis stood? Was she on the left—that is to say, between him and Mrs. Trentham, or on the right between Sir Eustace and Doctor Carrington?"

Helen hesitated. Desmond cut in impetuously. "I can answer that quite definitely. I happened to be looking at the time and saw Purvis bending down as Sir Eustace spoke to her. Purvis stood next to Ruby Trentham."

"So that I should be quite justified in assuming that whatever words passed between Sir Eustace and his butler might very well have been overheard by Mrs. Trentham—yes?"

Desmond nodded in strong affirmation. "I should say so—without doubt. Certainly they might have been."

"I have no more questions to ask at the moment, Inspector," exclaimed Anthony, turning to Craig with abrupt suddenness—"let's have that word we were going to have with Hammond."

When the maid appeared, it was plain that she was still showing signs of last night's terrifying experience. She had been very thankful to have been spared the ordeal of the Inspector's questioning upon the occasion of his first arrival, although she was sufficiently sensible to realize that the ordeal had been merely postponed and not abandoned, when he had been called away. Albeit at the time of her temporary respite she had fully subscribed to the belief—"Sufficient for the day is the evil thereof." She had remarked to her fellow-servant, Palmer, that she fervently wished it hadn't fallen to her lot to have given the original alarm.

"What will you say you was doin' in the grounds?" had rejoined Palmer ironically, but yet with a turn of seasonable wit—"gatherin' winter fuel?"

"I shall tell the truth, of course, Palmer," had been the indignant Hammond's reply—"if I did have a few words with my Albert, what else does it matter to anybody else? There's no crime in that that I can see—and what's more, nobody ain't goin' to make out that there is."

"H'm," had been Palmer's non-committal response—"some of these policemen can read crimes into anything you do—innocent though it may be. And it's worse since good old Edgar Wallace showed 'em up so in *The Ringer*. Now take that Cora Ann, to give an example—"

Hammond didn't wait for Palmer's masterly exposition of that lady's personal qualities, but presented herself in the study in obedience to the summons that had called her there.

"I don't intend to keep you very long, my girl, or to ask you a great many questions," commenced the Inspector—"as I already understand fairly clearly what happened to you when you gave the first alarm. But there is just this fact—about which we desire a little further information and if possible a little more explanation—shall we say? If we feel that the latter should be needed. Perhaps everything will be all right and it won't be. But will you tell us as accurately as possible what it was exactly that brought you outside the doors of this room last night at—well, what time would you say it was yourself—eh?"

Hammond answered with ready composure.

"About ten minutes to twelve, sir," she said. "I was coming back from the kennels, as I told the mistress last night. I'd been down to feed Boris, the wolfhound—Stevens, the chauffeur, gave me the orders to do so. If you ask him—you'll find what I say is quite true."

"But surely the direct way back from the kennels wouldn't bring you past these French doors?"

Hammond pursed her lips defiantly but withal determinedly. "If you must know then—I had a few words with my boy," she conceded.

"Ah," murmured Craig—"now we're getting to it, and how long did those few words take?"

"I wasn't with him longer than half an hour. I should think I was in his ar—company, I mean—from about a quarter-past eleven. His watch showed a quarter to twelve when we said good-night. I know that because he happened to look at it. That's how I reckoned the time at about ten to twelve when I came back past here."

"What is this gentleman's name?" demanded the Inspector.

"Mr. Albert Fish," replied Hammond—half-defiantly and half-timorously—"of His Majesty's ship *Semiramis*. He's home on Christmas 'leaf,' so we've been making the most of our opportunities as you might say, and small blame to us, say I." She tossed her head challengingly to give emphasis to this last remark.

"I see," said Craig nodding—"a Mapleton man, I believe?"

"Born and bred, Inspector—and his father and mother before him."

"Address?" queried Craig.

"Fourteen, Summerland Cottages, Rodding Road." As she spoke Hammond gave the Inspector a look of keen scrutiny. "Anything else you want to ask me, Inspector?"

"Not at the moment. Tell Palmer I want her."

Anthony smiled engagingly. "Two questions from me, if you don't mind, Hammond, before you leave us. I want a little more information regarding two matters."

The look of relief that had passed over Hammond's face upon her dismissal by Inspector Craig vanished instantly, to be replaced by a look of annoyance.

Mr. Bathurst smiled again to put her at her ease. "Nothing to worry you. Just two very ordinary questions. When you were in the grounds was there a light in this room all the time? Or did the room ever appear to be in darkness—I mean before you approached it on your way back?"

Hammond shook her head disclaimingly. "I never noticed, sir. I was occupied over other things. Albert doesn't like anything to—"

"Quite so," said Mr. Bathurst, with intelligent sympathy. "I understand perfectly why you can't help me over that. Now for my second question. This woman, who touched your face and frightened you—why do you think she carried a knife in her hand?"

Hammond shivered. The memory of that terrible moment was too imminent for her to remember it unemotionally. Her shiver was very real—Anthony was quick to see that fact.

"I *think* it was a knife," came the slow reply—"it flashed like a knife."

"She made no attempt to strike at you with it?"

Hammond's white face grew whiter. "No—and a good job for me that she didn't. For I couldn't have lifted a blessed finger to have stopped her—I was that scared I was."

"I've no doubt you were. It was a very nasty and thoroughly unnerving experience for you to have to undergo—quite of the type to upset the stoutest heart. You've nothing at all with which to reproach yourself as far as that goes. But this skirt or frock of hers that you say you felt—could you describe the material in any way? Was it of light texture—or heavy—for example? Any point about it that struck you may prove eventually to be of the highest importance. Can you recall?"

"I don't think I could. But I think it was of dark colour—else I should have been able to have seen it better, for I can't remember that I ever *really saw* it. Light colours are more easily seen in darkness, aren't they? Don't you think so, sir?"

"Perhaps they are. So you think this lady's dress was dark in colour?"

"As far as I could say—I *do* think so—but please understand, sir, I wouldn't swear to it or do anything like that."

"I quite appreciate that, of course." Anthony addressed himself to Miss Ashley. "I have no doubt, Miss Ashley, that you will find it easier to answer my next question than some of the others I have asked you," he declared. "What were the colours of the dresses worn by the various ladies last evening?"

"I wore a buttercup yellow, Mrs. Prendergast and Mrs. Venables black georgette—Ruby Trentham a *café au lait crêpe de chine*—we four were the only ladies present."

"There's a little problem in colours for you, Craig," said Bathurst with the momentary flicker of a smile on his face. "Two blacks, a yellow and a coffee—and on this occasion—just as is usually the case—two blacks won't make a white."

Craig grunted evasively.

"Tell Palmer we want her, Inspector," ordered Sir Austin—giving way to a strong feeling that it was incumbent upon him to take charge of the proceedings. "We shan't want you any more, Hammond," he added.

Palmer seemed to face the ordeal of the inquiry with a greater measure of equanimity than had been exhibited by her predecessor. She was of different calibre. She was a girl that possessed more than the normal share of self-confidence. Among her fellow-servants she had the reputation for rather prodigal drawings upon her imagination. Perhaps her critics were just a little too hard upon her. Actually she was blessed with what Anthony Bathurst, in a lighter moment, would have described as "an eminently natural gift for exaggerating things which never existed"; certainly, this power, which has gone so far upon its solitary way towards the establishment of the reputation of many of our greatest men and women, always served as an invaluable asset to her. She entered the study somewhat truculently and met Sir Austin's glare of antagonism—always ready at a moment's notice—with an indignant mien, worthy of the "British Warrior Queen" herself.

"Ask her what you want to ask her, Craig, as quickly as possible—we've a lot to do here, you know."

Craig got to work without more ado. "Tell me the exact circumstances under which you found Purvis, will you?"

"That's not much to tell, Inspector," she answered with ready alacrity. "I was going by his room—what was known as the butler's pantry, you understand—the door was open—and as I passed I couldn't but help seeing how strange he looked—unnatural-like, and all huddled together—he gave me a fair turn, he did. Something made me go in to have a closer look at him—I wasn't altogether satisfied—something seemed to tell me that there was something the matter with him. When I got up to him as he sat in his chair, I knew he was dead. Then I screamed and ran out of the room and along the corridor. I hadn't got far before I ran into Mr. Desmond here and Doctor Carrington—that's all I can tell you."

"How did you know he was dead?"

"Well, of course, Inspector, I didn't *know* in the manner of being certain of it—I wouldn't presoom so much—it wouldn't be my place to do such a thing—I *thought* it *was* so from the horrible look on his face. Such a dreadful colour he was, too."

"What time was it that this happened?"

Palmer gave the question careful consideration before she permitted herself the perilous adventure of reply.

"About a quarter-past twelve," she said.

"H'm! When you made this discovery were you aware of what had happened to Hammond?"

"No, sir. I hadn't heard a word about it. Nobody had breathed a syllable to me."

"Or about the absence of your master, either, I suppose?"

"I had no idea of it."

"What do you think of it, Bathurst?" asked Sir Austin—"want to ask her anything?"

"I do, sir—as a matter of fact. Something suggests itself to me." His grey eyes travelled across to Palmer and held hers as he asked his question. "When did you last see Purvis before you found him dead?"

"When did I last see him alive?"

"Exactly!"

"When he left the dining-room just before Sir Eustace did. I didn't see him again anywhere else after that."

Anthony, so it seemed to the Commissioner, experienced disappointment at the answer. He tried again. "Did you happen to see Sir Eustace again after he left the dining-room?"

Once again she shook her head in denial. "Neither of them, sir. I never set eyes on them again, sir, at all. But I heard them talking in here."

"You did!" exclaimed Mr. Bathurst—his eyes alive with keen interest. "And what time was that?"

"Round about ten o'clock, sir, I should say—as near as I can remember."

"And whom did you hear talking in here? Do I understand you to mean—Sir Eustace Vernon and Purvis?"

"I think it was them, sir! I distinctly heard a voice say—'That's something very special, Purvis—don't forget,' and then I heard Purvis reply, 'Very well, sir'—just as though he had been ordered to do something very important—then I heard a third voice say something."

"What!" yelled Craig—"what's that? A third voice?"

"That's what I said, Inspector," rejoined Palmer, with the utmost composure—"and that's what I mean, and there's no call to jump down my throat either. A third voice! A man's voice, too."

"Did you recognize it?" demanded Mr. Bathurst.

"Not to say *recognize* it, sir. That's worried me a bit, ever since, trying to recognize it, and I've been trying hard—I can tell you. I *can't* place it, and that's a fact. What worries me really is the fact that *I've heard the voice before—often.*"

"This grows interesting," observed Mr. Bathurst—"where?"

"I can't say where—that's just the trouble."

"When?"

She pondered over the question. He forced the issue to a decision.

"Recently?"

Her eyes flashed with excitement. "Yes! Recently! Within the last week or two!"

"Have you been in the Vernon House district all the time?"

"Yes, sir—haven't been farther than Mapleton since Michaelmas. Don't get much chance of gadding about in this district."

"Then the voice shouldn't live far away," remarked Mr. Bathurst. He walked across the room, away from her—then turned suddenly on his heel and spoke to her again. "The association of a voice may be a most elusive matter. For all you know," he declared, "you may have even heard it since—and *not* recognized it—it's quite possible—you know."

Chapter XII
THE DOCTOR AND THE MAJOR

"I feel very much more comfortable since lunch," remarked Sir Austin—"very much more comfortable—I always think the hour following upon lunch in an English country house one of the most agreeable and delightful moments of the day. It can be made so restful. Eh—Bathurst?"

"That and the luncheon-hour itself, Sir Austin. I must say that I find the latter extremely diverting upon quite a number of occasions during a normal year. Much more so than the tea interval."

"Quite so. Quite so. Whom do you propose seeing first, Craig? Are all the other people that you have asked to come along, here?"

"They are all here, sir. Mr. Desmond informed me to that effect a few moments ago. Everybody is present and it's simply a question of your convenience, sir, to commence the inquiry. Have you any particular desire, sir, as to the first person to be seen?"

"I do not intend to—er—take the spade-work of the case out of your hands, Craig—in any shape or form. That is very far from my wish—proceed just as though I was not here. You will carry on—regarding me simply as an interested—er—supervisor. Send for Doctor Carrington."

"Be seated, Doctor," declared the Inspector, as that gentleman stepped in briskly. Craig motioned towards the seat in which it was his intention that Carrington and all the others that were to follow, should sit.

"Good afternoon—gentlemen," said Carrington—"thank you."

"I wasn't able to say much to you last night about Sir Eustace Vernon, Doctor Carrington—I was concerned more then with the strange death of Purvis. But I understand, Doctor, that you were the late baronet's medical adviser."

"That is so, Inspector—quite true."

"Was he in good health?"

"Yes—and no. What I mean is this. He was organically sound—and constitutionally quite strong. But his nervous system had been impaired by a severe attack of influenza. And influenza leaves many legacies. He was in an acutely nervous condition a few weeks before Christmas and called me in to prescribe for him. I pulled him round a bit and in time would have tuned him up altogether."

At that moment he became aware for the first time of Mr. Bathurst's keen scrutiny. He shifted his seat—just a trifle.

"Was his condition at all consistent with suicide?"

Doctor Carrington shrugged his shoulders. "Do you mean would such an event have surprised me?"

"Something like that."

"As a medical man, I have learned to be surprised at nothing. But I can safely say this. I shouldn't have *expected* it."

Craig nodded his acceptance of the Doctor's point. "Did anything in Sir Eustace's manner at dinner, for instance, suggest to you that he was on the verge of what I will term—breaking-point?"

"Well—he was highly nervous—undoubtedly—but I wouldn't go so far as to answer 'yes' to your question, Inspector. To exemplify my point—one of the maids dropped a tray during dinner—the incident shook him visibly, but 'suicide' is a big proposition for any man to consider—let alone accept."

Mr. Bathurst leaned across the table towards him. "I understand, Doctor," he said, "that Sir Eustace declared at dinner that he had been the recipient of very bad news. Did you hear him say that?"

"Quite true. I did."

Mr. Bathurst continued. "I am also informed that you were Sir Eustace's immediate neighbour at table—that you were seated upon his immediate right—is that correct?"

"Quite right, again."

"Have you any idea, then, as to the *medium* through which Sir Eustace received this bad news of which he spoke—did he receive a letter, by any chance—or a note of any kind—or a verbal message from anybody? Sitting next to him, as you did, you surely would have seen had there been anything of that nature. You see my drift, don't you?"

"I appreciate your point, certainly. But I saw nothing at all. I was perfectly astounded when Sir Eustace rose in front of us all and made the announcement as he did. It was a bolt from the blue. I was staggered."

Mr. Bathurst spoke in a low whisper to Sir Austin. The latter frowned and nodded, and then gave what was apparently an instruction to Craig. Mr. Bathurst waited for Sir Austin to finish whatever it was he was saying. Facing Doctor Carrington again, his next remark stung and startled that gentleman much more than he had anticipated. "You remember the red bonbon found on Purvis, Doctor, don't you? Did you happen to notice if Sir Eustace—when he left the dining-table, carried such a bonbon away with him? Carelessly perhaps—or even absent-mindedly?"

Doctor Carrington shook his head. "Not to my knowledge. But if I may be allowed to say so—that occurs to me to be an extraordinary question."

"Not so extraordinary as you may imagine, Doctor," responded Mr. Bathurst somewhat nonchalantly—"for a similar red bonbon to that found on Purvis has also been found upon the dead body of Sir Eustace Vernon—who we have strong reasons to believe has been murdered."

Carrington sat bolt upright in his chair, his perplexity vying with his sense of horror. "Murdered?" he repeated, tonelessly.

"Unhappily—yes," returned Anthony—"although his body was found on the line near the level-crossing known as Dyke's Crossing, showing undoubted signs of having been run over by a train. But we have very good grounds for belief that he was shot in the head from behind by somebody and then carried to the crossing."

"Good heavens!" cried Carrington—"you can't mean it, how terrible—how was he taken to the level-crossing—how could a dead body be carried—"

"As far as we can tell, in his own car, Doctor," said Bathurst.

"You take my breath away—it seems unbelievable."

"I must conclude then, Doctor, by assuming that you can throw no light upon the matter at all? You know of no enemies that Sir Eustace might have had?"

Carrington raised his eyebrows semi-protestingly. "As his medical adviser I hardly came into very close contact with some sides of his character. That I think must be obvious. I simply called upon him when he was ill and sent for me. We were certainly getting to be on more intimate terms. But I know of nobody who had cause either to harm him or to wish him harm." He paused—only to proceed immediately. "I should like to put a question to you, gentlemen, in my turn, if I may be allowed? You assert that a similar red bonbon was found on Sir Eustace Vernon to that which we discovered on poor Purvis. Am I to understand also that it bore the same message? Or at least a similar message?"

The Inspector answered him readily. "That is so, Doctor. The message was exactly the same—that is to say—it was couched in similar words—'one hour to live—you pay your debt to-night.'"

"In the same handwriting?" rejoined Carrington, countering rapidly.

"To the best of our information—no."

"They appear to be two victims of the same diabolical plot," muttered the Doctor—"except, of course, for the fact of Vernon's letter, hinting at suicide as it did. That's hard to explain—at least so it seems to me. I'm not a professional investigator, of course—but—"

"The case presents strange features certainly," interposed Sir Austin. "I'm in complete agreement with you, Doctor. Tell Major Prendergast we should like to see him, will you, please?"

"One question before you go, Doctor Carrington"—Anthony Bathurst came in with quick and incisive eagerness. "From your knowledge of Sir Eustace, would you describe him as what is usually termed 'a ladies' man'?"

Carrington reflected for a moment before he answered. "I should describe him, without any hesitation, as a man who *admired* the opposite sex—tremendously. But I would not go beyond that. I might be doing him an injustice if I did."

"Thank you, Doctor," remarked Mr. Bathurst cordially.

Major Prendergast received the news of Sir Eustace's death with stoical calm. The details with which he was previously, presumably, unacquainted, awoke within him less emotion, possibly, than they had done in the case of Doctor Carrington. When the Inspector mentioned the fact of Sir Eustace having been shot from behind, he shook his head sadly.

"I can't honestly say that this information surprises me, Inspector. I felt from the first—or rather from the discovery of Vernon's farewell letter, that his intention to commit suicide could only have been engendered by a desire to escape from perhaps a worse fate which he knew was hanging over him. He was a brave man, you know, Inspector, who had proved his bravery."

"So I understand, Major. You know of nothing, I presume, likely to help us in our investigations or to throw any further light on the matter? No facts worth mentioning?"

Major Prendergast shook his head slowly. "I'm afraid not. It seems to me that your difficulty, Inspector, is going to be the time-honoured question of 'motive.' I know, of course, that remark applies to most crimes, but in a damnable murder like this it's—" He broke off with sudden abruptness.

"By Jove, Inspector! Now that's very remarkable to say the least of it. When I fired those remarks off relative to 'motive' I thought of people as possibly guilty who might have benefited by Sir Eustace's death. And by Jove! I've just thought of one."

"Who was that?" demanded Craig curiously.

"Myself, sir, and that's a solemn fact!"

Mr. Bathurst began to consider an absolutely interesting situation.

"You?" queried Craig—"in what way do you mean?"

"I'll be perfectly frank with you, Inspector, because I don't believe in keeping anything bottled up. I've always believed in direct methods, and consider that nothing can ever be gained by keeping relevant facts a secret. But as you know, Sir Eustace Vernon and I are—or rather were—close neighbours. My place—Camberley House—is next to Sir Eustace's estate. But part of my estate was once part of the Vernon House estate. But there were sales of land at various times, and at the present moment the two estates are separated by a piece of land known as the Forest Waste. Both Vernon and I were extremely anxious to purchase it, and we had, in turn, opened up negotiations to that effect with the owner. Had either of us been out of the way, the deal would have gone through, but as we remained in the market together, the owner seemed chary of coming up to scratch and finishing the business off. I believe there was a clause in the title deeds or something that permission to sell and also approval of the identity of the purchaser must be obtained from the estate holders of both Vernon House and Camberley House. Originally, you see, the whole thing was one estate and all the interests were wrapped up together. Now the most important thing of all is, *why* we each desired to buy Forest Waste." He paused abruptly as though seeking to discover the effect of his statement upon his audience.

"Let's have it," urged Craig.

"One moment, Inspector and Major," intervened Mr. Bathurst, very quietly. "To whom does the Forest Waste belong?"

"To Oliver Venables—elder brother of the Mayor of Mapleton—the Alderman Venables who dined with us last night."

"Thank you, Major. Proceed, will you?"

"*Why* both Sir Eustace and I desired to purchase the Forest Waste was because there is a vein of *tin* under it. I had the tip from a very reliable and influential quarter, and there is no doubt in my own mind that Vernon had heard pretty much the same information. As it is, I hope to conclude the deal with Venables this week—he's getting quite a good price for the land. But if good judges are right, there will be an annual output of tin ore from Forest Waste of about a thousand tons—equivalent to something like one hundred and twenty thousand pounds in hard cash. Then—but *not* till then—Oliver Venables will wish he hadn't sold." Major Prendergast coughed in apparent appreciation of his own unusual business acumen.

"During the time that elapsed between the conclusion of dinner and the first intimation you had of anything being radically wrong—where did you spend the time, Major?"

"Mostly in the music-room, Inspector—with Miss Ashley, Father Jewell and Mrs. Trentham. For a short time I was in the billiard-room watching Desmond and Doctor Carrington trying a few fancy shots, but I spent the whole of the time in the two rooms. I went nowhere else."

"I understand from Desmond," put in Craig, "that nobody played billiards last night beyond Doctor Carrington and himself. Doctor Carrington confirms that statement. You did not play, of course?"

"I told you, Inspector, I only watched. Put my time in the billiard-room at a matter of twenty minutes or so—you won't be very far out. I didn't murder Sir Eustace Vernon—if that's what you're—"

"Really, Major," said Mr. Bathurst—"I'm sure Inspector Craig will be the last to—but there—I want to ask you something else. When you examined the inner apartment, over there, in conjunction with Doctor Carrington"—Anthony pointed in the direction of the library—"I understand you were smoking a cigar—is that so?"

Major Prendergast showed signs of bewilderment upon his heavy face. "I was, sir. What of it? I put it on to serve as a steadying influence upon my nerves. Things looked damnably uncomfortable."

"I don't doubt that for a moment, Major. I have an altogether different motive for asking you. I'm confirming the fact in the first place, that you *did* smoke a cigar. But tell me this. When you and Doctor Carrington entered the library over there and found the safe door wide open—were you compelled to pull the *portière* to one side to make your entry?"

Major Prendergast looked puzzled, but nevertheless attempted to remember. He nodded his head slowly in affirmation. "Yes—I remember, I drew the curtain to one side."

"Thank you. Did the curtain remain drawn to that side during the whole of the time that you and the others were in the library?"

"Yes—as far as I can recollect—the curtain wasn't touched again by anybody. Nobody had any reason to touch if. But I don't see to where all this is leading."

"Don't be discouraged at that, Major. Somehow I don't fancy that you're the only one in that predicament."

Inspector Craig, sensitive apparently to the irony of the remark, glanced sharply in the direction of Mr. Bathurst—but Mr. Bathurst's eyes were elsewhere. Which fact brought a frown to the brow of the Inspector.

Chapter XIII
AND SOME OTHERS

Sir Austin Kemble took up the threads with an air. "I suppose Mrs. Prendergast won't be able to tell us more than you have, Major?"

Mr. Bathurst watched the expression on the Major's face as he answered.

"My wife, sir? Not by any means. Goodness gracious! The whole affair has upset her thoroughly. I can tell you that. But as to being able to give you any evidence—you can dismiss the idea at once, sir. You're very wide of the mark. She sat next to me at dinner and played 'Auction' afterwards all the time. The party consisted of the Mayor, Alderman Venables, and Mrs. Venables—Trentham and my wife. When the upset came—the first upset of that infernal night—Venables was on the point of getting ready for home."

Sir Austin pursed his lips and nodded. "I see. Then I won't detain you any longer. Be good enough to tell Father Jewell when you go out that we would like to see him in here, will you, Major?"

Major Prendergast bowed and departed. Scarcely had the door shut behind him than it opened again to admit Father Jewell. His tall, gaunt figure afforded a striking contrast, not only to those before whom he appeared, but also to the two men who had gone before.

"I have the honour, I believe, of addressing Sir Austin Kemble—the Commissioner of Police." His voice was the voice of the trained elocutionist, and Anthony instantly made a mental note to that effect.

"I am Sir Austin Kemble. This gentleman is Mr. Anthony Bathurst—a personal friend of mine—and this is Inspector Craig. He wishes to ask you one or two questions, Father Jewell, with regard to last night's affair. There is, of course, no need for me to emphasize the necessity."

Craig made his usual opening. "You know of no fact, I suppose, Father—likely to help us—in relation to what took place here last night? It is our duty to get at the truth of the case if we possibly can—and anything may serve to put us on the track of things, you know."

"I do not think I can help you at all, Inspector. Sir Eustace's sad end—the death of Purvis—and the discovery of the strange sex-secret in the case of the latter—have in turn completely mystified me. The whole thing affords me amazement. Profound astonishment! I don't see from where light is coming to you either, Inspector. The ways of the Almighty are inscrutable. Many dark weeds grow in the garden of the human soul unfortunately, and He moves in a mysterious way very often to effect His Divine Purpose. As a member of His Priesthood—"

"Quite so, Father. What you say is very true. You know of nothing then worthy or important enough to be mentioned?"

"Nothing whatever, Inspector."

Father Jewell clasped his hands with their long quivering fingers, behind his back. Craig tried a different tack. "Unfortunately we have cause to believe that Sir Eustace was murdered, Father, and that his intended suicide was—"

"I am aware of that, Inspector," came the priest's unruffled reply. "Sir Eustace was shot from behind, I understand."

"Where did you hear this, may I ask?"

"From Doctor Carrington a few minutes ago. He gave me the facts as far as he knew them. He told me he had been informed by you in here."

Craig frowned his annoyance. He had not intended that the Doctor should broadcast the news. The element of surprise in any form of attack is always far too valuable to be neglected or despised. He had meant to surprise more than one of the Christmas house-party with the true story of Sir Eustace's death in the hope that he would be rewarded with some response or rejoinder that would hold some definite tangibility. His frown deepened. Anthony came to his assistance.

"It seems to me a very strange thing, Father, that anybody should have harboured murderous thoughts against such a man as Sir Eustace Vernon. I should say his place in Mapleton, from what I have already heard, will be very hard to fill."

"I appreciate what you say, Mr. Bathurst. But at the same time you will permit me to point out that there is none of us whose place could not be filled. And it is meet that every one of us should realize that fact from the depths of our humility. It would be better for the world if we did so. We are tiny atoms in the sight of Almighty God. As to Sir Eustace having incurred the enmity of anybody—violent passions are only too easily aroused, and when they are aroused, they play havoc with the best natures. 'To err is human'—every day I live I am made more conscious of Human Frailty." His voice shook with the tremor of earnestness. "The world with its heritage of Sin still chooses Barabbas, and Christ is crucified daily. He occupies the scaffold far more than He does the Throne." Father Jewell raised his right hand fervently. Mr. Bathurst remained silent for a moment or two. He always respected anything that came from the heart. But his next question took an unexpected turn. The point of attack was completely changed, and even Sir Austin Kemble awaited the priest's reply with more than ordinary interest.

"When Hammond told you her story of having been attacked by a woman—whom did you suspect?"

"Suspect?" thundered the priest—his voice resonant with surprise—and just a *soupçon* of indignation.

"What do you mean? Why should I have—"

"Which woman?" returned Mr. Bathurst, with infinite coolness. He went on. "There were several in the house, remember. And we have no adequate reason for disbelieving Hammond's story—have we? When she accused a woman—surely the thoughts of all of you turned to the women in the house at the time?"

"Several in the house? I fail to see—"

"Just let us consider the *personnel* for one moment, if you please. There were Miss Ashley, Mrs. Prendergast, Mrs. Trentham, the Mayoress of Mapleton—Mrs. Venables—the other maid Palmer—and we mustn't overlook Purvis, the butler. Did you suspect any one of them—for example—Mrs. Prendergast—or Mrs. Venables, or—"

"I did not for the very good reason that I had no grounds to do such a thing. I imagined that Hammond's accusation was directed against a stranger. But if there is one lady about whom I can stifle suspicion immediately, it is Mrs. Prendergast. It is not too often that the Creator sends one of His pure angels upon earth to lighten our load and to illumine the way. It is not too often that He spills His Divine Goodness into the mould of human form so wastefully. Diana Prendergast is a lady for whom we should return our most blessed thanks."

"You are not alone, I take it, Father Jewell, in thinking like that?"

"Alone—Mr. Bathurst?" The priest's face shone with the cold radiance of heartfelt and celibate enthusiasm. "There are hundreds of souls here—"

Mr. Bathurst cut in—regardless of ceremony. "May I take it, for instance, that Sir Eustace Vernon shared that view?"

Father Jewell paused—he drew himself up to his full height—then seemed to check himself. There was a hint that he was retreating from what he had been about to say. He even appeared to allow himself the suggestion of a shrugged shoulder, "I have no doubt that Sir Eustace Vernon appreciated and viewed Mrs. Prendergast's qualities in the same way that I—that we all did. If you mean anything more than that, I regret that I cannot travel so far. I find the suggestion somewhat unpleasant."

Mr. Bathurst affected a certain indifference. "He was a brave man, you know, Father. And brave men—" He turned to Craig. "I shan't want to ask Father Jewell any more questions, Inspector. I don't know whether you do."

"No?" queried Sir Austin, as Craig dissented—"then perhaps Father Jewell would request Mr. Trentham to step this way. Thank you." The priest withdrew rapidly yet with dignity.

Morris Trentham looked as though the events of the previous night had shaken him considerably. He was not the sort to meet trouble with serenity. His fattish face was creased and lined with something more than care. He proved singularly uncommunicative, and had accepted the fact of Sir Eustace's murder with a quality that was as akin to stolid resignation as to anything else. It was as though he said to them, "After the happenings of last night that thoroughly and most inconsiderately upset my Christmas for me—I am prepared for *anything*, and nothing you can say in here now can in any way surprise me." He was a member of the Stock Exchange, he informed them, and had had business associations with the murdered man—associations that had a great deal to do with the cementing of their friendship. What? Did he know a Mr. Paget-Colvin? He looked at Mr. Bathurst—the inquirer, with some show of surprise. He certainly had known a gentleman of that name some four or five years back—in fact, Mr. Paget-Colvin had introduced Sir Eustace to him. Mr. Paget-Colvin had conducted some very successful operations upon Sir Eustace's behalf. Rubber—he believed! But Mr. Paget-Colvin had retired since then and had gone to live in the south of England somewhere—either in Hampshire or in Dorset, he believed, but he was not sure. In reply to Inspector Craig, he had played "Auction" after dinner with Alderman and Mrs. Venables and Mrs. Prendergast. He had certainly noticed the fact that Sir

Eustace had failed to rejoin his guests and had wondered what it could be that kept him away for so long. It was he who had observed that Sir Eustace's car was missing from the garage during the hastily-improvised search through the garden. But beyond that he could tell them nothing. Mr. Bathurst rose from his chair and conferred with Sir Austin Kemble. He spoke in low tones. The Commissioner listened attentively and appeared to extend approval to what Mr. Bathurst was suggesting.

"Certainly, Bathurst, by all means."

"Thank you," said Anthony. "Will you—"

"Mr. Trentham," declared the Commissioner—"we should like to interview Mrs. Trentham. She occupies a somewhat important place in our investigations by reason of the fact that she sat next to Sir Eustace Vernon at dinner last night. We are prepared, however, to allow you to remain here during her examination. I have no wish to try her unduly. Inspector! Call Mrs. Trentham in." The Commissioner's attention to Inspector Craig as he uttered his last remark caused him to miss the expression of annoyance that flitted across Trentham's face. He had evidently not expected that his wife would be subjected to any questioning from Scotland Yard. His eyes met hers as she entered, but even such an acute observer as Mr. Bathurst was unable to assess accurately what the message was that they intended to convey. Ruby Trentham's face was excessively pale, which only seemed, however, to accentuate her dusky, almost Southern beauty. Her raven hair and dark lustrous eyes suggested senoritas—guitars—and latticed casements half-opened to the seduction of the serenade. Mr. Bathurst, proof against feminine allurement, schooled himself to remember that this was the lady who had sat next to Sir Eustace at dinner at that gentleman's especial request. It was upon these lines that he desired to question her. It seemed to him to be fraught with a great deal of importance to the case.

"Sit down, Mrs. Trentham, will you, please?" He indicated the chair, into which the lady sank with a hint of relief. "You have no doubt heard by now of the circumstances in which your late host met his death, Mrs. Trentham. Unfortunately we believe him to have been murdered. Very treacherously murdered. Shot in the head from behind. A most distressing affair and one which will require all our abilities to elucidate. What I desire to ask you is this. You occupied the chair on Sir Eustace Vernon's immediate left at dinner last night. Now—this is my point. Can you possibly tell me if Sir Eustace received any letter or note during dinner—anything to cause him to make the startling announcement that he did? The announcement that he had received bad news."

"Nothing at all," replied Ruby Trentham with decision, but yet coldly. Her voice was pitched very low—but was nevertheless perfectly audible to all of them in the room as they listened to her. She proceeded. "Sir Eustace had seemed in excellent spirits—although I should say—if my opinion's worth anything—undergoing some severe nervous strain. He had been talking quite cheerfully to me—and to all of us—and saying how old-fashioned he was to enjoy Christmas as whole-heartedly as he did. I saw no letter of any kind brought in to him."

"Good," replied Anthony—"did you happen to hear anything of what it was he said to Purvis subsequently—or alternatively perhaps—of what Purvis said to him?"

"Not a word. I didn't listen, of course—not a syllable of the conversation reached my ears. It was obviously of a private nature."

"Thank you, Mrs. Trentham. Then I have only one more question to ask you. When you saw Sir Eustace walk down the dining-room to make his exit—did you happen by any chance to notice if he carried such a thing as a red bonbon with him? If he did—you, as the person sitting next to him, would stand the best chance of anybody, I fancy, to see it."

Ruby Trentham's hand travelled tremulously to her lips. "Oh—but he did! He did! He took *two away with him! His own and the bonbon that had been laid beside my plate for me!*"

"We progress, Inspector," remarked Mr. Bathurst, rubbing his hands. "I think I begin to see a little light at last." As he turned towards Sir Austin Kemble he was able to observe the combative frown on Morris Trentham's coarse, puffy face. It was very evident that something Ruby Trentham had said annoyed him, and Mr. Bathurst, serenely confident as usual, fancied that he knew what that something was.

Chapter XIV
THE MAYOR OF MAPLETON IS UNUSUALLY RETICENT

WHEN THE study door had closed upon Morris and Ruby Trentham, plain husband and beautiful wife, at the conclusion of the interview, Inspector Craig approached Sir Austin Kemble deferentially and disconsolately. "It seems very plain to me, sir, that we're very little 'forrader' as you might say. After all these people's stories we're no nearer knowing who the woman in the dark dress was—and it seems to me that we're no nearer knowing what caused Sir Eustace to decide on committing suicide. I agree with Mr. Bathurst, there's something we've missed. I think, in all probability, that I shall have to start on fresh lines all over again."

The Commissioner grunted. It would be difficult to assert if the grunt were in assent or dissent. Perhaps its best description would be "non-committal." It was a grunt that occupied a comfortable seat upon the mental fence. Anthony Bathurst thrust his hands deep into his trousers pockets and paced the floor of the room . . . backwards and forwards . . . two or three times. "In some respects, Sir Austin," he declared, "I'm disposed to agree with Inspector Craig. We are still very much in the dark, undoubtedly. There is so much in the story that has been presented to us that seems impossible of explanation—that is to say, with our present knowledge. From some points of view it appeals to me as the most difficult case of my career. On the other hand, we've been able to establish two or three facts at least. Any one of which may well prove to be our starting-point." He paused suddenly in one of his brief promenades. "A starting-point is a great thing, Inspector. When I get a starting-point, I invariably progress. And I've known it come from something that in its inception appeared to be absolutely infinitesimal or seemingly irrelevant. A chance word spoken—a stray remark here or there—a phrase in a written letter—an apparently insignificant incident—any one of these may put the investigator on the track that leads to ultimate success. In that pretty little problem at Considine Manor, for instance, it was the disposition of the bedclothes that established my previously purely tentative theory as absolutely definite, while in the very intriguing case of 'The Peacock's Eye' an even more trifling matter became the foundation-stone of the case that I eventually constructed. You see what I mean—don't you?" His grey eyes—eagerly interrogative—embraced both Sir Austin and Craig as he put his question to them. Without waiting for a reply from either—he continued upon the elaboration of his argument. "For example—consider just three things that we've been fortunate enough to establish this afternoon. Three points of definite progress. Palmer, the maid, is prepared to swear that she heard a third person in conversation with Sir Eustace Vernon and his butler—Purvis—both of whom are dead, mark you—*and—more important still—that the voice was—she feels sure—the voice of a man who is familiar to her.* You can't gainsay the importance of Palmer's statement—from any point of view—because it's so definitely *relevant.*"

Craig permitted himself a nod of acquiescence. "I agree there, Mr. Bathurst I admit that, willingly, but we don't—"

"Just a minute, Craig—think of something else. Take Major Prendergast's story of the coveted piece of land—he was almost self-accusative—a quality with which one seldom meets—especially in investigations of this nature. I wonder! I wonder!" He caressed his upper lip with his finger-tips . . . reflective and considering. Turning to Sir Austin with a chuckle, "'Pon my soul, sir," he exclaimed with that *éclat* that was peculiarly his—"we shall stimulate *'Entente Cordiale'* and give our French cousins a new proverb in exchange for that famous one of their own."

Sir Austin's eyebrows went up—somewhat askance. Then his face cleared somewhat. "I see your meaning, Bathurst. The new version will be *'Qui s'accuse, s'excuse'*—eh?"

"Assuredly," said Mr. Bathurst—"my meaning exactly. I don't say that it will be—although the Major intended that it should." He swung round on Craig. "Moreover, Inspector—and I'm inclined to rate this as our most important discovery since we entered Vernon House—Sir Eustace Vernon carried two red bonbons away from the table with him when he left the dining-room. Note what I say! *He took the two of them!* By the way, Craig, here's another point for you. Where do you place Sam McLaren's assailants in all this? Have you thought of them? I see no reason at all why we should doubt his story, do you? Why were they after the letter Sir Eustace had sent him? Also what was it that Vernon knew to benefit Sam? When we can answer all these . . . I think . . ." His face changed. "How about seeing this Mayor chap, Venables, Sir Austin? There's this question of the Forest Waste. It's on the cards he might know something."

"I think so. Send for him, Inspector, will you please?"

Craig went to the door.

"And I should also like to have a few words with Stevens, Sir Austin," mentioned Anthony—"that's the chauffeur—I should like to check up one or two points in connection with Sam McLaren's story."

The Mayor of Mapleton acknowledged the open door that the Inspector held for him with a somewhat solemn wave of the hand. It was a gesture upon which he rather prided himself, for it was based upon much observation of Army officers acknowledging salutes during the four war-years of 1914 to 1918. It was the only thing for which he would have liked to have held commissioned rank. This magnificent gesture, coupled with a genuine lack of understanding of most things, had been his two strongest claims to represent the burgesses of Mapleton for a great many years. At the present moment the predominant thought in his mind was one of distinct annoyance—in which respect he resembled Morris Trentham. But the annoyance rose from another reason. Truth to tell, he had never been too fond of his dead host. In the Council Chamber, Sir Eustace had rather "shown him up," as his own secret admission had it, and like most men of his type, he was acutely jealous of people possessing greater ability than had fallen to his own lot. Which fact caused him to be jealous of everybody! Now Sir Eustace was dead, Venables wished nothing more than to be well out of the whole business. Free from any unpleasantness that the inquiry might bring in its wake and rid of all the tragedy's associations! He found the intimacy of it abominably irksome. Actually he had complained to his wife that afternoon before returning to Vernon House, at the behest of this infernal Police Inspector, that he sincerely wished he had never been prevailed upon to accept Vernon's Christmas invitation. He walked to the seat that the Inspector selected for him with the feeling that the whole business as represented in its present conditions was nothing more or less than a distinct affront to the Civic dignity of Mapleton, He took his seat with the stern determination that more should be heard of it. On one occasion he had told the Ministry of Health auditor—his reminiscence was interrupted.

"You are acquainted, I take it, Mr.—er—Mayor, with the fact that Sir Eustace Vernon was murdered?"

"Yes, Inspector Craig. But I have known it only since I arrived here this afternoon. When I came to-day I was under the impression that he had committed suicide—the impression under which I left Vernon House very early this morning." There was a sourness in his tone that he made no attempt to hide.

"Quite so, Mr. Mayor. Well, now, the point is just this. Can you help the police at all? Do you know of anything that you imagine we may be in ignorance of?"

Craig was at his best here and maintained a perfect suavity of manner and tone. Venables, however, resented bitterly the fact that he should be questioned at all. It usually fell to his lot to ask questions of others, an occupation which appealed to him far more than the reverse position in which he now found himself.

"I am a Justice of the Peace, Inspector Craig, as you know. I have administered justice for more years than I care to remember. That fact alone should be sufficient to tell you that, if I knew anything that I considered important, I should immediately share that knowledge with the police—of that you may be assured." His face indicated severe disapprobation as Craig accorded him the suggestion of a bow.

"Quite so, Mr. Mayor—quite so. I think I can truthfully say that I appreciate that. But in a case of this kind—" He stopped, seemingly at a temporary loss for adequate words to describe the situation effectively.

Anthony at once took up the parable. "If you are unable to tell us anything, Alderman Venables—you will I am sure help us and support us to the full hilt of your power. You will be delighted to work with us. Do you know anything about a piece of land adjoining the late Sir Eustace Vernon's property, known as the Forest Waste?"

"Naturally," came the quick reply. "It would be strange if I did not—seeing that the piece of land in question is the property of my brother, Oliver Venables."

"Following up my first question then—do you know anything about that piece of land being sold—or your brother, for instance, negotiating with any prospective client in regard to such a sale?"

Alderman Venables' rather prominent teeth closed with an unmistakable snap. "I make it a rule, sir—and an inviolable rule at that—never to interfere in any way with anybody else's business—least of all my brother's."

"Come, Alderman Venables—surely you go too far when you say that? Surely it would be possible to have such knowledge as I suggested without laying yourself open to the charge of interference—probably you might have heard it from many—what I may reasonably term—justifiable sources?"

"I might—but I haven't. That ends the matter, I think. My brother's way in Mapleton and my way lie apart. It is not my intention that they should ever do otherwise." He rose from his seat.

It was evident to all of them who watched that he wished this remark to terminate the interview. For a moment, however, the Mayor stood in the centre of the room—irresolute and undecided—awaiting as it were the acquiescence of the others in this desire. It came at last from Sir Austin Kemble, and immediately upon its reception Venables withdrew.

"H'm," muttered Craig—"nice companionable sort of fellow to be sure. I always thought, sir," he continued, turning to Sir Austin, "that Mayors and Aldermen were jovial gentlemen—'hail-fellow-well-met' as you might say. I couldn't say that much, sir, for Mr. Alderman Venables."

Sir Austin ignored the Inspector's remark and addressed Anthony. "Where was Venables after dinner last night? Refresh my memory."

"Playing Auction Bridge, with his wife, Mrs. Prendergast and Trentham."

"Puts him out of the reckoning then, I remember now—Trentham told us. Still, you never . . ." He stopped—evidently considering some feature of the case very deeply.

"Is there anybody else you would like to see now, sir?" appealed Inspector Craig. Sir Austin shook his head.

"I think not, Craig, I think not. It seems to me that we've been able to exhaust most of the—"

"There *is* one more person with whom I would like to have a word, Sir Austin," broke in Mr. Bathurst—"as I mentioned just now. Perhaps if we sent for Mr. Desmond again he would see to it. The man I want to have a word with is Stevens—Sir Eustace Vernon's chauffeur. Firstly—there is Sam McLaren's evidence and secondly the fact that he figures rather prominently, I think, in the general story."

"I agree, Bathurst. Craig! Tell Mr. Desmond to send for this man Stevens, at once. Tell him we want to see him in here. Tell them to lose no time. I'm getting impatient."

A matter of a quarter of an hour brought the man that Mr. Bathurst required. At a sign from Sir Austin, peremptory at that—Anthony commenced the examination.

"You are Stevens, the late Sir Eustace Vernon's chauffeur?"

"Quite right, sir. And I served a good master, too."

"I've no reason to doubt your word, Stevens. And in a way you can still serve him. By telling us all you know. If you do that you will help the police to avenge his murder. Do you understand what I mean?"

Stevens jerked his dark head with some show of indignation; his thin face betrayed emotion.

"Very well indeed, sir. I shall be only too pleased to tell you all I know. Not that it's much. The first intimation that I had as to anything being wrong or out of the ordinary last night was about half-past nine. I was just going down to the kennels to give some special food to Boris, the wolfhound. The dog's been queer—and been under the vet.—and has been placed on special diet. Well—about half-past nine, as I said, I got a message from Sir Eustace."

"Who brought it?" interrogated Anthony sharply.

"Purvis—the butler. He came to tell me that the guv'nor wanted me in his study. I thought it was funny at that time of night, but I told Hammond to go down to the kennels and feed the dog, and I went straight off to Sir Eustace. When I got there—into the study—he gave me a note to take down to Sam McLaren—the old boy that runs the coffee-stall in Mapleton. I was to take the letter to Sam's place in Mafeking Street at once. Then, sir, I got a proper shock. Sir Eustace told me it was a matter of life and death."

"Were they his exact words, Stevens?"

"They were, sir. The absolutely exact words. And what's more, that I was to tell no one—which is why I haven't spilt till now. I haven't known quite what to do, but I reckon him being dead releases me from my promise, don't you, sir?"

Anthony made no reply to the chauffeur's query, but Sir Austin flung a question to Stevens that everybody had been expecting for some little time.

"Did Sir Eustace give you any inkling as to what his letter to Sam McLaren contained?"

Stevens shook his head vigorously. "None whatever, sir. I know no more with regard to that than you do, sir."

Anthony ran his forefinger along his upper lip. "When Sam McLaren received this message and read it—did he show any signs of surprise?"

The chauffeur turned the question over very carefully. "No," he announced at length. "I wouldn't say that he did."

"When you returned, Stevens—did you report again to Sir Eustace?"

"No, sir. I don't see that I had any reason to. I hadn't been ordered to do so. I had delivered the message, which was all I had been told. I put the car away in the garage and went indoors to enjoy a 'fag.'"

Mr. Bathurst approached the Inspector. "Do you want to ask the chauffeur anything, Inspector Craig?"

"No, Mr. Bathurst—I don't think so—you've covered most of the ground, I think."

"I've finished then, Sir Austin—with your permission."

The Commissioner nodded approval. Stevens touched his forehead and went out—Craig closing the door behind him.

"Well, Bathurst," demanded Sir Austin—"what do you make of it all?"

"I can't balance one or two important points, Sir Austin. I can't make them tally at all. I'm puzzled. But the ray of light that makes all the difference may come at any moment."

Craig nodded to emphasize his agreement. "But what I can't understand," he urged, "is this. Why did Hammond delay feeding that wretched dog for nearly two hours and a half? Here we have Stevens telling us that at half-past nine or thereabouts he told her to—"

"That doesn't puzzle me at all, Craig," interrupted Mr. Bathurst. "That will be easily explained, you will discover eventually. I'm considering a much more important point than that. If Sir Eustace Vernon wanted Sam McLaren last night on a matter of 'life and death' (to use his own words, mark you) and sent his chauffeur in his car with a message to that effect to Sam—why on earth didn't Sam *come back in the car with the chauffeur*? Why did he *wait* and *walk back*, thereby *wasting time*, to say nothing of the inconvenience? Was he obeying Sir Eustace's instructions? The two things don't coincide at all. And I'm hanged if I know why! There's something we're still missing, Sir Austin, and as Craig said just now, it's a vital something."

Mr. Bathurst began to pace the room—industriously. For his reason told him that, if the chauffeur's story were true, Sam should have returned in the Wolseley. But Sam had walked! And the question hammered on Mr. Bathurst's brain. Why had Sam walked—*had he been told to?*

Chapter XV
A LITTLE MORE LIGHT

Mr. Bathurst walked up the gravel drive and crossed the beautifully-kept stretch of grass that fronted Vernon House, somewhat absent-mindedly. For he was very much preoccupied. Two days had elapsed since the occurrences related in the preceding chapter, and he was very far from feeling easy with regard to the case upon which he and Sir Austin Kemble had stumbled so unexpectedly and in such strange circumstances. He was anxious for the time being because he found himself unable to separate the mass of information that had been presented to him into "facts that mattered" and "facts that didn't matter"— which process of separation he always contended was the first duty of the intelligent detective. So many people seemed to touch upon this latest case from some angle or another—more people perhaps than in any of his previous cases. He had heard from Inspector Craig that morning to the effect that that worthy had formulated a theory upon which he was concentrating very thoroughly. Mr. Bathurst had not been informed as to what the theory actually was, although he had definite suspicions. But he had telephoned Sir Austin Kemble at "the Yard" that he was travelling down to Rodding again that day in the hope of picking something up at Vernon House or in its vicinity that would enable him to essay his usual "summary of the case"—a task that he had not yet felt competent, even, to attempt. He rang the bell upon his arrival at the front of the house and handed in his card. Helen Ashley, emerging from the dining-room, was quick to greet him.

"Come in here, Mr. Bathurst," she said—"what have you to tell me? Is there anything? Have you discovered anything?" She led the way into the study.

Anthony shook his head disclaimingly. "I have nothing of any consequence to report, Miss Ashley. I am sorry to admit it—but it is so. Up to the moment we have made little progress."

"I am afraid the mystery is too deep," she replied, sadly. "Too deep to be solved by anybody. We shall never get to the bottom of it."

"I wouldn't go so far as to say that, Miss Ashley. Hope springs eternal, you know. A little thing might serve to help me—or any of the others working on the case—towards a solution. That is the kind of thing or the kind of idea—to put it more happily—that has brought me to Vernon House now. I'm hoping against hope." He paused and she looked up inquiringly. Mr. Bathurst warmed to his work. "You remember telling me that both you and Mr. Desmond were of the opinion that prior to his death, your uncle had seemed to be sorely afraid of something. That is so—isn't it?"

"Yes—that's quite true."

"Well now—a little point has occurred to me in connection with that fact. When your uncle was found on the line at Dyke's Crossing he was, of course, dressed as he was when he left the dinner-table. Just as one would expect him to be dressed, in fact. But tell me this. Was he a man who wore many suits? Did he often change his suit or did he usually stick to one for some time because he liked it, and probably found it comfortable—men differ in these matters—you know?"

Helen reflected over the question. "I think I know exactly what you mean, Mr. Bathurst," she said. "Of course, my uncle was in the habit of wearing several suits—for different occasions. But latterly he had been wearing a lounge suit of blue serge very regularly. It had a double-breasted jacket which fitted him rather well, and which he liked."

"Good," said Anthony—"now I should very much like to have a look at that particular jacket. Is it convenient, Miss Ashley?"

"Quite—I will get it for you, Mr. Bathurst." Before that gentleman could move to prevent her she had slipped from the room, which was not quite what Mr. Bathurst had intended should happen. She quickly returned, however, with the blue serge jacket that had been requisitioned by him. Anthony took it from her.

"I am going to be inquisitive, Miss Ashley. I want your permission to do something. I am going to ask you to allow me to look through the pockets."

She nodded in complete acceptance of the position. Save for a box of matches—half-filled—the side pockets were empty. From the inside pocket Anthony took a leather wallet. He opened it in front of her. It contained five penny stamps and four one-pound currency notes. In the opposite section to that which contained the four latter there were various pieces of paper—of various shapes and sizes. Mr. Bathurst extracted them with the utmost care—there were seven of them in all. The first was an ordinary envelope with an address scribbled on it in pencil—"Cornelius Van Hoyt, Letchworth Mount, near Leighton, Shropshire." It occupied Mr. Bathurst's attention for a brief space before he discarded it. The second was an account—unpaid—from a local veterinary surgeon—Mr. Blake-Dewhurst, of Mapleton—in respect of attendance upon "the wolfhound Boris." Mr. Bathurst noticed the dates. The third, fourth and fifth that Anthony extracted were hotel bills of various dates—the hotels being situated at Cardiff, Shrewsbury and Derby. The sixth caused Mr. Bathurst much more serious consideration. It ran as follows—"Suggest wanted for repertory 'The Only Way'—'The Prisoner of Zenda'—and 'The Lyons Mail'—all of which may be termed 'romantic drama.'" Anthony handled this creased note very carefully and looked up to find Miss Ashley watching him intently. He turned the paper over. On the back was written "J. Vincent Damery—Agent—Shaftesbury Avenue. Any time after ten." The seventh and last slip of paper was a piece of a page carelessly torn from a pocket diary—dated the 26th of November—it bore the word "Painswick," and underneath that two more words or portions of words, very faintly written. To Anthony's eyes they looked like "Page" and "Col," but he was forced to inspect them very closely before he could come to that conclusion.

"Well, Mr. Bathurst," interjected Helen Ashley—"are you any the wiser?"

"That's a question which is never too easy to answer, Miss Ashley. That is to say—to answer it in the way that you expect it to be answered. One can never tell, you know. But, speaking broadly, all additional information that an investigator is able to acquire as he proceeds upon a case, must make him wiser in a way—mustn't it?" He replaced the several papers in the wallet and handed it back to her. She took it and watched him with anxious eyes.

"Is Mr. Desmond still here?" he asked.

"He had to go home on important business. But he is returning here to-morrow, if he can possibly manage it. It is very kind of him, but he realizes, of course, that I need him."

"I understand perfectly. It is what I should have expected of him—no more and no less."

His eyes roamed round the room. "One more point, Miss Ashley, before I get back to town. Will you allow me to glance through your uncle's cheque-book?"

"Why do you ask me that, Mr. Bathurst?" She faced him with a strange mixture of what he described to himself at the time as composure and courage.

"It might help me, Miss Ashley. You would not deny me access to anything that might help me to avenge your uncle's murder—I am sure!" He raised a deprecating hand.

"You are right, of course, Mr. Bathurst, when you say that," she admitted. "But as it happens, you have asked me an impossibility. Or at all events something that amounts to an impossibility. I can't show you the check-book, because my uncle had no banking account."

Mr. Bathurst was at once keenly interested. "Really, Miss Ashley! And how do you explain that—er—anachronism?"

"My uncle refused to open an account at any bank. It was a whim of his. He used to say that anybody who wanted somebody else to mind his money for him ought to be minded himself. I realized that it was a perfectly ridiculous attitude for a modern man to adopt and I've remonstrated with him many times over the absurd position which he took up. But to no avail. My uncle was adamant. It was impossible to move him in the matter. I should say he was born with more than his fair share of obstinacy, and the experiences of later years only served to develop it more and more. So you see that I can't show you any cheque-book, Mr. Bathurst."

"How did your uncle pay his accounts then, Miss Ashley?"

"Nearly always by bank-notes."

"Then where did he keep them—there's that to be considered?"

She looked startled at the meaning his question held. "You mean—" she stopped, as though fearing to proceed.

"The safe—Miss Ashley—the safe! It might conceivably have held a fortune—with bank-notes of high denomination there." He rose from his chair as this new aspect of the problem presented itself to him. "With regard to yourself, then, Miss Ashley. This may make a tremendous difference to you—to your future. You see what I mean, don't you? If that safe contained bank-notes that comprised your uncle's financial resources—his fortune, if you like to describe it as such—what is there left for you?"

The girl's face was very strained and white as she made her reply. "I realize your meaning only too well, Mr. Bathurst. As a matter of fact, Mr. Desmond and I have discussed it between us since we have been faced with the situation; and of course it is made very much worse for me because of the fact that the parcel that my uncle mentioned in his last letter to me has gone too. Perhaps I shall never know now what it actually was that Uncle Eustace intended me to have so specially." Her eyes brimmed with tears, but Mr. Bathurst, although he was looking directly into them, was very definitely unconscious of the fact. His thoughts had winged a way elsewhere. Her last thoughts had given him the embryo of an idea for which he had been unsuccessfully groping for some time. "You refer, of course, to the second letter your uncle wrote on the night of his death.

Might I be permitted to glance at that again—do you happen to have it handy?"

She crossed to the other side of the room and took the letter from a drawer. "I shall keep this always," she said. "Apart from what it intended to do for me—these were the last words my uncle wrote. On that account alone I value it greatly."

Anthony glanced at her searchingly. A new thought had come to him from one of those spontaneous processes that always seemed to serve him so well, but deciding rapidly, he determined to mask it for the time being. Mr. Bathurst had profited more than once through the withholding of important information. He read the letter through. "This Cornelius Van Hoyt who is mentioned and whose address we happened to chance upon just now—you've never heard your uncle mention his name before, I suppose—in the course of conversation—or at any—"

"Never, Mr. Bathurst," she interposed—"I can safely say that the name is quite strange to me. I have never heard it. Neither had Mr. Desmond. I thought of the possibility and asked him the question myself."

"Thank you, Miss Ashley. Now you must pardon me asking you one more question—a question of a rather delicate nature."

A touch of colour tinged Miss Ashley's cheeks. "Yes, Mr. Bathurst?"

"This Mr. Desmond—who and what is he? What actual position does he occupy in the household?"

Helen Ashley's reply came with studied dignity. "Mr. Desmond is my friend, Mr. Bathurst. I have known him for nearly two years. He has done me the honour to ask me to be his wife."

Mr. Bathurst bowed. "Thank you, again, Miss Ashley. That was all I desired to know. I just wanted to be able to place his actual relationship—that was all. I don't think I need trouble you any more at present. The next time we meet perhaps I may be in a position to give you news. Take heart, and remember that it is always the darkest hour before the dawn." He held her hand in his for the briefest of moments. "Also, Miss Ashley—be assured of my most sincere sympathy."

Half an hour later, reclining luxuriously in the corner seat of a first-class carriage *en route* for London, Anthony Bathurst summed up the results of the day. He had come to Rodding optimistic about finding something that would help him to a greater understanding of the case. He was not absolutely sure, even now, as to the actual value of what he had managed to discover. His thoughts toyed unceasingly with the correspondence—if it could be correctly called such—that the dead man had thought of sufficient importance to retain within his private wallet. After a time he decided that the hotel bills might be discarded, although he would remember the three towns of stay—Cardiff, Derby and Shrewsbury. That left him with four items for consideration. It seemed to him, as he sat there and smoked, that the page torn from the pocket-diary should receive the first investigation. Sir Eustace Vernon had obviously deliberately extracted it and retained it for some definite purpose. This fact perhaps gave it an added importance. "Painswick—Page—Col." The last two words, he thought, might conceivably be abbreviated forms of "Page and Column" in reference to a book—newspaper—or even anything of a printed nature. But "Painswick!" What was meant by "Painswick"? The only Painswick that he knew was a village in Gloucestershire. He fancied that he had heard it described somewhere as the "Queen of the Cotswolds." Beyond that he could recall nothing about it of the slightest importance. He then turned his mind to the paper bearing the address of Cornelius Van Hoyt. He considered this to be an eminently useful discovery. The significant sentence of the dead man's letter to his niece came back to him. "He has been after it for years." There was a line of definite investigation clearly marked out for him to follow. But should he follow it before he attempted to follow others? What about "Mr. J. Vincent Damery, Theatrical Agent," of Shaftesbury Avenue? What had Sir Eustace to do with him? What had happened in the course of his career to develop or perhaps to stimulate Sir Eustace's interest in romantic drama? This seemed to him to be a most surprising development. Lastly, but by no means negligibly on that account, why had the veterinary surgeon's account been put with the other papers? True, it was unpaid, but surely it was not the only account of the Vernon House *ménage* that was in that position at that period of the year? That fact in itself should not have caused its segregation. Also it was a very recent account. "To attendance upon Boris, the wolfhound." The very dog which Hammond had been to feed before the incident with which the tragedy was presumed to have opened. The very dog which Stevens, the chauffeur, had been prevented from feeding by Sir Eustace himself when he had commissioned the chauffeur to deliver the message to Sam McLaren. Was there anything in these facts? "Strange—very strange," muttered Mr. Bathurst to himself as he stepped out of the train on to the platform at Victoria. Those three romantic dramas! Wasn't there a "Boris," a hound, in the book version of "The Prisoner of Zenda"? Or was it in its sequel—"Rupert of Hentzau"? In the latter, he believed from memory—certainly not in the play version of "Zenda." A coincidence—no doubt! Somebody touched him on the shoulder. He turned quickly.

Chapter XVI
A MAN WITH A JOWL

"Good evening, Mr. Bathurst. I've been waiting for you," said Inspector Craig, with some show of geniality. Mr. Bathurst returned the greeting.

"What is it, Inspector? Got any news for me—or have you come to assist me in seeing the Old Year out?"

Craig shook his head. "Not the latter, sir. Certainly—not that. The truth is that I've just been up to report to Sir Austin Kemble, and he's instructed me to get into touch with you at once. He told me where you had been to-day and that you would probably be returning from Rodding by this train. That's all there is to it, sir. I came up here and waited for you."

Anthony looked at his watch. "Very well, Inspector. I shall be delighted to hear what you have to tell me. Inasmuch as Sir

Austin has sent you to find me, I've no doubt it's well worth hearing. There's a nice, quiet little bar not far from here. Come along with me."

A few minutes later, Craig—after disposing of a third Guinness with the touch and gesture of the master—took a cigarette from Anthony Bathurst's proffered case and leaned over the table which divided the two of them—with an extremely business-like look in his eye.

"You asked me when I first accosted you to-night, Mr. Bathurst, if I had any news for you. As a matter of fact I have! That's the real reason why I'm here."

Mr. Bathurst nodded approvingly and encouragingly. "Naturally," he murmured.

"Do you remember the piece of 'hard' tobacco that Mr. Desmond stated that he had picked up in the grounds of Vernon House on the night of the murder? During the time that the search-party was conducting its operations."

"Very well, Inspector. It measured about six inches by three and had a little yellow strip of paper on the bottom—at the left-hand side. The strip of paper bore the words 'Dark Willie.' I saw your photograph of it in the papers on Tuesday, Craig. I thought it an excellent idea to broadcast it in that way. Any results, Inspector?"

"That's what I've been sent to talk to you about, Mr. Bathurst. You saw my advertisement, and you saw then, of course, my appeal to the tobacconist fraternity generally. Anyhow, I'll refresh your mind with the words that I said." He thrust his hand into the pocket of his overcoat with a very grave expression on his face, and took out Tuesday's edition of *The Morning Message*. He opened the newspaper—found the page that he required, and then folded it conveniently for reference. "Listen to this, Mr. Bathurst. The above photograph," he quoted, "is of a piece of slab-tobacco that the Mapleton Police believe to have been dropped by the murderer of Sir Eustace Vernon on Christmas night. They will be grateful to any tobacconist who recognizes it as having been possibly sold by him (or her) recently if he (or she) will come forward and give them any information that he (or she) may remember as to the identity of the purchaser." He laid the paper down on the table. "What do you think of the idea, Mr. Bathurst?"

"Very useful, Craig. I thought it quite within the bounds of possibility that you would hit on something. Well, what's happened? Have you struck oil?"

Craig allowed a gratified smile to pass over his face. "Well, there was just this about it. The tobacco was *unusual*. You must admit that. Not what you would term the popular taste, was it? It wasn't like broadcasting 'Mr. Gold and Mr. Flake'—or even 'The Hon. Bob' was it? To come down at once to brass tacks— I've had five replies."

"Four too many, at least," remarked the laconic Mr. Bathurst.

The Inspector waved a hand in semi-protest. "Hear me out, Mr. Bathurst I haven't finished yet, you know. I think you'll be surprised. The first four replies I got were all from what I may call the London area. There was one from Poplar, one from Silvertown, one from Islington and one from Crutched Friars. I don't fancy any one of them hits the mark. It's the last of the five that I'm attaching some little importance to. As I think you will too—when you hear it."

"Let's hear it, then," observed Anthony—more interested now that he was able to discern the Inspector's undoubted faith in the importance of his discovery.

"It's from Weymouth—in Dorsetshire. The tobacconist in question took the trouble to come up by train this morning to 'the Yard' and request an interview. So *he* evidently thinks it's worth something. Sir Austin had left instructions that if anything transpired it was to come on to me. So I was sent for. The man who came up is a man by the name of Cridge. He keeps a 'stationer's, sweets and tobacco' in Park Street, Weymouth. Now, listen to his story, which he tells quite confidently. He says that early in the morning of December the twenty-fourth—Christmas Eve— mark you—a big, powerful-looking man entered his shop and asked for a cake of 'ship's tobacco.' He said he wanted it to chew. It appears that Cridge was exhibiting some slabs of this 'Dark Willie' stuff in his window, so that there was nothing surprising about this man—or any other customer come to that—asking for it. Cridge is prepared to swear that the cake that Mr. Desmond picked up in the garden—I let him handle it this afternoon—is the very cake of tobacco that he sold in his shop on Christmas Eve to this man that he's described. So that's that! What have you got to say about it, Mr. Bathurst?"

"Can he describe the man that bought it with any detail?"

"He described him as a tall, heavily-built man, of about six feet in height. In age—between fifty and sixty. One of the expressions Cridge used in describing him was 'a man with a jowl.' This man Cridge is no fool, I assure you. I'll tell you another thing he said in the course of our interview. He said that his customer gave him the impression of being very nervous. He was wearing a heavy, blue overcoat—quite good—it might even have been new, Cridge says—and as he stood in the shop he kept putting his hands in his pockets and taking them out again."

"What's that?" demanded Mr. Bathurst with rapid intentness—"say that again, Inspector." Craig repeated his last statement to the accompaniment of a smile from Anthony. "Well, you've certainly got some job on hand, Craig, to trace a chance customer in Weymouth—a week old. I don't envy you the job, I tell you candidly. How do you propose to start about it?"

Craig looked at him curiously. "Has anything struck you about this customer of Cridge's, Mr. Bathurst?" He went on to outline his suggestion more clearly. "Of course, I'm conjecturing, I'm willing to admit—but you must conjecture a bit to be any good at my particular game. Do you see what I'm driving at? Think the facts over."

"I didn't, Craig, but I think I do now. And I shouldn't be surprised if you're not far out. You're identifying this customer of the Weymouth tobacco shop as one of the men who attacked Sam McLaren in order to secure Sir Eustace Vernon's letter. Though for the life of me I can't see any sane reason why anybody should want it. I wish I *could*!" He paused and lit another cigarette. "And I've given that particular matter more than a little attention, too."

Craig eyed him with a kind of grudged admiration. He was beginning to realize very strongly that Mr. Bathurst let very little escape him. "You're on the spot I meant, sir. That's the line I am taking. It came to me in a flash when Cridge was telling me his story. I thought of old Sam's woebegone expression and his epithet of 'a couple of "White 'Opes."' I know it was a shot in the dark, but all the same, I believe I'm on the right track. Funny that it should have struck you, too." He stroked his cheek with his fingers. Mr. Bathurst also became contemplative.

"Very likely you *are* on the right track, Inspector. I'm certainly not going to contradict you—or even to argue with you against your theory. But my difficulty is this. I can't link the incident up with Sir Eustace's murder. I don't see to where it tends to lead us."

"Can't reasonably expect to link everything up at once, Mr. Bathurst, with all respect that is. I'm well content to discover additional facts with a bearing on the case. It makes me feel that I must be getting nearer to a solution."

"That's all very well, Craig—up to a point. How about when the new facts *conflict*? That's the time that I begin to worry and to realize that the threads in my hands aren't being controlled properly. Have another cigarette, Inspector? And in return for the information you've given me, I'll tell *you* something." He struck a match and held it for the use of Inspector Craig. "I've been to Rodding again to-day—as you know. As Sir Austin Kemble told you, I went down because I wasn't satisfied with regard to one or two things. I'll pass on to you—for what it's worth or for what you may choose to make of it—one very interesting and at the same time very peculiar piece of information that I was able to gather from Vernon House while I was down there. My informant was Miss Ashley herself, so that it's genuine enough. Sir Eustace Vernon, Craig, was what you and I would term 'well off.' A comparatively rich man, I imagine—despite his own statement to the contrary in the letter that Miss Ashley discovered in her bedroom. Do you agree with me?"

Craig expressed acquiescence. "I should say the same as you, sir."

"You will be surprised to hear, then, Inspector—that he had no banking account. He seems to have kept all his money in the house and paid all accounts by bank-notes. What do you make of that? Prehistoric sort of idea, don't you think?"

"Strange—certainly," conceded Craig—"and where in the house was the money kept—does she know?"

"Well, as to that—now that she has had time to think things over—I think she discussed it with Mr. Desmond—she imagines it must have been kept in the safe."

"I'm beginning to see," remarked the Inspector—"so the safe was also robbed of money that in the beginning Miss Ashley was not sure was in there. I see—this makes a difference—doesn't it?"

"I told her it did. It alters the complexion of the case considerably. That's why I've told you. That safe might very well have held a small fortune in bank-notes of high value. Miss Ashley is beginning to fear that there is almost nothing left for her. Her position seems moderately serious. Her special legacy—whatever it was—has gone as well—remember."

"It's an 'impossible' case," declared Craig, vindictively—"I can't see a real glimmer of light anywhere—and we're almost a week old on it by now." He looked anxiously at his companion as though seeking a lead.

Mr. Bathurst rose from the table and carefully buttoned his heavy overcoat before plunging his hands into the depths of the pockets thereof. "Things aren't quite as bad as that, Inspector. As a matter of fact I feel that I'm two-thirds of the way towards a solution. But one of the points that worries me most is the identity of the woman who flashed the knife at Hammond and caused her to scream. The woman whose dress—no, whose skirt, she—" He stopped suddenly—his grey eyes alight with the illumination of an idea. "I wonder," he murmured to himself—"I wonder."

Chapter XVII
ONE FOR JACK

MR. ALBERT FISH, A.B. of His Majesty's torpedo-boat destroyer *Semiramis*, strode to the gate outside his parents' residence at Mapleton and spat solemnly into that particular portion of the King's highway that fronted Summerland Cottages. He was a Mapleton man, born and bred, and had performed similarly skilful feats of expectoration on many occasions that belonged to the past, throughout His Majesty's Dominions. His ten days' Christmas "leaf" (so described by himself and the particular social stratum to which he belonged) was "up" to-morrow, and he was unable to restrain completely a strong feeling of resentment against the *habitués* of Vernon House, Rodding, for having allowed a murder to take place there during his vacation, and which by reason of its close proximity to Gracie Hammond had interfered considerably with the tranquillity of his amorous relations. As he said to himself, ruefully and disconsolately, "it was just like his ruddy luck." He proceeded for the next few moments to apostrophize and anathematize the before-mentioned luck, with a completeness and precision worthy of the best traditions of the Senior Service. His attention was so completely and artistically employed with the procedure that, as a result, he was not aware of the figure of Mr. Bathurst approaching him from the rear, until that gentleman was almost upon him.

"Have I the honour to address Mr. Albert Fish?" Mr. Fish eyed his interrogator truculently. Then he rolled the "chew" upon which he had been actually employed for some little time, from one cheek to the other.

"Come orf it," he countered, delicately.

Mr. Bathurst smiled in appreciation. "Miss Hammond, up at Vernon House, told me that I should probably be fortunate enough to find you at home if I came down here at once. These are Summerland Cottages, are they not?"

"All day long," returned Albert, morosely.

Mr. Bathurst smiled again. "I know you're a busy man, Mr. Fish," he continued, "and I shall be prepared to pay you handsomely if you will be kind enough to extend to me—say ten minutes of your most valuable time. I need your services."

"'Arf a minute, guv'nor. You took the liberty of mentioning a certain young lady's name in your conversation a moment ago. If you've come to see me about 'er—you can pack it up before you kick-off. It's no go. Na-poo! Nothing doing. That girl belongs to—"

"You misunderstand me, Mr. Fish. I've no desire to alienate that young lady's affections. I realize that it would be sheer waste of time on my part to attempt it. I want to talk to you about the murder of Sir Eustace Vernon. And as I said before, I'm perfectly willing to pay you for the information that I think you can give me."

The sailor accepted the two pound notes offered to him with careless *bonhomie*. "I'm afraid, then, you won't find it worth two 'quid,'" he grinned. "Still," he proceeded—"that's your funeral, not mine. I never fixed the price—and you can't say that I did."

"You must allow me to be the best judge of that, Mr. Fish. Standards of value vary, you know."

Albert grinned his expansive grin again. "You ain't lorst for wot the cat washes 'erself with, are you, guv'nor? I reckon you couldn't 'arf describe a bandmaster. Still—get on with it. What is it exactly that you're after? Give it a name!"

"You can assume for the moment," rejoined Anthony, "that I'm representing Scotland Yard."

"Wot!" cried the sailor—"then you'd better take this 'ere couple o' quid back. I'm not falling for that. You ain't going to have me for bribery and corruption. The Navy's above that sort of thing—you can bet your life on it."

Mr. Bathurst extended a protesting hand and waved the Fishers back to the Fish. "Don't worry, Mr. Fish," he declared—"let me assure you that you are in no danger, and your personal integrity will remain unimpaired. Call me an unofficial representative of Scotland Yard, if you like—if it will make you feel any the easier."

Albert showed signs of relief. "All right then—but you put the breeze up me—you did and no mistake. What is it you want to know—because as I warned you just now, I don't think I've got very much to tell you? Shouldn't like to pay a couple of quid for it myself."

"According to your friend, Miss Hammond, you must have been in the grounds of Vernon House on Christmas night about half an hour. Is that a true statement?"

"If she says so it is—because I should have to say the same. I've learned to do that—it comes quicker in the end."

"Somewhat enigmatic," commented Anthony, "but I'll take your word for it. I think I know what you mean. I'll go a step further, however. According to your young lady friend, also, you were there from about eleven-fifteen to eleven-forty-five. Is that about right?"

"Quite right," declared Albert "The church clocks was striking twelve as I was coming home to Mapleton down the Rodding Road. So it would be about a quarter to twelve that I said 'goodbye' to Gracie."

"Now then," said Mr. Bathurst—"as you walked home—you came by the main Rodding Road you assert—did you happen to meet anybody on the road?"

"Not a solitary soul!"

"Did you overtake anybody?"

"Not me—guv'nor—I never met a soul between Vernon House and here."

"Do you know a clump of trees on the left of the road as you approach Vernon House—that would be on your right as you were coming away from it?"

"Very, well—I've done more than one bit o' courting in them there trees—they're very convenient—and you needn't tell Gracie about it either—they're just as you pass Major Prendergast's place—but why?"

"You didn't see anybody hiding in there for instance—one man—or it may have been a couple of men?"

Albert shook his head.

"I never saw no one there," he said, "but that isn't to say they couldn't have been there—it's pretty thick in there and very dark—and I wasn't lookin' out for blokes playin' 'ide and seek."

Anthony made a rapid mental calculation. According to Sam McLaren's story he had lain in the ditch from about ten-fifteen, when the assault took place, to twelve-fifteen or thereabouts, when he picked himself up. But it was quite on the cards, he concluded, that the sailor mightn't have seen the prostrate figure of the old man in the ditch.

"When you left the grounds of Vernon House, Mr. Fish, which side of the road did you walk—on the left or on the right?"

"On the left," replied Albert promptly—"I always does."

Anthony put on his thinking cap again. "What time was it when you walked down *to* Vernon House?"

Fish considered the question for quite a long time. At length he replied. "Put it down about a quarter to eleven."

"Ah!" volunteered Mr. Bathurst—"did you notice anybody about then?"

"That," he thought to himself, "should be more about the time when he *might* have run into somebody—timing the assault on Sam McLaren from his own version at a quarter-past ten."

But Albert shook his big head again. "Can't say as 'ow I did, guv'nor. No—nobody."

"Didn't see anybody lying by the side of the road, for instance?"

"No, guv'nor, I told you—I didn't see nobody—I don't believe I passed a single—" He paused in reflection. "I tell you what, though, now you come to ask me these 'ere questions—I'll tell you what did happen as I was gettin' near to Sir Eustace's place—a motor-car passed me."

"Overtook you—do you mean?"

"No—overtook me—no! What I said, passed me! A car coming from the opposite direction—I can remember how blindin' the headlights were. And I'll tell you something else, sir—it's funny how I remember it now, how it's coming back to me. I'd clean forgotten all about it—but your questionin' 'as brought it all back to me. Down there by that belt of trees that you spoke of—

near Major Prendergast's—about a hundred yards behind me it would be I should think, blest if the old car didn't stop. All of a sudden I heard it pull up and I turned round. I wondered what he was pullin' up for. There was a moon you know, sir, and you could just see a bit—even at that distance. I fancy I saw a man get out of the car as it stopped. At any rate—somebody did—I'll swear—and it looked to me like a man."

"You interest me, Mr. Fish—you interest me undeniably. How far are we from Dyke's Crossing? Or let me put it like this— how far is Dyke's Crossing from that particular clump of trees where you think the car stopped?"

"Put it at two miles," said the ubiquitous Albert, "and you won't be a couple of 'undred yards out."

"H'm—I know I'm asking you to remember a lot, Mr. Fish, but you're an exceptional man. Have you any idea what the man did when you think he alighted from the car?"

"You're askin' too much now, sir—I 'ardly gave it a thought. I was lookin' forward to seeing my girl, you see. My mind was a-runnin' on my little bit of cuddle. All I could say was that 'e got out of the car and walked into the trees."

"Then you walked on, I suppose?"

"Then I walked on. If he was goin' to play 'ide and seek—it was no concern of mine, was it now?"

"I suppose not." Anthony stopped short and apparently thought the matter over, before lighting a cigarette.

"Cigarette?" he invited his companion.

"Don't use 'em," replied Albert—"don't smoke a lot, as you might say. Give me a bit of 'Spearmint' and I'm happy." He chewed on complacently.

"Most of us smoke too much," ventured Mr. Bathurst. "Busy for an hour or two?"

Albert considered the question with becoming care. "Why?"

"Care to walk towards Rodding with me—taking the road just as you did on the night of the murder? I'd like to have a look inside that clump of trees. Just to satisfy my curiosity. Of course, I shall suitably recognize the fact that I'm taking up *even more* of your valuable time. I'm going down there in any case and if you could see your way to accompany me your knowledge of the country and the lie of the land generally would simplify matters for me considerably."

"I'm your man, sir—but you mustn't keep me too long. I'm playin' in a 'Dart's' Championship later on up at the *'Cauliflower and Crumpet'*—"

"Tell me when you want to part company," intervened Anthony—"and the job's done. You only have to say the word—make your own time to suit your own convenience. I can't say fairer than that, can I?"

Albert vaulted the front gate behind which he had conducted the latter part of his conversation and took his place by the side of Anthony.

"Quick march, guv'nor. I'll sign on for the voyage with you on those terms. Foller me."

Anthony swung into step alongside the rolling gait of the nautical Mr. Fish. Conversation was intermittent—Mr. Bathurst being content to take a good look at his companion. But Mr. Fish never turned a hair. Half an hour's journey down the road brought them to cross-roads. Mr. Fish jerked with his thumb to the left. "Dyke's Crossing is away there to the left," he announced—"the main line to London runs parallel with this road we're on now."

Anthony pointed to a stream away in the same direction. "That, I suppose, is the Rodd? Is that right?"

"Quite right, sir. But although it's called the Rodd—it's no manner of use for fishin'!" He grinned broadly—showing his beautifully white and even teeth in appreciation of his own sally.

"You ought to be glad of that, then," countered Mr. Bathurst.

"Me? How do you mean?"

"Doesn't a fellow-feeling make us wondrous kind—you as a Fish—"

"You were a bit too smart for me there, sir," acknowledged Albert, good-humouredly—"I didn't quite cotton on to—there's the trees, sir—you can see 'em from here. Away there to the left of the road." As the road bent a trifle, Anthony could see them. "And there's Vernon House—or rather the smoke from it." The far-seeing sailor shaded his eyes from the rays of the winter sun and pointed far ahead in the distance. Anthony could just see the chimneys of Vernon House away in the distance.

Ten minutes' brisk walking brought them to what Mr. Bathurst intended should be their destination.

"Now, of course, sir," announced Miss Hammond's fiancé—"a lot of this is in the nature of guesswork. Chancing your arm so to speak. It was dark—the only light was the moon—and I was a pretty good distance away. But look here—let me take my bearings a bit before I start." He glanced up the road—calculatingly. Then, twice pacing the entire length of the belt of trees, returned to Mr. Bathurst's side. That gentleman was thinking very deeply.

"What trees are these, Fish—alders?"

"Expect so—the ground's very damp and marshy round this quarter, as you see. Down there's the valley of the Rodd. Look how it runs down." The A.B. returned to his task of measurement. After a few moments he seemed to reach a decision. "Now, as far as I can judge, guv'nor, lookin' back as I was from somewhere up there"—he pointed to an imaginary spot up the road—"the bloke stopped the old car abaht 'ere and wandered dahn the mountainside somewhere abaht there." His carpet-bag-like hand indicated the place that he mentioned, and as he did so Mr. Bathurst was unable to refrain from thinking that Mr. Fish would probably pick up many unconsidered trifles off a fast bowler at fine slip. Anthony walked into the group of trees. Six yards inside he looked down the shelving ground away on to the shining waters of the sequestered little Rodd, placid and undisturbed. He measured the distance with his eyes. "Too far away," he said to himself, "if my theory be correct. Only a very powerful man could—"

He retraced some of his steps—eventually beginning to work round in a series of circles. Suddenly he stopped and gazed interestedly at the ground. Close to the river as it was, the ground was comparatively soft and the grass of that mossy, springy nature usually to be found under such conditions of environment Mr. Bathurst's attention had been attracted by—and was now riveted on—a distinct track of footprints. There were at least eight standing out quite plainly that he was enabled to count, and they undoubtedly came from the direction of the road. "Come here, Fish!" he called. "Look at those tracks down there. Do you think they might have been made by your midnight motorist?"

Albert gave them the benefit of his closest scrutiny. "Quite likely, sir." The sailor attempted to follow them back to the road. Then he returned to Mr. Bathurst. "Very likely, sir. In fact—more than likely. They do seem to me to be just abaht in the right spot for where he would have struck off."

"I may as well be frank with you, Fish. I've formed a little theory of my own in connection with Sir Eustace Vernon's murder, and I'm going to put part of it to the test. Follow those prints with me, will you?"

Albert Fish nodded obedience. His curiosity had been stimulated, and as a consequence his interest had grown considerably. The task was comparatively easy. The tracks led straight to what was, perhaps, the biggest tree of the belt. Beyond that they appeared to stop. Mr. Bathurst did likewise.

"Well, Mr. Fish," he exclaimed, "does anything strike you?"

Albert shook his big head blankly. This was taking him a bit out of his depth. "Can't say as 'ow it does, guv'nor. Sorry if I'm disappointin' you. But the idea was yours, you know."

"Look!" Mr. Bathurst pointed somewhat imperatively at the bole of the tree before which he and his companion were standing. Again Albert failed to come up to the scratch—except as regards his head. Mr. Bathurst prepared therefore to instruct him. "In what way, Alberto Poissonnio, does this tree differ from most of those that surround it? Have a good look at them all before you commit yourself. Take your time, my friend."

Albert let his eyes wander round the trees with a solemn inspection—his big round face becoming almost owlish. For a time he seemed impervious to idea, but at length happy light broke in upon him and spread over his spacious countenance. "The big hole in the trunk," he declared—"most of the others ain't got one. Or nothing like the size of that one if they 'ave."

"You're improving, my dear fellow," observed Anthony, "you thrive on encouragement—you've said just what I wanted you to say. Now we'll see if my theory will stand its first test." He bent down and looked carefully at the curiously shaped hole in the bole of the tree. It was full of the black moss-like substance that one usually finds in tree-holes of this sort. Mr. Bathurst carefully inserted his hand. To the left of the hole there was quite a good-sized cavity from where the black mossy substance had evidently been recently pulled away. The sailor saw the face of his companion gleam with undisguised satisfaction. Then he saw him draw his hand away.

"'Struth, guv'nor," he cried, in genuine amazement—"a revolver!"

"A revolver, most certainly, Mr. Fish—more than that—*the* revolver, I fancy." He turned it over in his hand. "Hallo—what's this?" On the butt were scratched two letters—initials.

"T.D.!" exclaimed the sailor. "Then that must belong to Mr. Desmond—the chap wot's expected to marry Sir Eustace Vernon's niece—Miss Ashley."

"Looks like it, Fish—without a doubt." Anthony regarded the sailor gravely. "Fish," he said—"I'm going to ask you to keep absolutely silent about this. I don't want you to breathe a word about it to a soul. Not even to Gracie Hammond. In fact—least of all to Gracie Hammond. Understand me? Can I rely upon your promise?" Two more currency notes exchanged company.

"You may, sir," affirmed the impressed Albert. He wiped his mouth with the back of his massive hand. "You may indeed. And thank you very much, sir. Rely on me. You're a gentleman."

"I wouldn't go so far as to say that," responded Mr. Bathurst.

Chapter XVIII
MR. BATHURST RENEWS AN ACQUAINTANCE

"That'll be fourpence—Nobby. And take your sleeve off the counter. Here's your slice of cake. And what can I get for you, sir?" Sam McLaren peered over the ledge of his counter at the tall figure standing back in the shadows—away from the lighted area of the coffee-stall. Then from his one visible eye there came a gleam of sudden and surprised recognition. "Why—bless my 'eart, sir!" he exclaimed, with a touch of jocularity—"I didn't recognize you for the moment. If I ain't mistaken you're one of the gentlemen what I saw up at the police station after my little adventure on Christmas night I'm not making a mistake, am I, sir?"

"You're quite right, McLaren," replied Mr. Bathurst—"I could see that you didn't recognize me in the first instance. Give me a cup of coffee and one of those hard biscuits, will you? I shall be stopping a moment or so with you. I want to have a chat about one or two things. I shan't be in the way, shall I? You're not too busy, are you?"

"Never too busy to talk to a gentleman, sir. My old grandfather from Aberdeen taught me that. He used to say, 'Sam—never lose no opportunity of conversin' with a gentleman. It's an h'education in itself and you never know what you may learn—moreover, it costs nothing.' He was a fine man, too, my grandfather," added Sam, reminiscently—"and we was all prahd of 'im. He 'ad a reputation in the place where 'e lived, too. On one occasion that I can remember, it took 'arf a dozen coppers to get 'im to the station. And then 'e laid four of the perishers out. Properly out they was—too."

"A man after my own heart, McLaren," contributed Anthony—"I like a man that can hold his own when the occasion demands. But as you may guess, I haven't come to talk to you about your ancestry. Although I've no doubt that I should find it to be both interesting and instructive. What I desire to do, if possible, is to continue our conversation of Christmas almost at the stage where we left off. Do you follow what I mean, McLaren?"

Sam looked a bit puzzled for a moment. "Can't say as 'ow I do, sir. Not exactly—that is. Put it a bit plainer—can't you?"

"Perhaps if I ask you a few questions you'll understand better what I mean. In the first place—have you anything further to tell me in regard to what I will term the 'Sir Eustace Vernon affair'?"

Sam slowly shook his head and shifted the position of a coffee-cup on the ledge of his stall. "No, sir—nothing. In what way d'yer mean?"

"Has anything more happened?"

"Nothing."

"You've received no communication from anybody—for example. No letter—or message?"

Sam turned on his heel and spat disgustedly. "Not a perishin' line, sir! I told you on Christmas night that Sam McLaren's little dream of Paradise was a thing of the past. Over the 'ills and far away. It's still the same, and what's more, I've got the 'orrible feelin' all the time that I shall never 'ave the satisfaction of knowin' 'ow much I've lost. That 'urts you know—that does. Gives yer a pain all over. For weeks after the old toff spoke to me I was a-seein' visions and dreamin' dreams. And do you know wot my favourite dreamland h'excursion was?" He paused—giving Mr. Bathurst the possible luxury of a reply. Instead—the latter shook his head in sufficiently doubting wonder. "I'll tell yer, sir. A little place dahn in the country—with a bit of grahnd close 'andy—a few fowls and p'raps a pig or two, and a nice little 'boozer' not too far away. A little 'boozer' where yours truly would ha' been the first boy in school every mornin' what came—punctual and regular. I should have gorn to evening school, too. And got medals into the bargain." A look of pathetic resignation pervaded Sam's countenance as he contrasted the roseate hues of expectation with the drab shades of the actual. His face reflected sadly that it was a far cry from a "boozer" to a coffee-stall.

Anthony made a gesture of sympathy. "Don't abandon hope too quickly, McLaren. A game's never lost till it's won—you know. Remember that 'tomorrow is also a day.'"

"Yus—and very similar as far as I'm concerned, sir. That's the very thing wot I'm grieving abaht." He bent over to attend to a customer.

"That night that you walked up to Sir Eustace's place, McLaren"—continued Anthony, a moment later, "do you happen to remember if any motor cars passed you—either coming or going?"

"Not a single one, sir. The only signs o' life that I come across were them two stable-companions wot waylaid me. Call 'em my "sparrin'-partners" if you like it better." He rubbed the bridge of his nose reminiscently.

"With reference to that—Inspector Craig can't trace either of them, McLaren. He's made inquiries all around here, not only in the district but within the surrounding neighbourhood as well—entirely without success. He's drawn blank everywhere. Nobody seems to have caught as much as a glimpse of them." Sam rubbed his head ruefully, and his one eye shone with dissatisfaction. "I caught more than a glimpse of 'em, sir. I was introduced to 'em properly. I—"

"By the way, Sam," interjected Anthony—"was one of them wearing a heavy overcoat—probably dark in colour—were you able to see as much as that?"

"'E was, sir! They both was! You've 'it the nail there all right and no mistake—'ow did you know?"

"Spare my blushes, McLaren. To deduce an overcoat on a cold winter's night—and the colour at that—"

Sam seemed to ignore Mr. Bathurst's implication. "If my opinion's worth anything—which I suppose it ain't, them two blighters wot 'anded me the Christmas greetings looked as much like h'escaped convicts as anything I can think of. It wouldn't surprise me to 'ear any day that they were the blokes wot done poor old Sir Eustace in. Not a bit—it wouldn't." He juggled dexterously with a cup of coffee before handing it to a customer. "Any more news abaht the crime, sir?"

"Hardly any, McLaren. The Inspector seems to be as much in the dark as ever."

"'Ow's the young lady gettin' on? The young lady wot lives up at Vernon 'Ouse—the old boy's niece, wasn't she? 'E's left her all right, I suppose?"

"On the contrary, McLaren, as far as we can tell at present—just the reverse. Wholesale robbery took place at Vernon House that night as well as murder. Miss Ashley has sustained a heavy loss, far greater than was at first realized. Even a special legacy—if we may so describe it—appears to have been stolen with the rest of the stuff." Anthony looked up to catch a sympathetic frown on the old coffee-stall keeper's face,

"Wot!" he exclaimed—"you don't say—now if that ain't real bad luck. Worse than mine—and I was thinkin' mine was bad enough. There's always people in the world worse off than ourselves if we only take the trouble to look for 'em. Dear—dear—dear!" He clicked his teeth in sympathetic annoyance. "Wot's she goin' to do abaht it?"

"What can she do? The police have the matter in hand. At any moment they may hear of something. We are all working to that end."

Sam shrugged his shoulders in obvious pessimism. "And they may *not*! I don't 'old too 'igh an opinion of the police. 'Cept for regulatin' traffic! I don't reckon you need to be a 'sooperman' to 'oodwink the majority of His Majesty's Constabulary. Thank you, sir." He took the proffered cigarette and promptly lit up.

"I suppose you hear a bit of local gossip at this stall from time to time—eh, McLaren? Ever heard anything that touched upon the murder?"

"Only wild talk, sir. Most of 'em wot I get as customers don't need no encouragin' for that—neither. They open their mouths and the wind blows their silly tongues round. I ain't 'eard anything worth repeatin'."

"I see. Nothing to which you attach any importance! Well—I'll take your word for it." He looked at his wrist-watch. "You'll be getting busy from now, I suppose?"

"I shall, sir. Business'll be brisk from now on. My best time's coming from now."

"How long have you been here, Sam?"

"Five years on the second of June, sir. And I've built up a good stall. A stall that's got a good steady trade." He grinned at Anthony, and the latter was reminded of Pew more than ever. "So good, sir—that I'm considerin' of an h'offer for it. I've 'ad inquiries from a local man, and if 'e'd agree to my terms I think I shall close with 'im. I ain't so keen on the place as I was. This last business 'as made a difference to me—I'm disappointed as you might say."

"I can quite understand your point of view," conceded Mr. Bathurst—"after all it's only a natural one. Most people would feel the same as you do. What's your address if I should want to have a word with you again?"

"Care of Mrs. Croucher, eighty-three, Mafeking Street, Mapleton. Just dahn by the tram depot—anybody in Mapleton 'ull direct you to it. I'm a well-known character."

"Thanks, I'll remember the address. Oh—one more question, McLaren, before I leave you. While you have resided in Mapleton—can you recall any private theatrical performances at Vernon House or at anywhere else in the neighbourhood?"

The coffee-stall keeper knitted his brows. "I can't, sir. Although, of course, I mightn't get to hear of anything like that. The news mightn't reach me—it's 'ardly in my line—so to speak. But why do you ask, sir, if I may inquire—what's your reason?"

Sam's face seemed to be quite a study at what he evidently considered the amazing nature of Mr. Bathurst's question.

His interrogator laughed. "Just for curiosity, Sam—that's all. Good-bye." He pushed the usual *pourboire* into McLaren's unwilling hand and swung off down the road before the latter could frame a reply. Mr. Bathurst travelled a hundred yards or so in deep meditation. "'The Only Way,'" he muttered to himself—"'The Prisoner of Zenda,' 'The Lyons'—" At that moment the astounding truth came home to him!

Chapter XIX
£500 FOR THE LATE MR. DAMERY

It was at this stage of the case—destined eventually to occupy a big space in the various organs of the daily Press under the title of "The Red Bonbon Murders"—that Mr. Bathurst began to put his house in order. As he explained afterwards to a chosen circle that contained not only Sir Austin Kemble but also Lady Fullgarney and her husband, Sir Matthew, it was at this definite juncture that he realized what he himself designated as the "kernel" of the nut that he had been called upon by Fate so whimsically—to crack. He was willing to admit, he told them, that up to this moment he had been perilously near to wandering. He decided that he had at least three most important calls yet to make. He wanted to make the acquaintance for one, of Mr. Cornelius Van Hoyt, of Letchworth Mount, near Leighton, Shropshire, for the very good reason that he anticipated with some degree of confidence that Mr. Van Hoyt would prove to be a veritable mine of information with regard to one very salient point of the mystery. And besides Mr. Van Hoyt there were two others. It was gradually coming home to Mr. Bathurst—forcibly and unmistakably—that he was engaged upon the investigation of an unspeakably facinorous crime—that for sheer callousness and cold-bloodedness would be extremely difficult to approximate. The same feeling had permeated him during the closing stages of his inquiry into the strange circumstances surrounding the "Mystery of the Peacock's Eye," but he felt that this last case that had come his way was, in some respects, at least—more devilishly conceived and, if anything, even more hellishly perpetrated. The realization flooded his brain with pellucid certainty that once again the clutch of circumstance had summoned him to cross swords with one who was undoubtedly a master criminal. A criminal who had made no mistake worth mentioning and who had left no stone unturned in his attempt to defeat the ends of Justice. This fact, however, did not deter Mr. Bathurst in the least. He was gathering the threads of the affair into his efficient hands slowly but surely, and he was quite hopeful that in a few days from now he would be in a position to complete his case. He would therefore make his first call upon J. Vincent Damery, Esq., of Shaftesbury Avenue. An examination of the current London directory revealed no such name as a resident there. Undismayed and not entirely surprised, Mr. Bathurst fell back upon a little telephonic communication with the publishers of the same excellent directory. Five minutes' rapidly effective research supplied him with the information for which he was seeking. A "J. Vincent Damery" had occupied a floor of Number thirty-four Shaftesbury Avenue until about three years ago, but at the present moment the premises that he had tenanted were occupied by a Mr. Spencer Sanderson. Mr. Bathurst thanked his informant with commendable brevity—he never allowed himself to be pleonastic on the telephone. When he reached the place indicated he discovered that it was a shop—the floor above the shop bearing a window lettered "Spencer Sanderson, Theatrical Agent." Mr. Bathurst entered at the appropriate side of the establishment and ascended the stairs. He rapped upon a window that obviously bore an invitation for "Inquiries." A middle-aged man appeared in quick response to the knock. Mr. Bathurst handed him his card, which he examined, and then tapped somewhat interrogatively.

"Mr. Spencer Sanderson?" murmured Anthony in mellifluous tones.

"He's in, sir, certainly. Must you see him personally?"

"I think I had better—if it's all the same to you. Is he free at the moment?"

"I will inquire, sir. Wait one moment, will you?"

The man vanished and reappeared with surprising celerity.

"Mr. Sanderson will see you, sir. He happens to be disengaged. Step this way, will you, sir?"

Mr. Bathurst proceeded along a narrow corridor that confronted him and entered a room where sat a cadaverous-looking man—bearing an obvious acquaintanceship with *the* profession.

"Sit down, Mr. Bathurst," he exclaimed, in a pleasantly deep voice—"what can I have the pleasure of doing for you?"

"Very possibly nothing at all, Mr. Sanderson. It's quite on the cards. My errand is certainly an unusual one. As a matter of fact, my business I should say, was more with the gentleman who was your predecessor than with you—I refer to Mr. J. Vincent Damery."

"Mr. Damery died about three years ago, I regret to say. But possibly I may be able to help you, if you outline the nature of your business."

"That's very kind of you—but I doubt it. I've called in connection with the late Sir Eustace Vernon, of Vernon House, Rodding.

I have reason to think that he had business with Mr. Damery—but I don't know when—and I don't even know for sure what the business was."

"Sir Eustace Vernon—isn't that the man who's just been murdered—about a week ago? May I ask, then, whom you represent?"

"You are correct in your assumption, Mr. Sanderson, about the gentleman's identity—and you can put me down as a Scotland Yard 'Auxiliary.'" Anthony smiled engagingly.

"Well, if I do or if I don't, Mr. Bathurst—I'm sorely afraid, now that you have mentioned your business, that I shall be unable to help you. When I bought the Agency, I made a clean sweep of nearly all the old files and correspondence. Personally, I've had no dealings at all with Sir Eustace Vernon."

"My quest, then, seems destined to failure. I was very much afraid that it might be. But nevertheless there seems to me to be just one possible ray of hope. Did you retain, by any chance, any of the late Mr. Damery's staff?"

Mr. Sanderson's face brightened considerably under the warmth of Mr. Bathurst's suggestion. "That's an idea—certainly. As a matter of fact I did—his clerk—the man whom you encountered just now. His name's Payne. You can see him, if you wish to, with pleasure." Sanderson rang the bell. "Payne," he said to the man in question—"you were here a good many years with the late Mr. Damery, weren't you?"

"I was, sir—over twenty. I'm fifty-seven now and I was thirty-two when I first came here—"

"Very good, Payne. See whether you can help this gentleman over what he wishes to know."

"What I want to know is this," delineated Mr. Bathurst—"can you remember whether your previous employer, Mr. Damery, had any business dealings with a certain Eustace Vernon at any time during your employment here?" As he spoke he could have sworn that he saw a flash of surprise enter Payne's eyes. But he answered Mr. Bathurst's question readily enough.

"Well, sir—I do—and I don't."

"Explain what you mean—will you?"

"I know it sounds absurd, sir," said Payne again—turning to his employer in extenuation as it were of his enigmatic position—"but it's true for all that. I can tell you this. Mr. Damery received a payment of five hundred pounds—I think it was—from Sir Eustace Vernon, but what it was actually for—I never knew. And Mr. Damery never thought fit to inform me. Several letters came here that bore either the Rodding or the Mapleton postmark, but the guv'nor never let on a blind word to me about it."

"I see," observed Anthony—"you are aware, I presume, that Sir Eustace was murdered on Christmas night?"

"I read the papers, sir, of course. A very mysterious business, too, wasn't it?"

"Very—and I was hoping to learn something as an outcome of my visit here to-day, that would throw some light upon the case. Unfortunately—primarily through the regrettable decease of Mr. Damery—"

"I'm sorry, sir," intervened Payne, with some show of eagerness—"but there's one thing I'd like to say before you go. Something I'd like to ask you. I never saw Sir Eustace Vernon in the flesh—he never called here at this office, for instance, to my knowledge—but do you think he was in any way connected with the theatrical profession?"

Anthony smiled.

"It's an idea, Payne—to be sure," he said. "At the moment, I must confess to a certain measure of doubt. Why do you ask me?"

"Well, sir—I'll tell you. Although, as I said, Mr. Damery never took me into his confidence over his business with Sir Eustace— that didn't prevent me doing a bit of conjecturing on my own. What I conjectured—you're very welcome to know. I was always confident in my own mind, that a man named Bradley Deane— an actor—was mixed up in the affair, somehow." Payne paused to reflect, and Anthony cut in briskly.

"Why? On what evidence do you base that statement? You must have some reason—"

"Hardly on evidence at all—at least not what you could reasonably call 'evidence.' But just this. On two occasions during the period I've mentioned, Bradley Deane called here and had an interview with the guv'nor, and on the second occasion when I happened to be passing the door of the room in which they were seated—I'm almost certain that I overheard the word 'Rodding' mentioned."

"This man—Bradley Deane—where is he now—do you know? Any idea of his whereabouts?"

Payne's voice sank to what was merely a whisper. "I never set eyes on him again, sir. Not that I ever really could have expected to. Still—I didn't. I'm fairly certain he never called here again. If he did—I never saw him."

"What sort of a man was he to look at? Could you describe him at all?"

Payne considered the question carefully. "I should have put him down as somewhere about fifty years of age. Clean-shaven, of course. Some people would have called him a handsome man. A proper artistic face he had—there could be no two opinions about that, at any rate."

Spencer Sanderson broke in upon his clerk's recital. "I remember the man you mention, Payne, now I come to think of it He's crossed my own path more than once. He was only a fourth-rate sort of actor, though. Never really got away from the provinces and 'fit-ups'—and did a lot of work on the 'halls' before he touched the 'legit.' I can tell you where he used to knock about a lot—where he had a regular 'house of call.' Down at the 'Brown Mouse' in the Commercial Road—there's still a nest of them down there of an evening who were by way of being on intimate terms with him. I've been in there recently myself and seen several of them."

"How long was this ago, Payne?" demanded Mr. Bathurst.

"About six years, sir—as far as I could gauge. I've got nothing reliable to go by—but six years wouldn't be far out. Certainly well within the last ten years."

Mr. Bathurst took out his pocket-book and extracted something which he pushed over to his two companions. "Allowing for the passage of time and general considerations of that kind—is that anything like Mr. Bradley Deane?"

Payne and his employer gave simultaneous exclamations—"that's the man!"

"That's Deane—right enough!"

"Thank you, gentlemen," declared Anthony. "You have assisted me tremendously. The *Brown Mouse* I think you said—in Commercial Road. Good-day, gentlemen, I will not take up any more of your time." Mr. Bathurst bowed to them and departed.

Chapter XX
MISSING!

The saloon bar of the comfortable-looking hostelry known as the *Brown Mouse* presented its usual animated appearance as Mr. Bathurst opened the door and entered. Its warmth and comfort were in marked contrast to the prevailing conditions outside. He had been informed by Mr. Spencer Sanderson that several old acquaintances of Bradley Deane still used the house and he was confident that he would not find it a matter of very great difficulty to run across at least one of them. Mr. Bathurst had sound reason for his confidence—for he knew that there are few professions that imprint themselves more plainly upon the faces of their devotees than that which owes allegiance to Thespis. Apart from such matters as particular forms of dress or the care of the hair, there is that inevitable result upon the face of the constant application of grease-paint and powder, and Mr. Bathurst, once a distinguished member of the O.U.D.S., was well aware of the fact. He felt convinced in his own mind that his luck would hold and that his labours of this winter evening would not be entirely wasted. He gave his order to a henna-crowned Hebe, by whom he was promptly addressed as "Angel-face." But Mr. Bathurst's serene equanimity was proof against disturbance by such happenings as that. He adroitly avoided her opening gambit of conversation, and glanced observantly round the saloon. There were many of the usual types forming the usual groups. It had occurred to Anthony that he might meet two kinds of acquaintances. He might encounter gentlemen who were "resting" and who would not desire to enter into details concerning the cause, and also he imagined he might run across, perhaps, one or two from the various "halls" in the immediate vicinity who might seek spirituous refreshment between the "turns." He looked at his watch, and decided that it was too early to expect any of the latter variety. He therefore essayed a second look around the somewhat meretricious apartment. His eye caught two men seated at a table in the far left-hand corner. There was no doubt whatever in his own mind that they both knew neither salary nor wages—they "drew their Treasury." He decided that he would try his luck with them. With that estimable intention he ordered a second drink, received a second sobriquet with it from the before-mentioned Hebe and sidled unobtrusively towards their table. When he heard the shorter of the two remark—"it flopped, Laddie, it flopped," he knew that the impression he had formed was perfectly sound. Mr. Bathurst took his courage in both hands. He struck while the iron was hot. The bar was by no means as crowded as it might have been, and nothing like as thickly populated as Mr. Bathurst astutely judged it eventually would be. Therefore he might not find a more favourable time or even opportunity. He approached the two seated men with a gesture of magnificence.

"Gentlemen," he exclaimed, with a sweep of his hat—"you will, I am sure, pardon this intrusion on my part, but I take the liberty because I believe you may have the power to help me. You belong, I think, to a profession that has always exacted my most sincere admiration and respect. But first of all—pardon my seeming neglect—you must accept my hospitality. What shall it be?"

The elder of the two men flickered his far eyelid in the direction of his companion with assumed *sang-froid* and replied laconically—"horse's blood."

Mr. Bathurst's grey eyes twinkled as he rose and gave the order. "G.H. Mumm suit you for the 'fizz'?" he inquired with perfect nonchalance.

"Too true, Laddie." A few minutes later he was being toasted—"Your health, sir."

"Thank you. Now, gentlemen, I will tell you of the particular direction in which I think that you may be able to assist me." He leaned across the table and uttered his next question very quietly. "Has either of you gentlemen ever met or ever known a man named Bradley Deane?"

The elder man drained his glass with definite approval and nodded in acquiescence. "I have, sir. Many a time and oft! But *not* 'upon the Rialto'! In here, sir, more times than a few. Why do you ask?"

"Let that wait for a moment or so. Where did you first meet him?"

"In Derby. I was fixed with him in the same show—a 'panto'—I think it was 'Aladdin.' I played the Widow Twanky. I never got over better. We played to capacity, sir, for over six weeks. I had some business with him into which I introduced some devilled sweet-breads. It was the hit of the show. I—"

"In Derby—eh? Any other places besides that?"

"Very many, Laddie! Besides having drunk from the goblet of Success with him, sir—I have also tasted the dregs. We travelled back from a Midland tour—from Leamington, I fancy—on our basket."

"You have my sympathy," murmured Mr. Bathurst—"but now tell me this. When did you see Deane last?"

Mr. Bathurst's informant became less voluble quite suddenly. Then he partially recovered himself. "In here, Laddie. In this identical saloon bar. I believe at this identical table. He borrowed half a crown off me. Or he tried to. I forget which. But you're getting on dangerous ground." His resonant voice became a whisper. He spoke into Mr. Bathurst's ear. "Bradley Deane disappeared! He was almost 'down and out' when it happened. I saw him one night in here somewhere about five or six years ago and he told me he'd got settled again. I formed the opinion that he was off on a southern tour. But he gave me no details and decency forbade me asking him. I never saw him again. From that day to this. No, sir—never again."

"Did he have any relations? Wife or anything?"

"Neither chick nor child! Nor wife of his bosom! But he disappeared, Laddie—suddenly and without warning. I have often wondered about it. It was a very strange thing to me that he should have gone so suddenly."

"Might that be he?" asked Anthony. The man addressed looked at what Mr. Bathurst held out to him and then nodded with certainty.

"It's some time ago, Laddie, and Time writes heavily upon the fairest and comeliest of us, but 'tis very like the Bradley Deane whom I knew. Very like."

"Thank you," declared Mr. Bathurst—"I was hoping you would say that."

"What have you to do with Bradley Deane—after all this lapse of years?"

"You'll see that question answered in about a week's time," replied Mr. Bathurst. "Good-night. I am sure you won't mind me going. The best of luck!"

Chapter XXI
THE CHOSROES CROSS

During the seventeen years that he had lived in England Cornelius Van Hoyt, millionaire and connoisseur of beautiful things, had resided in two counties. The first ten years he had spent in Devonshire and the other seven in Shropshire. His reason for so doing can be best given in his own words. "The two loveliest counties in the whole of England," he was fond of saying, "are Shropshire and Devonshire—and I'm not sure which is the lovelier."

Mr. Bathurst found Shrewsbury a most interesting and decidedly quaint old town. He was intrigued, for example, by the names of its thoroughfares—"Dog Pole" and "Wyle Cop." The inn into the stable-yard of which he drove his Crossley looked satisfying and comfortable. He manoeuvred the car into a convenient position, flicked a strip of mud from one of the pale primrose wheels, and was quickly upon the best of terms with his host. He dined alone, in a room of mullioned windows, and as he was indecently hungry (even for Anthony Bathurst) came to the conclusion very soon that never had he tasted mutton cutlets more succulent, or Camembert more delicious. He retired to bed—slept soundly, in a capacious four-poster bed with sheets fragrant of lavender, and woke to the cold and crystalline beauty of a perfect January morning in England. A morning clad joyously with the hues that can only come from the rosy-fingered Eos.

"Will you want your car early this morning, sir?" The solicitous landlord put the question to him as he was on the point of embarking upon the marmalade and toast section of that best of all meals—breakfast.

"I am not at all sure," replied Mr. Bathurst, as charmingly as he knew how. "Do you know—I'm almost tempted to walk to my destination. The morning seems so glorious—it's really the champagne of weather you know—this with which we've been favoured to-day."

"Very well, sir. If you should want the car let me know in time and I'll tell one of the men. Will you be back in time for lunch, sir?"

Anthony disposed of a corner of crisp brown toast with epicurean delicacy, before he replied to the question. "Probably not. At any rate don't expect me—and therefore don't make arrangements for me. If I should return later on, I'll content myself with a 'snack' down in the bar."

"Very good, sir. Going far, sir?"

Anthony regarded him curiously for a moment, but was able to see within that time that the landlord's question arose from solicitude rather than from mere inquisitiveness.

He smiled back his reply. "As far as Leighton. That's my destination to-day. Supposing I decide to walk as far as there—how long would it take me, would you say?"

"Starting after breakfast, sir, and taking your ease in a stroll—just jogging along nicely—you'd make Leighton about midday."

"Good. I think that's what I'll do, then."

Less than an hour later saw him over the Severn Bridge and well out of the town. For an appreciable time he found himself walking by the river on its lengthy journey to the west, and he began to understand more fully the true beauty of the "scrub" county through which he was travelling. The Wrekin—almost grotesque in the distance—kept him company temporarily and he stopped for a few minutes to glance over to his right at the historic ruins of Uriconium. A quarter to one found him at Leighton. The first question Mr. Bathurst put to himself was an alliterative alternative—lunch or Letchworth Mount? It may have been the effect of the walk—it may have been the "nipping and eager air"—it may have been mere force of the Bathurst habit—Letchworth Mount ran a bad second. An old and straggling hostelry, rejoicing under the sign of the *Moran Arms*, afforded him an adequate lunch. Mrs. Kinnersley was not used to catering for visitors, but the gentleman, if he cared to do so, could have a bit of lunch along with her in her own private apartment behind the bar. She couldn't offer him anything grand, but he could share a nice steak and kidney pudding that she had made *for* herself. But she was sure that there would be enough for two! In due time Mr. Bathurst complimented her upon its excellent quality. He placed it very high, he said, in the table of steak and kidney puddings—and he was no mean judge, he assured her! Did she know the direction of Letchworth Mount—the residence of a Mr. Van Hoyt? He thanked her for her explicit information, and to this day Susannah Kinnersley, relict of Josiah Kinnersley these last nine years, and mine hostess of the *Moran Arms*, still talks of the young gentleman with the nice grey eyes who shared with her a steak and kidney pudding on a lovely day one January. Letchworth Mount was an imposing mansion. It nestled within the comfort of magnificent grounds. Mr. Bathurst, at first glance, placed it as Tudor. In this estimate he happened to be correct. Cornelius Van Hoyt had purchased it from a Sir George Parry, whose family has held it since the first George Parry had helped to overthrow the Armada. Anthony was lucky enough to find the present owner at home and agreeable to seeing him upon the receipt of his card. He found himself ushered into the presence of a short man with a reddish beard—very carefully trimmed. Strange to say the beard was accompanied by a pair of piercing black eyes, and the strange combination attracted Mr. Bathurst's attention almost immediately. The black eyes sought the inscription on Mr. Bathurst's visiting card. "Mr. Bathurst?" their possessor interrogated. "To what am I indebted for the honour of this visit?"

Mr. Bathurst extended a courteously-deprecating hand. "To a certain extent, Mr. Van Hoyt, I feel very consciously that I owe you an apology. I feel that it is certainly incumbent upon me therefore to open with one. Frankly—I am trespassing upon your time and also upon your kindness. But I will state my business as speedily as possible. May I ask you if you keep abreast of the daily papers?"

The millionaire looked somewhat surprised. "I do. Certainly I do. Why do you ask?"

"You have read, then, doubtless, of the murder of Sir Eustace Vernon near Mapleton, in very strange circumstances, on Christmas night?" He watched Van Hoyt's face very carefully to see the effect of the dead man's name upon him. It instantly became alive with interest.

"I have, Mr.—er—Bathurst I very much regretted it—very much indeed. I may even go farther than that. It made a profound impression upon me. But there happened to be a definite reason for that. Sir Eustace Vernon and I were not unacquainted, I may say."

Mr. Bathurst's eyes gleamed with satisfaction. "It is with regard to that last statement of yours that you see me in the rôle of your visitor to-day, Mr. Van Hoyt. I did not actually know of its truth—but I suspected it."

"And you have come all this way upon mere suspicion?" Van Hoyt's face hardened perceptibly.

"I never suspect without a strong foundation of reason, Mr. Van Hoyt—believe me. I could not afford to work on those lines. But I will be explicit. Your name was mentioned in the last letter that Sir Eustace Vernon is known to have written."

The man addressed gave a start of surprise. "Indeed?"

"I admit," continued Mr. Bathurst, judicially, "that that inclusion of your name in that letter does not necessarily prove acquaintance. The name of any third party—completely unknown for that matter—might be found quite legitimately in any correspondence—I am quite ready and willing to concede that. But I formed the opinion, Mr. Van Hoyt, that Sir Eustace Vernon had visited you here at least once."

"He did, Mr. Bathurst. It is quite true, and there is no reason why I should attempt to deny it. Somewhere about two years ago." Van Hoyt made the admission with every appearance of willingness and as though the information was entirely ungrudged. His voice and his appearance tallied in this respect.

"Thank you," replied Anthony—"and I think I shall also be correct in saying that he offered you something for sale. Although I do *not* know what that something was. All I know is that the object he brought to you was a valuable one. Valuable not only to ordinary men for its intrinsic worth, but also doubly valuable and desirable to you as a collector. To you *in particular* as a collector. I am aware, you see, of your personal inclinations."

Van Hoyt rose from the chair that he had been occupying and walked across to the window. He stood there for a few moments looking out on to the beauty of the immediate surroundings. He was thinking deeply. Suddenly he swung round impetuously, having evidently reached a definite decision.

"I see no reason why I should withhold *any* information from you, Mr. Bathurst. I understand that you represent what I may call 'official inquiry.' Have you ever heard of the 'Chosroes Cross'?"

Mr. Bathurst wrinkled his brows. "You mean part of the—"

"The largest known fragment of the True Cross still known to be in existence. The sacred wood is enclosed with a gold mount and set in the most delicate enrichment of the finest filigree. It is believed to have been taken to Persia in 614 and returned by Heraclius in 628. It is supposed then to have disappeared for a considerable time and then ultimately to have found its way into the Church of the Holy Sepulchre. Some years ago it was rumoured to have been moved and to have been temporarily lodged in the Church of the Divine Compassion in London. From there it suddenly vanished." Here Van Hoyt paused to meditate again, but only for a brief period. "Judge then of my surprise, Mr. Bathurst, when I tell you that this most valuable Holy Relic was offered to me by Sir Eustace Vernon two years ago in this very room."

"He came to you because he knew you were a collector—of course."

"More than that, perhaps. It is well-known in what I will call the inner circles, that I have a special interest for objects with a religious significance. I have a really magnificent 'Via Dolorosa,' for example. This is a mediaeval burse in crimson silk damask, similar to the one in the Victoria and Albert Museum. I also possess two very fine Madonnas and a gorgeous Flemish cope depicting the Crucifixion. Sir Eustace Vernon was well aware of my inclination in this particular direction—that was why he came to me."

"Why didn't you buy the Chosroes Cross at the time—did you harbour suspicion concerning the validity of his title?"

Van Hoyt coloured to the roots of his hair. "It was not my business that I could see, Mr. Bathurst, to interest myself in that. Collectors cannot afford to be too squeamish. No—I didn't buy because I understood from Sir Eustace that he desired the actual sale to remain in abeyance for a time. He came to give me first offer as it were. I signified my willingness to complete the matter at his own personal convenience. In return he gave me a guarantee that he would approach nobody else as a possible buyer without first acquainting me."

"Didn't that strike you as somewhat strange?" asked Anthony.

Van Hoyt's answer came immediately. "It did. I mentioned my feelings in the matter, but Sir Eustace Vernon explained that he had very strong personal reasons for wishing the Cross to remain in his possession for some little time longer. Reasons that he regarded as impossible to be made public. I had to accept what he told me. I may as well admit, quite frankly, that I was very desirous of getting the Cross. That was my chief concern. I still am. If the offer still holds good, Mr. Bathurst, I shall be very willing—"

That gentleman raised his hand. "The offer does *not* hold good, Mr. Van Hoyt, for the very good and sufficient reason that on the night that Sir Eustace was murdered, the Chosroes Cross disappeared from his safe."

"Do you mean by that that he was murdered for its possession?"

Mr. Bathurst shrugged his shoulders evasively. "I should be perfectly justified in thinking so, shouldn't I?"

"But who could have done it? I have a distinct recollection of Sir Eustace telling me that not a living soul knew that the Chosroes Cross was in his possession."

"That may have been true then—but not now. Circumstances alter cases."

"Quite so—quite so," put in the millionaire, slowly nodding his head in affirmation—"he may have been indiscreet and allowed the news to filter out and to have reached the ears of the unscrupulous. When that happens—anything else may happen as a direct sequence. In these days scientific burglary is a lucrative profession."

"There is one other strange feature of the case, Mr. Van Hoyt. I think it only fair to tell you what it is. I have already informed you that Sir Eustace mentioned your name in the last letter that he wrote. I will now tell you of the connection in which it was mentioned. The Chosroes Cross, as you describe it, was his legacy to his niece, a Miss Helen Ashley, and the letter is thought to have been written very shortly before his murder. Miss Ashley is his only known relative, it appears, and this was all that he was able to leave her. In the letter he merely speaks of 'a parcel in the safe.' But I have no doubt, Mr. Van Hoyt, that that parcel contained the Chosroes Cross, because he went on to say that it should be brought to you. I take it that you would not be inclined to contradict me in that opinion?"

"I have no doubt whatever that you are right in your surmise, Mr. Bathurst. The Cross was the only reasonable association that there could be between Sir Eustace and me." Cornelius Van Hoyt stroked his beard with a movement of the hand that approximated to a caress, but Mr. Bathurst was able to ascertain the measure of the millionaire's disappointment from the expression in the depths of the black eyes.

Anthony rose from his seat. "I don't know that I need waste your time any longer, sir," he observed. "My visit to you has certainly not proved to be fruitless. I was working in the dark, you see, as long as I had no knowledge of what Sir Eustace's parcel actually contained. Now that I have acquired that knowledge, my path towards a solution of the mystery has been made very much smoother."

"I am glad to have been in a position to assist you, Mr. Bathurst. I have hopes that you will be able to recover the Cross. If you do—don't forget to inform Miss Ashley that she is still to consider me as a purchaser should she desire to sell. I sincerely hope that she will fall in with her late uncle's wishes—as expressed by him to me—and give me the opportunity of the first refusal. Good-bye."

Anthony shook him by the hand. "Good-bye, Mr. Van Hoyt, and—once again—many thinks! I don't want to destroy your hopes, but I am afraid you will never possess the Chosroes Cross."

"What? You think it's gone forever, then?"

Mr. Bathurst shook his head. "I didn't quite say that," he said, bowing on the point of departure, "although I wouldn't contradict your idea."

That same evening the pale primrose wheels of his Crossley were eating up the miles upon their way back to London.

Chapter XXII
SIR AUSTIN KEMBLE'S CONTRIBUTION

Sir Austin Kemble replaced the telephone receiver with an angry gesture. "Why the hell does Macmorran worry me over trifles like that?" he muttered to himself. "Haven't I enough to occupy my time without being troubled with matters of that kind!" He looked at his watch and saw that, according to arrangement, the next quarter of an hour should produce Mr. Anthony Bathurst in person. Arrangements as made held good, and Sir Austin rose to greet his visitor with outstretched hand.

"Damned glad to see you, Bathurst—and I'm sincere in saying that. What is it—Mapleton?"

"That's it, Sir Austin. Since I saw you last I've put in some very useful work down there, in more directions than one. I'll run over them with you in a minute. In the meantime, what's happened to Craig? I had a chat with him the other evening—the night I came back from seeing Miss Ashley at Vernon House—he was hard at work on the tobacco trail. How's he progressing—any developments of importance?"

Sir Austin produced his cigar-case. "To tell the plain, unvarnished truth, my dear Bathurst, I am very far from being impressed. Indeed, had I not known that you were at work on the case, I should have put Macmorran himself on to it. It requires the best brains that can be given to it."

Anthony's grey eyes indulged in a little twinkling. "'Pon my soul, Sir Austin, I am almost tempted to believe that you're descending to flattery." He took a cigar and qualified his last remark. "If I didn't know you better—that is."

Sir Austin grunted.

"I am intensely sincere, Bathurst," he said. "In fact, I was never more serious in my life. Still, you will be able to judge for yourself before very long. Then you'll realize what I mean. Craig's coming up here—he wants to see me very particularly about something—so I arranged for him to come when you were here. Thought I might be able to kill two birds with one stone."

Mr. Bathurst let the fragrant aroma of the cigar play delicately under his nostrils. He knitted his brows thoughtfully. "I see, sir. In relation to the phrase that you just employed, I should like to ask you a question. Do you think that the Vernon House murderer (or murderess) killed two birds with one stone? Do you think that the two deaths that we've been called upon to investigate were brought about by the same hand? I ask you the question, because your remark coincided very appositely with the run of my thoughts just at that moment."

Sir Austin looked a trifle uncomfortable. As had happened many times in the past, he could not quite see the subtle reason that lay behind a Bathurst question.

"You have me at a disadvantage, Bathurst, to a certain extent," he ventured at last, "I have not had time to give the case a complete review, but from what I saw and gathered when I was down at Rodding with you—I was certainly disposed towards the opinion that the two crimes were perpetrated by the same— agency—shall we say—if not precisely by the same hand. Have you discovered anything that would inevitably demolish this theory? I should be interested to know."

Anthony shook his head non-committally. "Don't misunderstand me, sir. I wasn't on the point of criticising your opinion. I merely wanted your view of the case to assist me—to add it, as it were to my own. I've learned to appreciate the value of your knowledge of personal psychology."

Sir Austin leaned back in his chair with unconcealed satisfaction. Anthony could almost hear him purring. "I think I know what you mean, Bathurst," he emitted. "It is only after years and years of experience, together with the closest possible application—and then only if a man has a *penchant*—" he stopped abruptly to unhook the receiver of his telephone. "Certainly," Anthony heard him say—"by all means. Send him in to my private office at once. Mr. Bathurst is with me, but it's all right. It's Craig, Bathurst," he said as he replaced the receiver.

A few seconds later saw the entrance of the Inspector.

"Good afternoon, Sir Austin—good afternoon, Mr. Bathurst. They told me to come along, sir," he explained.

"Quite right, Craig—quite right Mr. Bathurst and I were expecting you. I understand you have something important to tell me."

Craig sat down. "Well, sir—in a way I have, and yet in a way, I haven't But I certainly do want to see you. As far as the case proper is concerned, I may as well confess that I'm not making the progress that I should have desired, or even that I anticipated. The tobacco clue that I was following up has led me nowhere, beyond what you already know. I was very confident after I got Cridge's evidence that it would result in something tangible—but I was deceived. It has brought me nothing at all. Inquiries of a general nature in Rodding, Mapleton and throughout the district generally have proved equally unproductive. I can't trace the man I wanted to trace. I have even had a go at tracing Sir Eustace Vernon's antecedents—it struck me from the very outset that judicious inquiries in this direction—"

"That point appeals to me, too, Inspector," put in Mr. Bathurst—"I should be very interested to hear what success has attended your efforts in that quarter—if any."

"'If any,' is right, Mr. Bathurst," declared Craig, rather dolefully—"I have proved as unsuccessful there as I have in all the other directions. But—and here is something at least that should be better hearing to you than a recital of my lack of success—there are two things I do want to tell you."

Anthony raised his hand. "Hold on a moment, Craig, will you? Before you tell me what you are going to tell me—let me reverse the order of things and give you a piece of information first. It is only right that you should know now—because the knowledge of it may tend to affect your present view of the case. In the first place, have you given any thought as to the weapon with which Sir Eustace Vernon was killed?"

Craig scratched his cheek very thoughtfully. "I have that, Mr. Bathurst. According to Doctor Tempest, who extracted the bullet from the wound, the weapon used was probably a small 'automatic' of the American pattern. But I don't think it belonged to anybody in Vernon House. I've thought it over very carefully indeed. In my opinion it's what I should call an outside job—although it may have been *engineered* by somebody inside."

"Well, I can readily understand you thinking that way, Craig, and it's quite possible that you may be perfectly right in your theory, but before you leave here this afternoon, I shall have much pleasure in showing you the very weapon with which the crime was committed.

"I had the good fortune to stumble," Anthony continued, "if you like to put it that way, upon a piece of evidence that conducted me to it. I should be the first to admit that it was singularly fortunate for me." He smiled indulgently. "Doctor Tempest was a very good judge."

Craig lifted up his face in undisguised amazement. "Well, you surprise me, sir—it's no good my pretending that you don't. Luck like that hasn't come my way. May I see this revolver?"

Anthony took it from his pocket—handing it to Sir Austin Kemble, for examination, first Craig's eyes were open—widely incredulous—as the Commissioner took it in his hands and looked at it.

"How can you be sure about this, Bathurst?" he asked—then, as his eyes fell for the first time upon the initials which the butt of the revolver bore—"T.D.!" he exclaimed—"T.D.? That would be Terence Desmond—surely—eh, Bathurst?"

"I imagine that your suggestion would be entirely accurate, sir," replied that gentleman.

"Where did this weapon come from?" put in Craig with sharp anxiety—"from inside Vernon House do you suppose?"

"Looking for evidence of one particular kind caused me to run across this," said Mr. Bathurst in explanation, as he told the story of his call upon Albert Fish, and what eventually transpired from the encounter. "I was lucky, as I said. I thought Fish, having been in the grounds of Vernon House not very long before the murder, might be able perhaps to give me information of some kind—you never know in cases of this sort—I certainly wasn't prepared to obtain this. However, one thing brought up another—you have the result in front of you." He held out his hand for the revolver.

"What do you yourself make of it, Bathurst?" asked Sir Austin curtly.

"The ownership of the revolver—do you mean, sir?" Sir Austin nodded.

"Well, as to that—I have formed certain theories about the case that satisfy me—that satisfy my intelligence would be a better way of putting it—but there's still a missing link somewhere. Nobody realizes that fact more than I do. Frankly, sir—I can't get to the *Fons et Origo* of the affair." He looked up and smiled at Sir Austin, who was listening to him intently—then continued. "I'm near to it constantly though—and something in time will give it to me. In all probability it will come to me suddenly. When that happens I will answer your question with regard to the significance of the initials on the revolver. Till then—" He broke off and shrugged his shoulders.

Craig meanwhile had been staring fascinatedly at the object under discussion. Suddenly he seemed to come to life again. "I haven't followed the gist of all Mr. Bathurst's remarks. I don't quite understand for instance the reference he made to that foreign gentleman just now—all the same, there's no doubt in my mind that the story he's just told us—the evidence of the sailor Fish—is very important It would be idle for us to pretend otherwise. The man who hid the revolver in the tree was the murderer of Sir Eustace Vernon. It's all Lombard Street to a china orange on it, to my idea. At any rate I shall give Mr. Desmond a little close attention. However, that's as far as it goes—now for my two pieces of information. Are you ready to hear them, Sir Austin? Is it convenient?"

"Carry on, Craig. Let's have them."

"Well, sir—it's like this. I've had a fairly good loot round every one of the house-party that Sir Eustace had there on the Christmas night. I don't believe in taking any chances. I can't afford to. Although it entails a very wide circle of suspicion indeed, the fact that a number of people were round Sir Eustace on the night of the crime can't possibly be overlooked." The Inspector had commenced to speak rapidly, but by this time was slowing down. "Motive! All the three of us here in this room realize the importance of that, but how many of us can answer it in this case? What *was* the motive behind these two murders? You may have your opinion, Sir Austin, Mr. Bathurst, here, may have his—I may have mine. Very probably there will be three different opinions. Which again might *all* be wrong. But I've found out *something*! Inquiries that I have made tell me that one person in that house-party benefited considerably on account of Sir Eustace's death. To say the least of it—it came very opportunely. And I don't mean Major Prendergast. I refer to Morris Trentham."

"Be more explicit, Craig," interjected Anthony—"how do you mean that this was so?"

"Sir Eustace and Trentham were running a big oil deal—jointly. One of the conditions of their partnership was that if either died—the survivor was to take all the profits or correspondingly bear all the losses. The venture in question has turned up trumps. A nice little fortune has come Trentham's way. Moreover, he needed the money badly."

"How do you know?"

Craig smiled. "I've cultivated the acquaintance of one of his clerks these last few days—it's surprising the amount of beer that chap can drink before he gets properly garrulous. I've promised him, also, two or three things straight from the stable. It's wonderful how they'll come up for that. It's right enough, though, Sir Eustace Vernon's death was a bit of jam for Mr. Morris Trentham. I've established that fact beyond any contradiction."

Sir Austin glanced across at Mr. Bathurst, but the latter was oblivious of the fact. He sat in his chair with his two eyes firmly closed. The Trentham implication had evidently given him much food for thought. With his eyes still shut, he rubbed his finger-tips together.

"I, too, have an interest in the Trenthams, Craig—I've had it for some little time now. I've always felt—" He broke off. "Can you give me their private address?"

Craig chuckled. "I can that—easy. Twenty-nine Courtland Gardens, Kensington. Going to look him up?"

Anthony smiled whimsically. "There's a distinct possibility that I shall call there, Inspector. As a matter of fact—to be perfectly candid—it was in my mind before I heard your story."

Craig sniffed rather disdainfully. "There is such a thing as being wise after the event, sir—still I'll take your word for what you say. Now I'll let you have my second piece of news." It was his turn to rub his hands in pleasurable anticipation. "It concerns Miss Ashley."

"We're going through the card," muttered Sir Austin—"goodness knows where we shall get before we've finished What about Miss Ashley?"

"Nothing detrimental, sir. I didn't mean it in that way at all. But something very interesting has happened to her. And very surprising, too. The night before last she received a letter that had nothing externally to cause it to differ from any other letter. The postmark was London, E.C. The handwriting was unfamiliar. But the contents were ten thousand pound notes! They were enclosed within a smaller envelope. There was nothing else whatever—no sender's name—no address or initials—nothing at all. Nice little windfall—eh, Sir Austin?"

Mr. Bathurst sprang to his feet, as near to excitement as he had ever been. His eyes reflected his enthusiasm. "An unknown benefactor—eh, Craig?" he murmured.

"Either that or a conscience-stricken criminal," declared Craig.

"Or something Higher and Greater," announced Sir Austin Kemble, oracularly—"*à brebis tondue le bon Dieu mesure le vent*—"

"Call it what you choose," supplemented the Inspector—"you can't deny that it's a surprising occurrence."

Anthony smiled and shook his head. "Not so surprising as you think. I'm frightfully sorry to disappoint you, Inspector—but I'm not in the least surprised. I could almost—truthfully too—say that I have lived these last few days, in some expectation of it happening."

Craig allowed himself to cough. Sir Austin puckered his brows in an abortive attempt to reconcile all that had transpired, when his telephone rang insistently and put a stop to what he was essaying.

"Yes"—the others heard him say. "It is Sir Austin Kemble speaking. Who's that? What . . . Painswick dead? You astonish me! I had an idea he was ill. . . . On leave? . . . Dear—dear—how inexpressibly sad. . . . Give my condolences to all concerned. . . . I'm very, very sorry, Doctor. Many thanks for ringing. As you say—a tragedy—a great loss indeed—a man we can ill afford to spare." He turned to find Mr. Bathurst's face fixed intently on him—his eyes alive with superlative eagerness.

"Painswick—Sir Austin! You mentioned the name 'Painswick.' Who and what is 'Painswick'?"

For a moment Sir Austin Kemble stood with bowed head. "A very old friend of mine, Bathurst. Major Arnold Painswick. We were at Sandhurst together. Up to last night, when he died of lobar pneumonia—he was Governor of His Majesty's Prison at Portsea. He went on leave at Christmas, so I've just learned, up to his home in Leicestershire—near Syston—caught a chill and passed away last night. Doctor Carrington—the prison doctor—knew of his friendship with me—"

"Doctor who?" cut in Anthony.

"Carrington. Why? Oh—you're thinking of the doctor down at Rodding—very likely a relation—I've never met the one at Portsea—so I can't say."

"Sir Austin," said Mr. Bathurst—"I think I can say at last with a degree of confidence that my case is now nearly complete. You have helped me more than I could ever have anticipated. It will be necessary for us to act very quickly, I am afraid, Craig. I shall be communicating with you in a very short time from now. I can rely on you implicitly, of course?"

Chapter XXIII
CRAIG BEGINS TO UNDERSTAND

The Inspector, thus addressed, rubbed his lips with the back of his hand. "Naturally, Mr. Bathurst, I shall be prepared, I hope, when the time comes. But I'm still very much in the dark. What's this Major Painswick and this other Doctor Carrington to do with the case?"

"You can easily ascertain that, Craig. In fact, I was going to suggest that you did something of the kind." Anthony walked across to Sir Austin and spoke in a very low tone. The

Commissioner listened attentively and nodded agreement two or three times.

"As you wish, my dear boy. I trusted your judgment before—I was justified. I am willing to trust it again."

"Thank you, Sir Austin."

Mr. Bathurst returned to the Inspector. "Get away down to Portsea, Craig. Tell the prison doctor, Doctor Carrington, who you are—that you are engaged on the Mapleton case and that your visit to him is directed by Sir Austin Kemble himself. Find out *what* the communication was that passed between Sir Eustace Vernon and Major Painswick. For I'm pretty sanguine that there was one. Somewhere about the end of last November if I hazard an opinion. When you've got the required information in your hands—communicate with me. I shall be ready by then. I have still to test the last link of my chain of evidence."

The following morning saw Inspector Craig leave Waterloo, *en route* for Weymouth, with somewhat mixed feelings. For he had no very clear idea as to what he was going to discover in H.M. Prison at Portsea. The one fact that stood out strikingly clearly in his mind was that after all, he was returning—and returning in person—to the town—from where his witness Cridge had emanated, or at all events—next door to it. This fact served to afford him no small measure of satisfaction, and whetted his appetite for the task that he had in hand. Moreover, it gave him a certain *locus standi* in the case. The most remarkable and baffling case that had ever come his way, and a case that, taking all things into consideration, was not going to do him any harm. Indeed, it might benefit him considerably. To have been brought into such close contact with the Commissioner was an event not to be regarded by any means lightly.

His credentials, after a time, secured him admission to the prison and to Doctor Cyril Carrington's room in particular. It occasioned Craig no difficulty to see that the man and the late Sir Eustace Vernon's doctor at Rodding were either brothers or cousins. They had the same breadth of shoulder—the same lines of face, and hair of similar colour rising from the same high forehead. Craig fell to wondering whether Lionel and Cyril

Carrington were twins, as he was inclined to place them, at a first glance, at about the same age.

"I haven't the least idea why you desire to see me, Inspector—er—Craig." Doctor Carrington looked at the latter's card. "You have heard perhaps of the lamentable death of the Governor—the late Major Painswick? Is it on that account that you wish—"

"Not entirely, Doctor, if you'll pardon me for a moment. Although in a way it can be said to be something to do with him. I am in charge of the Rodding murder case."

A gleam of more than ordinary interest flashed into the eyes of Doctor Cyril Carrington. "Ah, yes. The murder of Sir Eustace Vernon? I am, to a certain extent, familiar with the main outline of the affair. The Doctor Lionel Carrington, who was the late Sir Eustace Vernon's medical adviser and who was present at Vernon House on the night of the murder, is my elder brother. He is just a year my senior."

Craig nodded. "I guessed almost as much, Doctor. There is a strong likeness between the two of you, if you will allow me to say so. Your partial familiarity with the matter will help on my interview a bit. Or it should do. When Sir Austin Kemble received your telephone message yesterday the significance of your name struck us, so I arranged to run down to see you. Now, Doctor, what I want to ask you is this. Had you been in touch with Sir Eustace at all before his murder?"

Doctor Carrington looked a trifle surprised. "Do you mean me—personally?"

"Well—not exactly—you or Major Painswick, shall we say?"

"I hadn't—I couldn't answer for the Governor—naturally. He wouldn't take me into his confidence over anything of that nature. Why do you ask? Do you suspect that anything of the sort had occurred?"

"Yes—we do. We should say that it happened about the end of November."

"Really—as a matter of fact—although I've been up to Rodding—to my brother's place—three or four times during recent years, I was never lucky enough to run across Sir Eustace. My brother thought no end of him—especially after his gallantry at that frightful fire, and took me with him to Vernon House on two occasions. But each time Sir Eustace himself happened to be absent. Is your errand to-day by way of being important?"

"It is rather, Doctor. Can you think of any way by which—"

"You might see Cannon, Major Painswick's chief clerk. He attends to most of the Governor's correspondence. Shocking thing, you know, the Major going off like that—only away a week."

"Is this Cannon available for me to see him now?" asked Craig.

"I'll inquire for you, Inspector, with pleasure, if you'll excuse me. Would you mind waiting here for a moment?"

While he was away Craig took a quick glance at the walls of Doctor Carrington's private room. There were three or four "group photos." Two were of St Bart's Hospital Rugger XV's and one of the cast of a Hospital dramatic performance. Craig found it easy to pick out in each the man whom he had travelled to see. The subject of his thoughts was not long away.

"If you will kindly come this way, Inspector—Cannon will see you at once. What's more, he is of the opinion that he can help you. He seems quite confident. I mentioned the line of your inquiry and he seemed to know something about it."

Much heartened at the news, the Inspector followed the Doctor into the office of Cannon, the clerk. The last-named was a young man evidently in the early thirties. He wore glasses, and as a further handicap was the possessor of an ill-fitting set of false teeth. When Craig entered he clicked these brightly as a sociable accompaniment to his "Good day, Inspector." Despite his appearance and his appalling style of dress, he proved to be eminently business-like.

"Doctor Carrington has told me of the direction of your inquiry, Inspector," he announced—"and of its connection with a matter of which I know something. I think I can help you at once. If not—if it touches upon anything else—I'm afraid you've drawn a blank. The sudden death of Major Painswick, who was a hale and hearty man when he left here on Christmas Eve, has, of course, made me very busy. It's a bad blow. I would have taken a lease of his life."

"Thank you, Mr. Cannon. The correspondence in question took place about November last, I believe."

Cannon nodded in affirmation. "That is so. I remember the correspondence quite well. Sir Eustace Vernon wrote to the Governor with regard to a matter of Prison Reform. He was a sort of philanthropist, I should say, and Prison Reform was one of his pet hobbies. Very interested in the future life of convicts and what was to become of them after their release. He found them suitable employment, I believe, wherever he was able. He wrote to Major Painswick concerning two convicts, whose time here finished at the end of December. Their names were Collins and Page. Perhaps you remember their case. There was a gang of three implicated—one turned King's Evidence. Their special line was what we should describe now as 'cat burglary'—and more than once they employed great violence with it. The Judge gave them a very heavy sentence—fifteen years' penal—I think. It was Mr. Justice Ivory. Now, I may tell you that Sir Eustace Vernon was particularly anxious to help these two men. Actually they were released a week before their time. They had earned full remission marks, and as it was Christmas—the Governor took the responsibility of discharging them on the morning of Christmas Eve."

Craig's brain began to buzz with excitement. The day was important. "One more question, Mr. Cannon. Have you such a thing as a 'photo' of Collins and Page?"

Cannon thought for a moment or so. "Yes, I can assist you there as well. Just a minute. There they are," he said five minutes later, pointing the two men out to the Inspector—"those two men standing there by the side of the big warder."

"I'll borrow this, if you've no objection," returned Craig. "Doctor Carrington, here, will make himself responsible, I feel sure—won't you, Doctor?"

"What's the idea, Inspector?" rejoined Doctor Carrington. "What connection have Page and Collins with what you came down—"

Craig's reply was in the nature of an interruption. "The connection that they formed the subject of Sir Eustace Vernon's correspondence with your late Governor—Major Painswick. That's just the point," he added grimly—"I've found out what I wanted to find out. I don't think I need take up your valuable time any longer, Doctor. Thanks very much! And you, Mr. Cannon." Inspector Craig shook hands with the two men and left the building.

On his homeward way he broke his journey at Weymouth for longer than is usual. It did not take him very long to find Park Street and the stationer's and tobacconist's kept by Cridge. That gentleman was actually behind the counter when the Inspector entered. The usual salutations followed, after which Craig whispered something in the other's ear. He then produced the photograph he had brought from Portsea Prison that included Messrs. Page and Collins. The tobacconist pointed instantaneously to the bigger man of the two. "That's the man," he exclaimed. "That's the man that bought the tobacco here on the morning of Christmas Eve. I could pick him out in a thousand."

"Would you swear to it?" asked Craig.

"I would that. I haven't the slightest doubt about it, Inspector."

"I'm very pleased to hear you say that, Cridge," said Craig, with a smile of intense satisfaction, "this information is going to make the Rodding murder case look a great deal simpler." He patted his pocket in which he had replaced the photograph. "The whole thing's as plain as a pikestaff to me, now. I shan't be taking any more lessons from anybody either. I'd wager a pony to a dried pea, Cridge, that the solution of the whole affair is in my hands. Watch the papers for the next day or two. Good-bye."

Many times in the near future George Alfred Cridge was heard to tell to an admiring circle that he was the first person in the whole world to know the inner history of the Rodding red 'bonbon murder.' "I was absolutely in Inspector Craig's confidence," he was wont to remark—"as perhaps I deserved to be. However, I'll speak fair—the Inspector always recognized it. You hear a great deal of talk against the Police Force and against its methods, but I'm going to speak as I find. I gave him the clue that put him on the trail, and he knew it, and what's more, he didn't mind saying as much. He was a sportsman. Same again, Miss, please!"

To Sir Austin Kemble, three days later, the news that two men had been detained by Inspector Craig in connection with the Rodding murders came as something in the nature of a surprise—as the Inspector intended it should. Sir Austin telephoned to Anthony Bathurst immediately upon receipt of the news. Judging by the way that Mr. Bathurst received his telephonic communication, Sir Austin was unable to be sure whether Mr. Bathurst was as surprised as he was.

"So he's detained a couple of men 'on suspicion,' has he?" commented Anthony. "Two ex-convicts, I suppose, Sir Austin?"

"That's so, Bathurst—how the devil did you know?"

"What are their names?"

Sir Austin referred to a paper on his desk. "Ralph Page and James Bernard Collins," he replied. "They were detained by Craig at a village in Essex—Kelvedon Hatch, somewhere near Navestock, I believe—Page's brother lives there. They're at Mapleton now. Craig wants to know if you'll go down and have a look at them. What do you say?"

Had Sir Austin been in a position to see what was happening at the other end of the telephone, he would have observed an enigmatic smile playing on Mr. Bathurst's face. The latter hesitated for a moment before he answered the Commissioner's last question.

"I may do—some time to-morrow—but I've a couple of calls to make before that—one of them in Mapleton. Thanks very much for ringing me, Sir Austin. By the way—it's just possible that one of the two men arrested has just lost 'a near relative.'" Mr. Bathurst replaced his receiver without waiting for Sir Austin's reply, and smiling still, opened his telephone directory. He turned to the "T's."

Chapter XXIV
MR. BATHURST AS A LADIES' MAN

Ruby Trentham turned quickly as her husband entered the room. It was almost as though she had been suddenly startled in the act of doing something that she fervently desired to keep secret. Morris Trentham, not for the first time these days, flung a nervously-suspicious glance in her direction. His wife swiftly raised her hand to her throat and turned away again with a gesture that bordered upon the height of nervous tension. It was obvious that she was labouring under the influence of great strain. Trentham was a man of gross and powerful face—a face that carried two heavy chins and coarse eyelids covering slightly bloodshot eyes.

"What the devil's the matter with you lately, Ruby?" he growled—"you creep and slink about the house like a damned ghost. You get on my nerves—I told you so yesterday. Why can't you walk about like a Christian?"

His coarse, heavy features were revealed at their worst. Ruby Trentham flushed suddenly. She swiftly and violently turned to face him. "I don't know what you mean, Morris. For goodness sake explain yourself. You seem suspicious of me. I turn suddenly and find you behind me. What is it? What's troubling you? My conscience is clear, at least."

"What do you mean by that?" he barked at her.

She shrugged her shapely shoulders. "If you don't understand I'm afraid I can't put it any more plainly." Her coldness met his glare with definite antagonism. But he was not done yet.

"May I ask to what you particularly refer when you speak of consciences?" he rallied.

She looked at him searchingly. "I spoke in defence," she said—"that was all. You have seemed to be so doubtful about me lately—so furtively inquisitive with regard to everything I do or say, that I simply defended myself. I told you that there was nothing on my conscience. I am not working in the dark against you, if that's what you're afraid of. I am sorry the word 'conscience' has caused you so much anxiety." She paused and then proceeded. "I will choose my words more carefully, next time I speak."

He mumbled something under his breath before breaking out again. "Look here, Ruby," he said, meaningly, "you can't deny that you've acted very strangely since Vernon's murder—any man in his senses would have noticed it. He couldn't help noticing it. I'm not exaggerating things. I wouldn't have been surprised if you'd garbed yourself in widow's weeds. They would have suited your particular style of beauty," he sneered. "Or perhaps you're wearing your black next your heart."

The pallor of her face seemed to be intensified under her crown of raven hair. When other women would have flushed Ruby Trentham grew white.

"The insinuation comes well from you," she countered, in a low tone. "I suppose you judge me, like all men of your type, from your own exemplary code of morals. The death of Sir Eustace was a great shock to me—as it would have been to any woman in the circumstances. I should have had to have been made of steel not to be upset by it. And, while we are on the subject, *you* haven't been altogether unmoved by it." She watched the effect of her words upon his heavy countenance. He shuffled his feet somewhat aimlessly. Before he could reply she attacked again, and moreover, realizing the invariable strategical strength of the move, changed the point of the attack. "I could also say—were I evilly-disposed—were I, for instance, as prone to flinging irresponsible accusations about as some people whom I could mention—that Sir Eustace Vernon's death hasn't been exactly a calamity for *you*!"

Again the glare flickered in his eyes and menaced her. "I can't help coincidences happening, can I? I suppose *somebody* benefits when *anybody* dies, if you could only find out. There's one thing—I can account for *my* time after dinner on the evening of the murder. You can't play cards very well by yourself—except 'Patience.' It isn't everybody at Vernon House has as good an alibi as I have."

She made no attempt to ignore the veiled accusation that his words contained. "If you're alluding to me, Morris," she said, with even more frigidity and hauteur than her tones had previously held, "I can account for any and every moment of my time just as satisfactorily as you can. I was in either the billiard-room or the music-room the whole time. You won't frighten me with remarks of that kind, if you think you will. Perhaps if the truth's known and while we're on the subject, my alibi could be established even better than yours," she hinted darkly.

"Perhaps—and perhaps not," he growled.

He flung out of the room and slammed an inoffensive door savagely behind him. Ruby Trentham watched his departure with icy disdain, and as the door closed upon his retiring figure shrugged her shoulders again contemptuously. Half an hour later she found herself contemplating Mr. Bathurst's visiting card with some trepidation. For what purpose was this man calling upon her now? She remembered the tall, lithe, grey-eyed man, who had questioned her at Vernon House the day after the tragic evening, and she recalled without taxing her brains very heavily that he had possessed that indefinable something that most people try to explain by the word "personality." She had been able to sense during that brief interview that Mr. Bathurst was not quite as other men are, and that she had as much chance of defeating him in a battle of words and wits waged upon equal terms as there is of the coming of the Greek Kalends. She told her maid, however, that she would receive him.

Mr. Bathurst made the usual dutiful overture and looked at his wrist-watch. "I must apologize for troubling you, Mrs. Trentham, but I have most important news for you. By the way—is Mr. Trentham in?"

"He went out about twenty minutes ago, Mr. Bathurst. Was it my husband that you wanted to see?"

"Not exactly, Mrs. Trentham—I can convey my message to you just as well as to him. As a matter of fact, Sir Austin Kemble, the Commissioner of Police, asked me to come along to see you. He was very anxious that I should. There is important news with regard to the murder."

A spot of colour appeared and burned scarlet in each of her cheeks. "Yes?" she murmured interrogatively.

"Yes. I have just been informed from Scotland Yard that Inspector Craig has collared a couple of men—Page and Collins by name—and that the evidence against them is pretty conclusive. He also desires me to tell you something else. Also very important and relative to the late Sir Eustace Vernon's estate. Sir Austin Kemble wishes all the people who were at Vernon House on the fatal night to assemble there again on Friday—at seven o'clock in the evening. It is essential that *all* those concerned should be there. There are, I may say again, highly important interests at stake. Sir Eustace Vernon, like most rich men, left a lot to be desired."

She looked up quickly—challengingly. "To what do you—?"

Mr. Bathurst smiled as the subtlety of his last phrase broke in upon her.

"I see what you mean," she said. "For the moment I was puzzled at your way of putting it."

Mr. Bathurst looked at his watch again. As he did so the telephone bell rang aggressively over on the side table.

"Excuse me for a moment," said Ruby Trentham as she crossed to answer it. As she did so a lancinating pain seemed to shoot through her breast. "What's that?" she said, with a strange catch in her voice. "Yes, yes, I'm listening." She stood waiting for a second or so—tense and very anxious. Her face was white with anxiety. Then it cleared. "It's quite all right," she said. "Don't apologize." She turned to discover Mr. Bathurst watching her curiously. "Somebody got the wrong number," she explained.

"'Tis a nuisance," he said commiseratingly—"but I suppose it can't be helped occasionally. You will tell Mr. Trentham about Friday evening, won't you?" He held out his hand. "Vernon House at seven o'clock. You won't forget, will you?"

Chapter XXV
SAM McLAREN BUILDS MORE CASTLES

NUMBER 83, Mafeking Street—just down by the Mapleton tram depot, was of the usual type of modern villa-residence, the erection of which, at inflated prices, has done so much to enable speculating builders to enjoy Continental tours and give their sons the chance to become Perambulators, Etceteras or Authentics. Mrs. Croucher, who had been left a widow some five years previously, had been forced to supplement a meagre income by "letting." She had found Sam McLaren an excellent investment. His hours it is true were irregular—but, if one may employ a seeming paradox—they were regularly irregular. His rent was always paid "on the nail" and his rooms were invariably kept scrupulously clean and tidy. When he told her that he had a chance of selling his "business" and clearing away from Mapleton, she had been grieved. Her grief, although to a certain extent not disinterested, was genuine. She had learned to value her lodger for his own sake. More than once she had been heard to remark to both friends and acquaintances that although old Sam was a rough diamond with his customers down at the coffee-stall—a lot of his crudity and roughness disappeared when he was at home by himself. "Take my word for it," she used to say with a waggle of the head intended to be *le dernier cri* as regards impressiveness—"old Sam can take a leaf out of St. Paul's book—he can be 'all things to all men.'"

When Mr. Bathurst called upon Mrs. Croucher she took an immediate liking to him. In which respect amongst her sex, Mr. Croucher in no way dwelt in splendid isolation. In the initial stages of the conversation she actually allowed herself the wildly imaginative flight that this gentleman might even be secured as Sam's successor, should the sale of the coffee-stall materialize and the worst come to the worst. But she did not hold to this idea for very long and ultimately was forced to abandon it— albeit with some reluctance.

"No, sir," she said, shaking her head in response to Mr. Bathurst's third question, "Mr. McLaren's not in just at the moment. Though I expect him any minute. He's very busy just now—as perhaps you know. January's one of his busiest months, in fact, sir, this cold snap we're having means a deal of trade to Mr. McLaren."

"I can quite believe that, madam. If I'm not troubling you, though, I'll wait a little while on the off-chance of Mr. McLaren turning up. I've got something to tell him."

"You come right in, sir, and wait in his sitting-room, and don't talk about it being a trouble. I'm one of the kind that's only too pleased to do anything for anybody."

Anthony followed the form of Mrs. Croucher with its ample proportions into "old Sam's" room. Having piloted him in there, the landlady let her conversation have its head.

"I hope you haven't got any news for him that will upset him, sir. You see—I'm in his confidence a little bit and I know how disappointed he was over that matter of poor Sir Eustace Vernon's up at Rodding. He's told me more than once how he built his castles in the air over what Sir Eustace had said to him, and how they all toppled to the ground. He ain't been the same man, sir, since then—not by any manner of means."

"How do you mean, Mrs. Croucher? Has Mr. McLaren been ill?"

She shook her head expressively. "Not what you'd call ill, sir, but like a man who's had a severe blow. You mightn't have noticed anything, but living with him here as I do, it was easy to see that he took his trouble a bit bitter, as you might say. Little things told me—after all straws show which way the wind blows—don't they now? His appetite's fallen away—things he was keen on in the food line, tasty little dishes I used to make for him—he won't hardly look at some of them now, sir. He's taken something to heart very much, sir—you can take my solemn word for it I've told him more than once not to sit and worry over what's gone or cry over spilt milk, but all he'll say to me is, 'You don't understand, Mrs. Croucher. Somebody's cheating me out of my lawful rights.' Only the other day he refused a dish of tripe and onions—done in milk at that. And there's nothing he likes better."

Mr. Bathurst nodded his head in sympathetic appreciation. This was indeed significant. "What was he before he started in the coffee-stall line? Do you know?"

Mrs. Croucher pursed her lips before she gave her questioner a triumphant reply. "A Government official, sir! Civil Service—if you ask me. I've heard him speak many a time of his days at the Treasury Office."

"Really, Mrs. Croucher! I suppose he must have been unfortunate enough to lose his position in some way."

"That's just what I think, sir. I've said to my cousin Maria Champion that is—her that was Maria Crabbe—she changed her name and not the letter, and the old rhyme came out true as true—her husband had the *Blind Beggar* over at Perringham—I've said to her—" Mrs. Croucher's recital ended abruptly.

"Here is Mr. McLaren," she said—"I'll let him in and you can talk to him yourself. I'll only ask you one thing—if you've bad news break it to him gently, 'cos he's a good old soul and one of the very best. No woman ever had a better lodger."

"Well, McLaren," said Anthony, in greeting, "how's the world treating you, now?"

"No different, sir! No different! It's going to be 'ard work for old Sam to the end of the blinking chapter—until 'e pushes the daisies up." He shook his head pessimistically.

"How's the coffee-stall business? Disposed of yet?"

Again Sam shook his old head. "Not yet, sir. Although I still 'ave 'opes. Was that what you wanted to see me abaht, sir?"

"Not exactly. I fancy that you may regard me on this occasion perhaps, as the harbinger of good fortune—the bearer of good tidings. But I am not at liberty at the present moment to divulge them to you. That must wait until this evening."

"This evening? Why—wot—?"

"Let me explain and you'll understand. Sir Austin Kemble, the Commissioner of Police, the gentleman whom you saw at Mapleton Police Station about your assault, desires you to be in attendance at Vernon House this evening at seven o'clock.

You can take it from me that you will hear something to your advantage."

Sam became the incarnation of incredulity. "I was 'ad once that way before," he remonstrated. He shook his head again. "I don't feel like gulping the bait down twice."

Anthony smiled. "Have no fear, Mr. McLaren. I can promise you, upon my personal word of honour, the surprise of your life." Sam looked at him searchingly. Mr. Bathurst proceeded to clinch the argument. "I want to tell you also, Mr. McLaren, that Inspector Craig has detained two men on suspicion for the murder of Sir Eustace Vernon. The two men are named Page and Collins. It is just possible that they are the two men—"

"That waylaid me! Well, I never!" Sam was trembling with an excess of excitement that he found impossible to conceal.

"Your evidence will doubtless be wanted before the police complete their case. There is one other matter before I go. You will not be the only visitor at Vernon House this evening. All the people who were with Sir Eustace on the night of his murder have been instructed by Scotland Yard to be in attendance."

Sam's one visible eye flashed a look in Mr. Bathurst's direction. "Everybody?" he murmured in interrogation.

"It is hoped that everybody will be there. The only doubtful person is Father Jewell."

"Why are the police doing that? What's their little game, eh?"

"A little idea of Sir Austin Kemble's—that's all. Perhaps I can plead guilty to being partly responsible for it. But Sir Eustace, you must know, was a rich man. Be prepared for some astounding developments."

"Will any of the ladies be there, sir?"

"They will, Sam. Every one of them. There's an added inducement for you." Mr. Bathurst rose from his seat and buttoned his heavy overcoat round him. "It's an appropriate night, you know, Sam. It's Friday night."

"Pay night you mean, sir, don't you?" grinned McLaren.

"Call it 'Treasury' night."

"'Treasury?'" queried Sam.

Mr. Bathurst smiled whimsically. "Treasury, Sam! Mrs. Croucher, your esteemed landlady, who entertained me here for a few minutes pending your arrival, tells me that you've often told her that you were an official of His Majesty's Treasury." Anthony smiled invitingly. The smile held allurement and the invitation was obviously for Mr. McLaren's confidence.

The latter hesitated for the fraction of a second—a prey to conflicting emotions. Then he crossed the Rubicon. "Quite right, sir. But I was only pullin' her leg about being an 'official.' That was only my way of puttin' it—just a joke that made me laugh inside. As a matter of fact, sir, between our two selves and the gate-post, I was only a messenger there."

Mr. Bathurst laughed heartily. "I see." He held out his hand to the old coffee-stall keeper and repeated verbatim the last words that he had spoken to Ruby Trentham. "Vernon House at seven o'clock. You won't forget, will you?"

Chapter XXVI
THE GUESTS RE-ASSEMBLE

It would have been difficult for the most astute student of psychology to have diagnosed accurately the various feelings that pervaded the breasts of the various people who re-assembled at Vernon House that evening at the "request" of the authorities who had the case in hand. Doctor Lionel Carrington seemed very cool outwardly—he was helped to his condition by the exigencies of his profession. The Mayor and Mayoress of Mapleton—Alderman and Mrs. Venables—disliked the position immensely, and the dominant partner of the alliance did not hesitate to express his opinion of the unusual procedure. To which, as usual, nobody paid any attention except perhaps to disregard it completely. Major Prendergast and his wife, Diana, were perhaps the calmest of all. They fell back upon that habitual quality of reserved aloofness which is the recognized prerogative of the English upper middle class. The Major was an Old Wykehamist of some distinction. He had been a member of the eleven for two years, and an innings of his against Eton on Agar's Plough that defied the Etonian attack for over two hours and a half is still remembered and spoken of with bated breath on many a pavilion from The Saffrons to Old Trafford. His wife relied upon a wholly natural serenity. Morris and Ruby Trentham seemed to differ radically from all the others present. To an acute observer they appeared to be distrustful not only of each other, but also of everybody else, and Sam McLaren, from his seat near the French doors of the study of Vernon House found himself watching the lady more than once and becoming fascinated by the tremulous anxiety that played in wistful waves upon the beauty of her face. The semi-arrogant poise of the head was still in evidence, however, and Anthony Bathurst was quick to detect it. Father Jewell, as austere and ascetically ecclesiastical as ever, and despite Mr. Bathurst's openly-expressed fear to the contrary, was present with the others and occupied a chair next to Mr. Bathurst himself. Helen Ashley and Terence Desmond stood side by side. Perhaps the most bewildered mind within the company belonged to Inspector Craig of Mapleton. He had received certain instructions from Mr. Bathurst via Sir Austin Kemble himself. These instructions had been rigorously repeated to him by the Commissioner upon his arrival at Vernon House, and the Inspector was conscious that there must be no mistake on his part. The Commissioner would forgive ignorances before negligences. The hands of the clock showed but a few minutes past seven when Sir Austin closed the door of the room and addressed the company. There was a generally perceptible stir at the first sounds of his voice. He spoke, let it be said, very quietly.

"Ladies and gentlemen," he said—"not very many days ago you were the guests here of the late Sir Eustace Vernon. It is not necessary for me to recount the manner of his death. It suffices for the time being to say that the police believe they have their hand upon the assassins of both Sir Eustace Vernon and Purvis, his butler. I also feel, personally, that an explanation is due to each one of you—because each one of you was, for a time at least, within the area of our definite suspicion. It was inevitable that you should be. Remember that Sir Eustace was a rich man and that his will—but I will call upon Mr. Bathurst to carry on from now."

Ruby Trentham's hand went to her brow and Diana Prendergast clutched momentarily and convulsively at her throat. The incisive tones of Mr. Bathurst compelled universal attention.

"I will preface my remarks by calling to your attention the statement just made by Sir Austin Kemble. This should effectively allay any apprehension that any one of you might feel at having been asked to be present here this evening. But Sir Austin and I are conscious that an explanation is due to each one of you. I will endeavour to the best of my ability to describe the events that took place here prior to the two murders and also some, at least, of the events that led up to them. It is incumbent upon me, however, to separate the history of the affair into two parts, because there were two parts—one of which was never expected to happen by the ingenious mind that had engineered what I will term the main portion of this most astonishing history. It is the old story over again of the inevitable miscalculation caused by the intervention of the unexpected. Although, I admit, that in this instance the intervention came subsequently to the happening of the more important events. Somewhere in the neighbourhood of fourteen years ago three men were sentenced by Mr. Justice Ivory. They were expert burglars and had been responsible for at least a score of the cleverest coups that ever baffled the ingenuity of the policy. One of the three, in fact, may be legitimately regarded as the first of 'the cat burglars.' His agility and athletic prowess were such that no building—however high—awkward or imposing—presented any terrors to him. When the arrests were made this man turned King's Evidence and received a very light sentence in comparison with the sentences received by his two confederates. The three men concerned were Ralph Page, James Bernard Collins and Charles Ramsay, and the last-named—the one of whom I have been speaking—knowing the desperate characters of the other two, knew also from information that they conveyed to him during the trial, that when the time came for their release from prison his own days were numbered. Collins is as strong as a lion, and he threatened to strangle Ramsay with his own hands if he had to cross two continents to do it. But Ramsay, who had been the brains of this unholy trinity, and although he went in abject terror of Collins, held different views."

Mr. Bathurst paused for a moment and the silence within the room became almost oppressive. It was broken only by the ticking of the clock. Diana Prendergast was staring at the speaker as though under some strange spell, while Ruby Trentham's face showed many emotions, among which could be unmistakably seen fear. The men were all relatively uneasy. Mr. Bathurst proceeded calmly and dispassionately.

"When Ramsay emerged from prison, about ten years ago—a free man—he disappeared. It was his firm intention to efface his former identity completely. He was a single man with only one relation in the world—his little niece—but he had ample means in reserve—the fruits of his evil deeds. He came to Rodding, where he lived originally as Eustace Vernon." Helen Ashley gave a little gasp, but Desmond drew her to his side and quieted her. The effect of Mr. Bathurst's declaration upon the others seemed electrical. "In Rodding he made good. He threw himself with all his heart and soul into the municipal activity of the neighbouring County Borough of Mapleton, and he capped many years of efficient and valuable citizenship with a deed that earned him a baronetcy. I have heard it described by one man as the bravest deed he ever saw. During those tense moments Vernon became Ramsay again, when no climb—hazardous and perilous though it might be—had any difficulty for him. He saved the lives of many children—the deed will stand to his eternal credit." Anthony made a sign to Craig which that gentleman evidently understood, for he acted upon it immediately. He took up a new position in the room. Mr. Bathurst once again took up the tenor of his narrative.

"But despite all this, Ramsay had to reckon with the day that would see the release of Page and Collins. He had hoped that his new associations would cover up his tracks and that he would be able to elude successfully the attentions of the avengers. But nevertheless he took no risks, and in connection with another man, to whom I believe that I shall be able to give a name, he evolved a most ingenious scheme that, if carried out successfully, would place him safe—high and dry—beyond the reach of his pursuers forever. This companion, whom I have mentioned, was not aware of the entire scheme—he was only apprised by Ramsay of part of it. Had he known the whole of it—the scheme would have fallen through. In the first place it was essential for Ramsay to know exactly when Page and Collins were to be released. To this end he posed as a benefactor to released convicts. You know the idea—'The Prison Walls Must Cast No Shadow.' He was in touch with Major Painswick, Governor of H.M. Prison of Portsea, in particular reference to Page and Collins. Major Painswick would have been very surprised to know that the avowed philanthropist, Sir Eustace Vernon, was the Charles Ramsay who had been under his care some years previously, however, and such was the machinery that Ramsay had set up that, provided he could get reasonable time between the release and their running him to earth, he would be able to outpit his two enemies. Even if they were successful in running him down almost immediately, an hour or two's grace was all that he required to put his plans into operation. But a tiny something upset them. He had learned that his two former associates were leaving prison in the early days of the New Year. Sentimentality, however, on the part of the Governor caused him to release them on Christmas Eve—a week at least before Ramsay expected them. Once again, however, and at a most critical moment, his luck held good. He was always, I may say, one of Fortune's favourites. *The other side made a mistake.* Purvis, his butler, whom I will call either Mrs. Page or Mrs. Collins—time will give you the correct answer—gave the game away. She gave him in the momentary passion and exultation of revenge, the very information that was vital to him. She had planted herself in his house, pseudo-sexed by means of forged references, and the pair at Portsea were hot upon his track directly they became free citizens of the King's Highway. They communicated their plans to her, but she gave them away to the very man who shouldn't have had them! She couldn't resist the temptation of making him suffer—of seeing him read the message of his doom and gloating over his terror! She wrote it and placed it in the red bonbon!"

"I begin to see," said Doctor Carrington—"that was when Sir Eustace received the 'bad news' about which he informed us at dinner."

"Exactly, Doctor," went on Mr. Bathurst—"and at that moment also, I imagine, he suspected the bona-fides of his butler. It may have been a look, it may have been that he recognized the handwriting—Purvis was doomed. Let me recall to you the evidence of the maid, Palmer. 'That's something very special, Purvis—don't forget.' She drank whatever it was that he gave her and with devilish ingenuity he conceived the idea of planting the red bonbon with its grim message upon its actual author. *But he had also had time to set the wheels of his machinery in motion!* Bare time, but just enough! His confederate—the other essential partner in the scheme—arrived according to plan, and when Collins and Page—their hands tingling with the lust for Ramsay's throat—entered the grounds of Vernon House and made their way into the study, with the topography of which Purvis had thoroughly acquainted them—they found their quarry dead at his own table! Shot through the head. It was easy for them to recognize him as the perfidious Ramsay despite the passage of the years and to read his farewell message. He had cheated them at the bitter end! But I fancy—I am only conjecturing now, I admit—that there was some solace for them on the study table. I should say it took the form of a substantial packet of bank-notes. The notes had been left there deliberately—they might very well help to hang the men who took them. Page and Collins decamped—who shall blame them?"

At this stage a police officer entered and asked leave to speak to Sir Austin Kemble. The Commissioner listened gravely for a moment and then motioned him to Inspector Craig. The latter in turn had a few words of conversation, with the result that the officer remained in the room. Mr. Bathurst waited for silence again before he resumed.

"For certain reasons that I cannot outline for the present I will omit details of what happened in this room after the departure of Page and Collins, and I will come to the moment when Hammond screamed—the moment we will say when this astonishing history really began for most of you here to-night. You will remember that the man whom I have described as Ramsay's partner had been in the study and that he had played the part that he had been well paid to play. Hammond was returning from the grounds when the open French doors attracted her attention. She entered. A woman dashed out upon her with a knife—placed an icy hand upon her face—and Hammond screamed and fainted. That was the story as you had it. The woman had come from the safe, ladies and gentlemen—the keys had been left lying on the table—but the knife was not a knife—it was the "Chosroes Cross"! It had been stolen by Ramsay in the hey-day of his adventurous campaign against the eighth Commandment and now was being stolen back from him. And the woman who touched Hammond is in this room." Mr. Bathurst paused.

Chapter XXVII
MR. BATHURST MEETS SUCCESS— AND FAILURE

ALL EYES were turned to the ladies. Diana looked indignant, Ruby Trentham was pale with excitement and fear, Mrs. Venables sneeringly scornful and Helen Ashley almost in a state of collapse. But not a word passed the lips of any one of them.

"Most of you here, I have no doubt, have some idea of the history and the value of the 'Chosroes Cross.' There is one *man* here, who coveted it. That *man* was Hammond's 'woman'! When the company rushed to investigate Hammond's trouble he came unnoticed in their rear—with the cross concealed on his person. He was not dressed as ordinary men are. She felt his 'skirt'! That 'skirt' was a cassock! His name is Father Jewell!"

Mr. Bathurst swung round dramatically and flung an accusing finger in the direction of the priest, who sprang to his feet white and trembling.

"I would alter your choice of words, sir—that would be my first desire. I did not covet the Cross, that is to say I did not covet it for myself. Sir Eustace Vernon—for I shall still continue to call him that—showed it to me some months ago. When I asked him questions as to how he obtained it, I was not satisfied. I was very far from being satisfied. I determined that I should be lacking in my duty to my Master and to Holy Mother Church if I did not replace it whence it had come. I therefore made it my especial mission to do so. I considered myself appointed to the purpose. I awaited my opportunity, which I knew was bound to come before very long. That opportunity came on the night that Sir Eustace met his death. I knew where the Holy Relic was kept and I found the doors open and the keys of the safe on the table. Am I to be arrested?" He drew his tall, spare form up to his full height and faced the ring of men and women with an air of proud disdain. Mr. Bathurst could see the fires of the Inquisition burning again in the depths of his eyes. He himself was no stranger to hagiology and had more than once realized the thin line between Supreme Devotion and Fanaticism.

"Where is the 'Chosroes Cross' now, Father Jewell?" he asked quietly.

"Back in the House of the Lord from where those iconoclasts stole it. I returned it—anonymously." His face wore a smile of quiet triumph. "Am I to answer any more questions? Permit me to point out that you have not yet answered mine. Am I to be arrested for 'stealing' what had been stolen? My opportunity was given to me from High Heaven. Or am I to be arrested for the murder of Sir Eustace Vernon? Perhaps that is your intention?" For a moment there was an intense silence. A silence which was eventually broken by the clear tones of Mr. Bathurst.

"That is not our intention, Father Jewell. When we make an arrest—we do not intend to make a mistake. We cannot afford to make one. We shall arrest the right man."

He made a quick movement with his hand to Inspector Craig and to the other police officer. But quick as his movement had been it was not quick enough. For it had been anticipated! Anthony's cry of "Watch him!" came a second too late, for Sam McLaren, with a sudden twist of his body, threw all his weight against the French doors, causing them to yield instantaneously at the impact. Five pairs of hands were impetuously outstretched to detain him—all unsuccessfully, and to the accompaniment of a woman's shriek, he disappeared—fiercely desperate—into the wintry darkness of the January night.

Chapter XXVIII
TO MEET SUCCESS AGAIN

"Got clean away," muttered Craig, despondently—an hour later. "But thank God he won't get far. We're bound to take him before very long. Mr. McLaren won't be long at liberty—his appearance is against him for one thing—what do you think, Mr. Bathurst?"

Anthony shrugged his shoulders. "I wouldn't be too sure if I were you, Inspector. All the same, I'll do my best for you." He turned to Sir Austin. "I want half a dozen of your best men, sir. You can take it from me that Sam McLaren won't be taken to-night. Or to-morrow," he added drily.

"You seem pretty sure of that, Mr. Bathurst," put in Craig. "What makes you so confident of the fact?"

"You underrate his ability and his resources, Craig. Those men I mentioned, Sir Austin. Is it all right?"

"You can have anybody you want, my boy. 'Phone right away. You can 'phone from here. The 'phone's in the hall."

"That's a good idea, sir. I'll pop in there at once. Perhaps though you'd better accompany me. They'll jump to it quicker coming from you."

The Commissioner put the instructions through as Anthony suggested "Ring me directly anything happens worth mentioning. Don't forget," he concluded.

"You gave me a free hand once before, sir," said Mr. Bathurst—"and I didn't let you down. I shan't let you down this time. Craig's a bit jumpy, naturally, but all the cards are in our hands now. I shall be able to put a hand on our man without any difficulty—and I think, before very long."

"That's different from what you told Craig," rejoined Sir Austin.

"I had a reason for saying what I did to him."

Sir Austin stared at him, wonderingly. "What's our next move?" he said, at length.

"Say good-night to everybody here and get back to town. I'm going too—for one very good reason, at least."

During the journey of the primrose-wheeled "Crossley" back to London the Commissioner of Police was strangely silent. Mr. Bathurst drove and seemed in no mood for confidences.

"When we have our man, sir," he declared ultimately, as he shook Sir Austin by the hand—"which will be early next week, I'll run the main facts of the case over to you. It has been distinctly interesting and far from simple."

With that promise the Commissioner had perforce to remain content, although he was not allowed to chafe under his impatience very long. In twenty-four hours the hunt was up! Mr. Bathurst received the news with his ordinary imperturbability, although it had come sooner than he had expected. But for all that he slipped a revolver into his pocket. "The train is timed to arrive at Parkeston Quay at ten-twenty to-night. Whittaker was next to her in the queue at the booking-office at Liverpool Street when she took her ticket. To all appearances the lady is travelling light and alone." Such was the tenor of the message that had reached him. He looked at his watch. It was just half-past eight. He had just time to pick up Sir Austin and make Harwich before the train arrived. He calculated the distance at just about seventy miles. Pretty good going, but once clear of London he could eat up the distance in the "Crossley" at that time of night. As far as Chelmsford they were well behind time, but between there and Colchester the "Crossley" began to make it up. Hatfield Peverel . . . Kelvedon . . . Colchester . . . Manningtree—the great car was well in its stride now and even seemed to be affected by the excitement of the chase. The engine fought eagerly for its head as it were, and as they made the last turn in the Harwich direction, Sir Austin glanced at the speedometer, and (to use the words that he himself employed) noticed that they were "knocking a cool fifty-six miles out of her."

"A near thing, but three minutes to spare," murmured Anthony, as they ran alongside the Quay. "The case started for us in a car and we've brought the same car down with us to be in at the death."

"What time does the boat leave, Bathurst?" queried Sir Austin.

"Almost immediately, sir, I understand. They probably hope to be in Brussels by ten o'clock tomorrow morning. How many of your men are on the train?"

"Three—to be on the safe side, I thought. Do you anticipate any trouble? An old man like McLaren shouldn't—"

"There's our train running in," interrupted Anthony—"come along—and be prepared for any emergencies."

The engine, sparks flying upward, began to slow down, and within a few moments ran slowly into the station.

"There are my men," muttered Sir Austin—"and there's the dainty bird they are trailing."

Anthony smiled, and suddenly pulled Sir Austin back into the shadow. As he did so Ruby Trentham passed them. She wore a smart, dark blue travelling costume. They watched her as she walked straight towards the landing-stage. "Even now—perhaps I've been a bit prem—"

The words were cut short on Mr. Bathurst's lips as Ruby was joined by a gentleman who had obviously been awaiting her. Only his back was visible to the five watchers. The Commissioner made a sign to his men and they carefully closed round the unsuspecting pair. Suddenly the man, faultlessly dressed and debonair to his finger-tips, turned round and they saw his face.

Sir Austin gave a startled gasp of astonishment. To the Commissioner's utter amazement the face was the face of the dead man at Dyke's Crossing. He raised his right hand but was too late. Craig—the leader of the three shadowers, was too quick for him—before he could move again he was handcuffed and helpless. Ruby Trentham swayed backwards, silent and swooning.

"What's the meaning of this outrage?" demanded the prisoner, with seething hatred in his voice. "Who are you?"

Mr. Bathurst stepped forward. "You are arrested, Charles Ramsay, or Sir Eustace Vernon, if you prefer to be so called, for the murders of Rose Collins and Bradley Deane on Christmas night of last year, and I warn you—"

Ramsay's voice rose in an infuriated scream. "You devil! If words could burn, I'd ransack the dictionary of Hell for your cremation—your blasted cleverness is inhuman—you—"

Craig swung him round viciously. "That's enough of that, Ramsay—see to the lady, Seton, will you?"

Mr. Bathurst watched him go. "Quite an unsolicited testimonial, Sir Austin," he murmured nonchalantly.

Chapter XXIX
A TELEGRAM FOR MR. BATHURST

"Draw the armchair up to the fire, Sir Austin, and make yourself comfortable. There are cigars over there and the tantalus is just to your right." Sir Austin Kemble obeyed the instruction of his host with a sign of complete contentment.

"You are fully cognisant," said Mr. Bathurst, "as to the events which took place at Vernon House up to the time when Ramsay, knowing that Page and Collins would be upon him, in an hour or thereabouts, put his machinery for defeating them into motion. Stevens, the chauffeur, you will remember, had been despatched for Sam McLaren. Firstly, I will tell you what transpired—then I will attempt to give you the various processes of deduction that enabled me to solve the mystery. Frankly, I think you will find them decidedly interesting. When Ramsay left Portsea he knew from his knowledge of the character of Collins that he would have to be extremely clever to escape the latter's vengeance. Also, *if* he escaped it—the fear of it hanging over his head eternally, like the sword of Damocles, would be more than he could bear. Life to him would be an everlasting nightmare of acute doubt and agonizing dread. He determined, therefore, not only to escape it, but also to rid himself of the constant menace forever. He would provide Page and Collins with the dead body of Charles Ramsay—they should *see* it themselves so that they harboured no doubts about it and if possible *he would get them hanged for his murder*. He, therefore, looked round for a man sufficiently like himself to deceive people, whom he could employ in a certain capacity. For, my dear Sir Austin, Ramsay was a most astute man. Clever, daring, and when he wanted to be—utterly callous. He saw one step farther than most people habitually, and he realized that when the time came for the 'death' of Ramsay there must be an identity to hand—*ready-made* and immune from conjecture or questionings—*going about its ordinary occupation undisturbed*—into which he could immediately sink his own. To that end he obtained the services of an impecunious actor, by the name of Bradley Deane. He went to an agent and told a certain story—left his photograph and in time secured the very man he required. I can only surmise that Deane was told to assume Ramsay's personality on certain occasions and Ramsay took over his, but I am certain that Deane never knew the real reason of the procedure. But if Deane were to be left free to become Ramsay in this way whenever Ramsay desired it, it was necessary that his own real identity and appearance should be generally hidden under another completely different guise."

Sir Austin gasped with astonishment. "I am beginning to see," he said. "But go on, my boy—go on."

"Ramsay therefore started the coffee-stall business and installed Deane therein as 'Sam McLaren.' To an actor, skilled in the delineation of 'character' parts, the task was fairly easy. A ginger wig, a black shade over one eye—the trim, grey moustache pulled out and made unkempt—these worked transformation wonders with his appearance. And he was well paid for his work. He entered the study at Vernon House on Christmas night as he had done before—prepared to play the part of 'Sir Eustace Vernon.' But on this particular occasion he arrived—not as McLaren—but actually made up and dressed for the other part. Ramsay had changed into his character of McLaren—he kept his own wig, etc., at Vernon House—and met Deane at the French doors of the study. Purvis was then sent for, and when she left the apartment she carried her death in her hand."

"Whose was the voice, then, that the maid, Palmer, heard?"

Anthony's reply came promptly and decisively. "In my opinion, Ramsay's—in his affected character of the coffee-stall proprietor. Deane probably gave the butler the poisoned whisky—without knowing, of course, the true nature of what he was giving her. I suggest that he could imitate Ramsay's voice moderately successfully. Very possibly, too, it was his last action, for Ramsay got him in the chair under some pretext or the other and shot him dead with a bullet from young Desmond's revolver. No time was wasted I assure you. It was the one part of the contract for which Deane had never bargained! The 'suicide' letter was placed in front of him and a comfortable bundle of bank-notes at his hand. The picture was all ready and complete for Comrades Page and Collins to behold. Ramsay was dead! Vernon had committed suicide! But 'Sam McLaren' watched from behind the *portière*—for *Bradley Deane* had been murdered! When Page and Collins arrived it is easy to see what happened. I told you the other night at Vernon House. Ramsay watched them go—planted the red bonbon in Purvis's coat— and wrote a similar one to be found on the dead body of Deane under the impression probably that it would serve to mystify the police when the time came for investigation. But he still had other work to do. He could not risk the dead body being identified by *Miss Ashley*—she would perhaps detect 'differences' in the two men that would pass unnoticed by others. His devilish mind would checkmate that possibility. A mangled body—found on the railway line—would be the very thing. He left the keys of the safe on the table for Helen to find her legacy and—perhaps wrote the second letter—it may have been written before—then Deane's body was conveyed to Dyke's Crossing by car and 'run over.' On the way the revolver was hidden in the tree. That was where you and I entered the case, Sir Austin—at Dyke's Crossing." Mr. Bathurst paused to light a cigarette.

"Fancy the old devil going up to the police station afterwards, with that fantastic assault-story," put in the Commissioner.

"That was a clever move on his part, sir. It brought Page and Collins into the arena, as he intended it to. And his touches with regard to Sir Eustace Vernon were extremely misleading—I had no reason to disbelieve his story, you see."

Sir Austin nodded. "Wily old fox!"

"He returned to Deane's lodgings as 'McLaren,' and of course, meant to retain the character till Ruby Trentham was ready to go abroad with him. She was in his secret and probably hates her husband even more than most wives."

"You're becoming a bigger cynic than ever, my dear Bathurst," declared the elder man, with a smile. He poured himself out a stiff peg of whisky. "Now let me hear your deductions. For the life of me I can't see how you got hold at all."

"I was coming to that, sir, and I will readily admit that for an appreciable length of time I was 'stone cold.' In fact, for a very long time, I was unusually blind and I deserve a good kicking for my dunder-headedness. I will trace my construction of the case, step by step. When we found the car abandoned at Dyke's Crossing you will remember that you helped me to take a good look at it. *There was a patch of blood showing on the fawn upholstery of the seats at the back, but no mud, grit, or dirt of any kind on the floor underneath.* I was certain that the car had carried a prostrate body, and eventually I decided that the man we found on the line *had been dead when he was put there*. My surmise was sound. We established that he had been shot. Then we got into the 'Vernon' atmosphere. I will not recount all of it again, but I was puzzled by those *two letters*."

"Why?" interrogated Sir Austin.

"Why should a man write *two* letters, sir, when he intends to commit suicide? Why isn't *one* enough? Surely Miss Ashley's letter would have sufficed?"

Sir Austin relapsed into meditation. "I see what you mean," he muttered.

"There was another point, too," urged Anthony. "Miss Ashley's letter was put by Ramsay in a place where she couldn't find it till she went to bed—till she actually *got into bed*. Had she found it *before*—during the evening—it might have interfered with his plans. I came to the conclusion therefore that the letter in the study had been meant for *somebody* to see. Why? And who? The problem grew interesting. I might have suspected a 'fake' suicide, but there was a dead man and the right man at that, apparently! Hammond's story was true—it was confirmed by more than one other—but unhappily it was but a complication. The 'Chosroes Cross' had been stolen after the murders, but it was an 'extra turn.' I have explained it. Then there came two incidents—trifling perhaps in themselves, but very helpful in putting me on the right road. Firstly, there was the cigar-ash on the *portière*. Craig's story that this ash came from Major Prendergast's cigar did not satisfy me. This is a piece of deduction on which I rather pride myself. Not only was the ash on the fringes of the curtain at the bottom, but there was a patch in the middle—on the inner apartment side—over five feet from the ground. Now inasmuch as Prendergast pulled the *portière* to one side when he entered—in which position it had remained all the time that he was in there—it couldn't have been made by *him*. It had been dropped—'knocked off' is the better term—as the man who was smoking the cigar *stood behind the portière and either listened or watched*."

"Good—Bathurst! A most palpable point." Sir Austin rubbed his hands in approval.

"Who was this man? was the question I put to myself. It was a question that for a long time I was unable to answer. I then found myself contemplating the very strange fact that although a car was sent to McLaren's and that McLaren himself was wanted in a hurry—the car was *not* used to bring him back! Doesn't that strike you as most unusual? It certainly did me. Again—*why?* There was something spurious about the whole thing somewhere. The 'fake' idea persisted. But where? Therein lay my difficulty. So I called on Helen Ashley again and I elicited the rather alarming fact that her dead uncle had no banking account. That set me thinking furiously. If you intend to disappear or to assume a new identity it's very convenient to be able to take your money with you at a moment's notice—that fact began to hammer at my brain. While with her I secured the Van Hoyt— the Painswick—and the theatrical agency clues. The first simply needed following up—the second beat me altogether—but the third—although I didn't see it at the time, eventually threw a flash of illumination into the very centre of my mental darkness. What in the name of goodness had Sir Eustace Vernon to do with the stage? 'Repertory' was mentioned—and three plays actually *named*. Consider them for a moment, Sir Austin."

"I can't remember—"

"I'll refresh your memory, sir. They were 'The Only Way'— 'The Lyons Mail' and 'The Prisoner of Zenda.' Know anything about them?"

"I saw Sir John Martin Harvey in the first and poor Harry Irving in the second. Did I see Alexander in—"

"That's not the point, sir. What can you remember as *common* to the three plays?"

"I think I catch your meaning, Bathurst. In each play there is a—"

"Double!" cried Mr. Bathurst, triumphantly.

"Damay and Carton—Dubose and Lesurques—The King of Ruritania and Rudolf Rassendyll. Speaking from memory, I rather fancy that one man usually 'doubles' the parts except in 'Zenda,' where for a brief period in the first act the two men actually appear on the boards together—but I don't suppose Ramsay knew this. He got his double from Damery on the strength of wanting him to take part in one of these plays. I followed the scent, it led me to Bradley Deane. An actor had suddenly disappeared! An actor—whom three people recognized when I showed them a photograph of *'Sir Eustace Vernon'*!"

Sir Austin chuckled. "Neat—very neat indeed!" Anthony smiled. "Even now I was partly in the dark. Who was who? Which one of the people still living was the man I wanted? It could only be one, I concluded at length—'Sam McLaren' the coffee-stall keeper. His appearance *might* be a triumph of 'make-up'—there was the patch over the eye with which to begin. Then something happened that told me I was bowling dead on the wicket. Helen Ashley received an anonymous gift of bank-notes! And I had told McLaren just previously—in reply to an *inquiry* from him—mark you—that she had been left badly off—that her special 'legacy' had been stolen. Everybody else had known this before—Sam McLaren was one who had not! The news worried him—he has a genuine affection for her—he sent her the money. All this time, however, I had not been able to touch the roots of the history. *Why* was all this happening? What was at the bottom of it all? Who *was* Vernon? It was not until I learned the truth of the 'Painswick' clue that I discovered the truth. Why was he so concerned with two convicts? Who were *they*? I sent Craig down to find out When he found the two men and detained them 'on suspicion' I made inquiries into their antecedents and came across the name of their treacherous colleague—Ramsay. You will find an excellent account of the case in *The Times*. Ramsay the king of cat-burglars—Vernon the daring climber of burning buildings! They were one and the same!"

"Another good stroke, Bathurst," interposed the Commissioner—"I certainly never considered a possibility of that kind."

"I only had one thing now to do, sir. I had to *prove* that McLaren was Ramsay and not Deane. Also I suspected the complicity of Mrs. Trentham. I couldn't entirely dismiss from my mind that there had been a strong attachment developing between 'Vernon' and the beautiful Ruby. He had been most explicit with Miss Ashley that Mrs. Trentham was to sit next to him at dinner on Christmas night. He was a man that delighted in the society of the gentler sex. I had a strong intuition that Ruby knew something. I kept my eye on her and determined to test her. I called upon her at her husband's flat in Kensington and arranged for a telephone message to be put through to her while I was with her. The message was this. 'Is that you? It's *Eustace* speaking.' I watched her carefully. She was agitated, but *not* surprised—certainly not surprised. My man at the other end then asked for another name—not hers—according to plan. She concluded that the 'Eustace' was just a coincidence and that the call had been put through to a wrong number." Sir Austin took another drink and handed one to Mr. Bathurst. "Thank you, Sir Austin. Well—I hadn't so very far to travel after that. The question at stake was proving Sam to be the man believed to have been Vernon. I called upon his landlady—a Mrs. Croucher, of Mafeking Street, Mapleton. She put the last cards into my hands. She spoke of a 'recent change' in her lodger. He was *different*. He had even gone off such delicacies as 'tripe and onions.' A dish, I understand, in which he had delighted! It all fitted in with my theory. Then she clinched matters. Deane—her original lodger—had spoken to her, in the course of conversation, of 'Treasury,' the name by which the acting profession knows 'pay-day.' She had misunderstood him—thinking he was referring to the Government office. When McLaren came along I put him to the test. 'Treasury' conveyed nothing to him—beyond the ordinary. The man to whom I spoke was no actor—he was unacquainted with the slang of his profession—he was not Deane—he was 'Vernon'—he was Ramsay the 'cat-burglar.' The rest you know, I think, sir."

Sir Austin nodded. "Yes. It seems to me though that when Ramsay fired the fatal shot he ran a risk that it would be heard. Don't you think so, Bathurst?"

"In a way perhaps. But the room where the crime took place was at the other end of the house—and the door was closed—remember. And there was music. At any rate—nobody *did* hear it."

"What would have happened, Bathurst, if anybody had walked into the study when what you call 'the machinery' was being put in motion?"

Anthony shrugged his shoulders. "He locked the door on the house side, only unlocking it for Purvis to come in and go out. That diminished the risk, didn't it?"

"I suppose it did. Well—I must be off. You've done well, my boy—I'm proud of you." Sir Austin rose. As he did so there came a tap at the door. Mr. Bathurst took in a telegram. He read it with a smile and tossed it over to his companion. "When did you see her?" he inquired.

Sir Austin read the message.

> "I have heard all about everything. Congratulations again. When are you coming to Dovaston Court? Soon?—PAULINE."

This time it was the Commissioner's turn to smile.

"Yesterday," he replied to Mr. Bathurst's query. He gave Anthony a shrewd glance. "Sir Matthew's an old man, Bathurst. I don't suppose you altogether rejoice over the fact of his existence."

"On the contrary, sir! I am profoundly grateful for it, I assure you."

Sir Austin growled and cast a lingeringly appreciative glance in the direction of the tantalus.

Anthony's eyes followed his. Gentle prompting becomes a host.

"Don't leave any, sir. You would disappoint me tremendously if you did."

"I should never forgive myself if I did that, my dear Bathurst. It would be damned ungrateful of me."

Sir Austin walked quickly towards his objective.

THE END

Printed in Great Britain
by Amazon